Kiss Me Under
the Irish Sky

Kiss Me Under the Irish Sky

A Love Always, Ireland Romance

Karen Foley

TULE
PUBLISHING

Dedication

For Caitlin Rose, who found her heart in Ireland…
and stayed.

IRELAND

Crohy Head

Ballylahane

O'Rourke
Sheep Farm

Fort Doon

Kilclooney
Dolman

Assaranca
Waterfall

Ardara

Glengash Pass

Slieve League

SEAFOOD SHACK

To Galway

Killybegs

BRENNA FOLEY · SILVER SOLSTICE PRINTS

Chapter One

NO AMOUNT OF jet lag could make Rachel Woods take a nap, not when the Wild Atlantic Way beckoned just outside the door of the cozy bed-and-breakfast she would call home for the next three months. Leaving her suitcase and her backpack on the bed, she quickly changed her shoes, slipping her bare feet into a comfortable pair of leopard-patterned ballet flats. Through the casement window, sunlight glittered on the distant ocean and she could hear the cry of seabirds overhead. Low stone walls edged the greenest fields she had ever seen and tiny blobs of white told her there were flocks of sheep grazing there. Grabbing a lightweight jacket and her phone, she locked her room and made her way downstairs.

Mrs. O'Leary, the owner of the B&B, appeared from the back of the house, her face wreathed in smiles. "Ah, there you are, Miss Woods! I just put on the kettle for tea if you'd like a wee bit of refreshment. You've had a long trip, all the way from America."

"Oh, thank you, Mrs. O'Leary," Rachel said, "but I thought I'd go for a walk. I can't believe I have a view of the ocean from my bedroom!"

Mrs. O'Leary laughed. "Oh, yeah, it's not that far. Turn left out the gate and follow the road until you come to the church, and then bear right. You'll see a livestock gate and, beyond that, a path through the fields. If you follow the path to the top of the hill, you'll have a fine view of the sea and the cliffs."

"Through the sheep field?" Rachel repeated doubtfully. "Isn't the land private?"

"Paddy Cullen owns the field and he will not mind you walking through; everyone does. Pay no mind to the sheep; they'll stay away from you. Stay on the path and you'll avoid the bogholes."

Rachel laughed, sure the other woman was joking. "Bogholes? What's a boghole?"

"The fields can be wet, especially this time of year. A boghole is just a hole filled with mud and water, but it's not very pleasant to fall into one."

"Maybe I'll just stay on the road," Rachel ventured. "I'm not really one for hiking through sheep fields."

"Well, it's up to you, of course, but the best views are from the top of the hill."

Rachel smiled. "In that case, if I'm not back in an hour, send out a search party."

"You'll be fine. I'll have the kettle on and tea ready when you return," Mrs. O'Leary promised. "Since it's lambing season, you'll likely see some wee lambies as well."

"That seals the deal for me," Rachel declared, holding up

her phone. "I'll gladly brave bogholes for a picture of a lamb."

Mrs. O'Leary laughed. "Very good, enjoy, and mind you close the gate behind you! We don't want our own sheep escaping."

Stepping outside, Rachel paused to breathe deeply. The air was tinged with salt, and fragrant with the smells of the ocean and the fields, and the peat smoke that puffed from the chimneys of the nearby houses. She still couldn't quite believe she was here. The landscape that spread out in front of her seemed surreal in its beauty, and so far removed from the glossy skyscrapers and urban sprawl of Chicago that she almost pinched herself to be sure she wasn't dreaming. She was really in Ballylahane, a small village in the heart of County Donegal, home of Ireland's oldest weaving mill. The McDermott family had been handweaving and manufacturing tweed and luxurious textiles in this village for nearly two hundred years. Tomorrow, she would begin a three-month internship at the mill as part of her graduate studies, the last step in earning her MFA in textile design.

The O'Leary B&B sat just on the edge of the busy town center, a little back from the road. The gravel parking lot in front of the house was surrounded by a low wall with a white iron gate. Several sheep grazed at the edge of the driveway and eyed her cautiously as she slipped out of the yard and pulled the gate closed behind her. She stood for a moment and looked up and down the main street, which was lined with brightly painted shop fronts. From where she stood, she could see the pub, the post office, a tea-and-bake shop, a small clothing boutique, and a locally owned supermarket. There were also two woolen and tweed shops and a small hotel. Rachel laughed softly. Ballylahane was certainly a far cry from Chicago, in every way possible.

Setting out in the direction of the church, Rachel turned her face toward the sun and smiled. Could anything be more lovely or magical than Ireland in the spring? Here she was, mere steps away from the quaint village center, strolling along a gravel lane edged with stone walls and green creeping vines. Overhead, the sky was a brilliant, cloudless blue. She passed an older couple walking in the opposite direction, each of them carrying a walking stick. They nodded politely and greeted her with a smile, but Rachel didn't miss how they stared at her leopard-patterned shoes. She could see the curiosity in their eyes, and wondered if she stood out as an American.

At the small stone church with its ancient graveyard, she turned right. The road narrowed to just two ruts, and she could see the wide expanse of field ahead and the steep hill that must overlook the entire countryside. The wide, metal livestock gate was closed, but there was an opening at the edge with a wooden step built into it for walkers to access the field, and a wooden sign with a crudely painted arrow that read, Ballylahane Head—2 km.

"This must be the way," she murmured, and climbed

through the opening.

From her window at the B&B, the field had looked like a uniform sweep of green velvet. Up close, Rachel could see the ground was wet and marshy, with tussocks of grass that grew in great clumps, surrounded by spongy earth. But the path was easy enough to follow, and she made her way upward for what seemed like an eternity, until eventually she had to stop when she became overheated and out of breath. Bracing her hands on her knees, she looked back the way she had come and realized she'd traveled farther than she'd realized. The church and the road now looked tiny, but she was barely halfway up the hill. She could see the B&B and the miniature white tufts that were the O'Learys' sheep in the front yard. Glancing upward, she saw a small flock slowly making their way along the ridge above her and among them were several lambs, cavorting alongside their mothers. Seeing them, she straightened, determined to reach the top. She stripped off her jacket and tied it around her waist.

"I can do this," she muttered. "And when I get back to the States, I am so joining a gym."

She continued on until she came to a shallow stream that was too wide for her to easily cross without getting wet. Gingerly, she stepped off the path and picked her way across the field in search of an easier spot to cross. The ground squelched wetly beneath her feet and she tested each footstep for firmness until she found a spot where the stream narrowed and she thought she could jump across. The ground on either side looked soft and mushy, and there were no hummocks of grass here as there had been near the path. Drawing in a breath, she leaped across the water, slipping a little as she landed in the mud on the other side, realizing her shoes were completely impractical. Regaining her balance, she searched for the best way back to the path, but everything looked marshy, and suddenly she felt less certain about continuing on. From where she stood, she could no longer see the path, although she knew where it must be.

Hearing voices, Rachel looked up and saw three men appear over the rise. They wore shorts and running gear, and she watched as they jogged easily through the field. Noticing her, one of the men lifted a hand in greeting and Rachel waved back. Aware they were watching her and feeling self-conscious, she took two steps forward and then shrieked as her feet sank into a murky quagmire. Thrown off-balance, she fell forward, but there was no solid ground to break her fall, only thick, wet mud that sucked at her hands and feet and threatened to pull her down. She scrabbled for purchase, reaching for something—anything—when a strong hand suddenly caught her beneath her arm.

"Easy, I've got you."

One of the runners had come to her rescue. Rachel clung to him as she felt herself sinking deeper into the hole, past her knees. "I'm still sinking! It's like quicksand!"

"Hold on, I'll pull you out." He was tall and strong, and in one easy movement, he hauled her upward. The mud made a wet, sucking sound as it released her, and then Rachel was free. Feeling unaccountably shaken, she collapsed against the man, her muddy fingers clutching the front of his jersey.

"Thank you, thank you," she gasped, and then started to laugh. The absurdity of the situation, combined with her relief at having escaped certain death, released something inside her and she laughed until tears streamed. Aware that her rescuer was watching her in bemusement, she made an effort to pull herself together. Wiping her damp cheeks with one hand, she managed to speak. "So that's a boghole!"

"It is, yeah. Have you hurt yourself?"

He was looking at her as if she had lost her mind, and aware that she was still clinging to him, Rachel pushed herself away, balancing on one foot. "No, I don't think so, but I seem to have lost a shoe."

Worse, she was covered in thick, reeking black muck up to her thighs, and her arms and front were wet and muddy from where she had fallen.

"Right, well, let's get you onto firmer ground first, and then we'll find the shoe." He held on to her arm as she half hopped beside him, back to the path where the other two men waited. "She's okay, lads. Why don't you go on ahead and I'll see her safe into town?"

With a wave, the other two men continued their run. For the first time, Rachel got a good look at the man who had rescued her. She guessed him to be no more than thirty. He was tall and lean and had bright hair that glinted with burnished gold and copper highlights in the sun, and the bluest eyes Rachel had ever seen.

"I don't know how to thank you," she said, feeling herself blush beneath his regard. "If you hadn't come along—"

"You'd be just another tourist gone missing down a boghole." Seeing her horrified expression, he grinned. "I'm joking. Truly. I'm glad I could help. You're American, yeah?"

She liked his accent and the way he rolled his r's, so that *tourist* sounded like *toor-rist*.

"Yes, I'm Rachel." She extended her hand, only to swiftly pull it back when she realized it was covered with black mud. The front of his jersey was also filthy where she had grabbed on to him. "Sorry." She gave him an apologetic look. "Looks like I owe you a new shirt."

He laughed. "It's fine, really. I've plenty more where this came from." Extending his own mud-covered hand, he grasped hers and smiled into her eyes. "I'm Conall. Pleasure to meet you."

"Same here." Aware that she was still smiling stupidly at him, she withdrew her hand and tried to pull her scattered thoughts together. "Mrs. O'Leary did warn me about bogholes, but I honestly had no idea they were so treacherous."

"They can be, yeah," Conall agreed. "Most folk take a stick with them when they go hill-walking, to test the ground."

"Well, that would make sense, but I only just arrived today and I've never been hill-walking." She laughed. "Until now, I've never even seen a bog."

"Right. Well, let's see if I can recover your shoe. Stay here, don't leave the path."

"Don't worry," Rachel assured him. "You don't have to tell me twice."

She watched as he made his way carefully back to the spot where she had fallen. He had an athlete's physique, with broad shoulders and long, muscled legs. Bending down, he plunged his hand into the boghole and triumphantly came up with her shoe, dripping with mud and water.

"Success," he said as he retraced his steps and handed her the shoe.

Rachel grimaced. Turning the ballet flat over, she poured out the mud. "Oh, that smells terrible! These are definitely ruined."

"Might as well put it back on," Conall said cheerfully. "You're already covered in the stuff and it will at least protect your foot from rocks on the way back."

Using his arm for balance, Rachel managed to push her bare foot into the wet shoe. "Ugh, that feels disgusting!" In fact, she was extremely uncomfortable with her jeans clinging wetly to her legs and mud squelching between her toes. And the smell was beyond anything she had ever experienced. "Why does it smell so bad?"

Conall laughed. "That's literally millennia of decomposed plant material."

"Oh, it's awful!"

"I agree. Let's get out of here."

Conall led the way back down the hill, reaching out to help her over the tricky spots, and checking to make sure she was able to keep up. "Doing okay?"

"Yes. I can't wait to take a hot shower."

"Staying at O'Learys' B&B, are you?" He took her hand and helped her across the stream at the point where she had previously left the path. He made it seem effortless.

"Yes. Do you know the O'Learys?"

"Oh, sure. Pauline's a good sort and she'll treat you well. You'll be sitting by her fire and sipping tea before you know it."

"That sounds like heaven," she confessed. "Then . . . a long nap."

"Where are you from, in the States?"

"Chicago, born and bred."

"Ah, the big city. This must be quite a change for you, then."

Rachel thought of the small apartment she shared with her cousin, Lori, in the middle of the city. She couldn't remember the last time she'd visited the countryside or had seen the ocean. Her apartment building was surrounded by other high-rises so she never saw a wide-open vistas unless she went down to the waterfront and looked out over Lake

Michigan. At night, she fell asleep to the sounds of sirens in the streets and the rumble of the Metra train that ran behind her building. It was the third week in March, but Chicago was still encased in ice, while Ballylahane was already vibrant with color. The only green she'd seen back home had been the Chicago River on St. Patrick's Day, when the local plumbers union had dyed it green in celebration of the Irish holiday just a week earlier.

"You have no idea," she said with a huff of laughter. "Ballylahane is like something out of time. It's so quaint."

"Yeah, it is that."

They reached the livestock gate, and Conall gave her his hand as she negotiated the wooden step through the opening that led to the road. Soon they reached the gate to Mrs. O'Leary's yard, where her three sheep still grazed. Rachel turned to Conall with a smile.

He stared at her for a moment, and a lopsided smile curved his mouth. "You have mud on your face. Quite a bit of it, actually."

"I do?" Rachel rubbed her fingers over her cheeks.

"Ah, you're just making it worse," Conall said, laughing. "Here, let me."

Carefully, studying her face with all the intensity of an artist surveying his subject, he swept a thumb over her cheekbone and came away with a thick dollop of black mud. "That's the worst of it."

"Thank you again," she said.

"Nah, don't mention it. But if I could make a suggestion, you might want to wear some proper trainers the next time you go exploring."

"Trainers?"

"Er, runners. Sneakers. Lace-up running shoes. They won't come off so easily if you fall into another boghole."

Rachel raised her hands, laughing. "No worries, I have absolutely no intention of ever climbing that hill again."

"I hope you don't mean that. The views from the top are spectacular. I could show you, if you'd like." He glanced at her feet. "Once you have a proper pair of shoes, that is. And I promise to keep you out of bogholes."

"Thanks, but as you probably noticed, I'm not much of an outdoors type," she confessed, her tone rueful. "I'm probably safer sticking to paved roads."

Conall tipped his head as he looked at her. "If you don't get off the beaten path, you'll miss all the best parts."

Rachel realized he was right. If she hadn't ventured into that field, they might never have met. She might have taken a nap, instead, and he would have jogged straight past the O'Learys' B&B and they never would have crossed paths.

"Maybe you're right," she conceded with a smile. "Can you recommend somewhere to buy a good pair of trainers?"

Conall grinned. "I can, actually. There's a shop called Heart and Sole on Drumbarron Road that can sort you out."

"Great, thanks." She turned toward the gate and then paused. "Maybe we'll see each other again."

"No doubt we will. It's a tiny wee town, after all."

Chapter Two

"AND THIS IS our weaving floor," Seamus McDermott said as he ushered Rachel into an enormous warehouse-sized bay, which was part of the McDermott tweed factory. In his early fifties, Seamus had an open, friendly face and blue eyes that crinkled when he laughed. The pride he felt for his company was evident in his voice as he talked about the weaving process to which he had dedicated his life.

The rhythmic noise of the powered looms was familiar to Rachel. At least a dozen industrial looms filled the massive space, separated by floor-to-ceiling open shelves that held hundreds of giant spools of wool thread which could be fed directly into the looms. When she had arrived at the mill that morning, she had been surprised and humbled to realize the owner had set the day aside for her, to personally show her the weaving operation. He could have turned the responsibility over to the factory manager, but she could see in his face how proud he was of McDermott Mills.

"This is amazing," she said, taking in the noise and colorful bustle. The air smelled like wool and machine oil, and she was surprised at the size of the McDermott factory. Being in such a small village, she had expected something on a much smaller scale.

Rachel was no stranger to the weaving industry; her family owned a textile factory in Chicago that manufactured high-end upholstery material and other home textiles. For as long as she could recall, Rachel had planned to work at the family business, designing fabric for Lakeside Industries. Her uncle, Jack Woods, was on the board of directors for the company, and had promised Rachel a position on the design team once she finished her degree. But McDermott Mills was vastly different than the Chicago-based company. This was no sleek, modern operation, and there were no robotics to be seen. The equipment was old-school and once again Rachel felt as if she had stepped back in time. The noise of the machinery was loud, but the workers seemed competent and happy, greeting them and moving with confidence among the weaving machines and spindles, ducking beneath lengths of thread and occasionally checking the warps.

As they made their way across the factory floor, Rachel admired the patterns being worked on the looms. The nearest one was a rich red fabric, woven with a deeper red windowpane pattern. She had expected to see brown and gray tweeds and plaids that reflected the earthy hues of the Donegal landscape. She had not expected to see such modern—and vibrant—interpretations of the traditional tweed cloth.

"How many weaving machines do you have?" Rachel asked.

"We have thirteen power looms, and can produce upward of five hundred meters of woven fabric a day, and that's just here in the mill," Seamus said. "We also send select patterns and yarn to local handweavers, who work out of their homes in the traditional fashion."

"I'd love to see that."

Seamus chuckled. "I'll arrange it. Our drivers collect and deliver the handwoven fabrics each week. If you'd like, you can go along one day and see the process. Come along, and I'll show you how we process the raw fabric and where we store the finished bolts."

The day passed so quickly that when Seamus suggested she go home and get some rest, she was surprised to see it was already midafternoon.

"I look forward to having you here, Rachel," Seamus said as they walked outside. "When I received your letter, you could have knocked me over with a feather. I remember your father and I'm sure he'd be proud that you've decided to follow in his footsteps."

A small knot formed in Rachel's chest, as it always did when she thought about her father. He'd died suddenly of a heart attack when she was just thirteen years old. Nobody had been prepared, least of all Rachel. One day he'd been there, and the next day he was gone. Rachel hadn't even had a chance to say goodbye. That had been twelve years ago, and she still missed him. Without conscious thought, her hand went to the necklace she wore beneath her blouse, a

Celtic knot on a heavy gold chain. She couldn't remember a time when her father hadn't worn the pendant, and she'd begged her mother for it after he had died.

"I actually had no idea he'd spent time here as a young man," Rachel confessed. "When I was looking for somewhere to do an internship, my uncle mentioned that Dad had spent a summer here working in this factory, so I was anxious to do the same."

She didn't add that coming to Ballylahane and literally following in her father's footsteps seemed a way for her to honor his memory, while fulfilling his dream for her to learn the family business. She hoped he would approve.

"Seems a long time ago," Seamus mused. "Probably going on thirty years. Of course, I didn't own the factory then. My father did. I was still a lad, learning the ropes, so to speak."

"Did you know my father?"

"I did." Seamus nodded. "He worked for us for a full summer. I thought he might stay here in Ballylahane, but in the end, duty called, and he returned to Chicago." He gave Rachel a sympathetic smile. "I was sorry to hear of his passing."

"Thank you. It was a long time ago," Rachel said, not adding that she still felt the loss as keenly as she did twelve years ago. "It may sound strange, but being here makes me feel closer to him. Maybe there are still people here in Ballylahane who remember him."

"Oh, no doubt," Seamus said, but his expression grew pensive.

"Well, thank you for taking the time to show me around," she said, smiling at him. "I'm looking forward to learning everything I can."

"I'll have you work with Fiona tomorrow," he said. "She's my oldest daughter and our lead designer."

"That sounds perfect." She gave him what she hoped was an endearing smile. "I'm looking forward to trying my own hand at designing a tweed pattern before I go back to the States."

Seamus looked at her thoughtfully. "I think we can work something out."

Rachel pulled a face, feeling suddenly awkward. "You're under no obligation to weave anything I come up with. I know the expense would be great."

"Well," he said, obviously amused, "let's see what you come up with. It's why you're here, after all. And I've no objection to you weaving a dozen new patterns, if they sell."

"That's the trick, isn't it? Well, I'll let you get back to work," Rachel said. "Thank you for an amazing day. Can you point me in the direction of Drumbarron Road? I need a pair of sneakers—er, trainers—and was told there's a shop there that can sort me out."

Seamus's smile grew wider. "Sure they can. Cross over the bridge and go straight. Drumbarron Road is just beyond the bank. Turn right and you can't miss it. Tell wee Conall I said hello. Oh, and before I forget, you're invited to join my family for supper tonight at the house."

"Oh, thank you! What time?"

"Half seven, and it's very informal."

"I'll look forward to it," Rachel said. "Thanks again."

She made her way out of the mill parking lot, which was surrounded by a tall stone wall, and stood for a moment to get her bearings. What had he meant about telling wee Conall hello? Could he be referring to the same Conall who had rescued her, or was there more than one Conall in the village? She decided it must be a different man, since nobody would ever describe the Conall she had met as *wee*.

Crossing over the bridge, she paused to watch a mother and her two children toss bread to a cluster of ducks below. Decorative iron street lamps marched across the stone bridge, adorned with flowering baskets that spilled over with colorful blooms. On the other side of the bridge, Rachel strolled along the main road and peered into the shop windows, admiring the woolen and tweed products on display. There were chunky sweaters from the Aran Islands, tweed caps and houndstooth capes, handbags, and handsome vests and coats. Even in the small town of Ballylahane, it seemed there were enough tourists to keep the shops in business. Past the bank, she turned right on Drumbarron Road and saw the sign for Heart and Sole ahead.

An overhead bell tinkled as she entered the shop, and it took her less than three seconds to realize she was out of her depth. The shop quite obviously catered to serious runners, and the sneakers she saw on display were high-end and expensive. A strip of red racing track ran the length of the shop, from the front door to a podium and a computer at the far end. Several racks of jerseys, shorts, and waterproof jackets stood near the cashier counter. She could hear the shopkeeper speaking on the phone, just out of her line of vision, and she quickly turned to leave before she was spotted. She had her hand on the door handle when a voice interrupted her.

"Hey, welcome to Heart and Sole. Is there something I can help you with?"

Too late, Rachel turned and then stared as she saw the man who had rescued her from the boghole the previous day. Today he was dressed in a pair of jeans and a dark blue pullover that emphasized his broad shoulders and the blueness of his eyes.

"Conall!" Rachel smiled, surprised and happy to see him. "You *work* here?" She wanted to laugh out loud. She hadn't seen that one coming. *He was a shoe salesman!*

He came forward, grinning. "I do, yeah. I was hoping you'd come in."

She looked around. "It's a great shop, but I think I'm out of my league here."

"No, not at all. In fact, I was thinking of what you said about not being much of an outdoors type, and I have a shoe that I think will be perfect for you. But we'll need to confirm your size first."

"I'm not sure. This looks like a serious running store and I'm not much of an athlete. A top-end sneaker would just be wasted on me." She pulled a face. "I'd probably just lose it in a boghole!"

Conall laughed and the sound was so deep and rich that Rachel found herself laughing in return. He really did have the nicest eyes. And smile. And everything else too.

"A good trainer—er, running shoe—is never a waste," he said. "It doesn't matter if you're training for a marathon or just getting out to enjoy nature, comfort is key. A good runner is the first step toward a happier, healthier lifestyle."

"You should make a commercial," she said, teasing him.

"I did, actually. We have a video on YouTube that I think is quite good." He gestured toward a row of leather chairs along one wall. "Have a seat and kick your shoes off. I'll get a quick measurement."

Feeling self-conscious, Rachel did as he asked, toeing off the Italian leather flats she'd worn for her tour of the mill. Underneath, she wore a pair of mustard-yellow socks with whimsical red mushrooms on them, and wished she'd opted for something a little more sophisticated. She watched as Conall grabbed a measuring device and went down on one knee in front of her.

"Stand up for me," he directed, and then guided her foot onto the device with one large hand on her ankle, and slid her foot against the heel cup. Even through the sock, his fingers were warm. Looking down at his bent head, she saw his thick hair was cut in short layers, as bright and shiny as a new copper penny. She curled her fingers into her hands to prevent herself from touching. He slid the rulers against her foot and then had her switch feet.

"Okay, you're a perfect European size thirty-eight," he said, standing up. "Give me a sec and let me grab those runners."

He disappeared into a back room and Rachel sat down again. She needed to get a grip on herself. She couldn't recall the last time she'd found a guy so attractive. Maybe it was the charming Irish accent, or the way a smile always seemed to lurk in the corners of his mouth. Or the way he looked at her, as if she'd just lit up his whole day. When he returned moments later, he had four shoeboxes stacked in his arms.

"Let's try these first," he suggested and withdrew a pair of black sneakers with bright orange and purple accents. "They're my bestseller and they're super comfortable. Perfect for a leisurely walk or something more strenuous."

Rachel slid her feet into the sneakers and allowed him to lace them for her. "They do feel good," she admitted, standing up and taking several experimental steps.

At his urging, she tried on two more pairs and finally settled on the first pair. "I like these," she said, admiring her feet in a nearby mirror. "I just wasn't prepared to spend so much money on sneakers. I usually reserve this kind of price tag for my leather skimmers."

"Which are terrible for your feet," Conall declared, picking up one of her discarded shoes. "Absolutely no arch support and the narrow toe box will give you blisters, or worse."

"Fashion hurts," she said weakly.

Conall chuckled. "If you say so. Let's do this; I'll give you the runners at cost, which will be a thirty percent reduction in price." He cast an amused glance at her. "I'll even throw in a couple pairs of good running socks, my treat. Do you want to wear them out of the shop?"

"Sure." Putting her own shoes into the empty shoebox, Rachel watched as he went to the counter and began writing up an invoice. "But you don't have to give me a break on the price. I'd hate for you to get in trouble with your boss."

"Actually, I am the boss," he said without looking up. "I own the shop. I opened it a couple of years after I graduated college, and I have three other locations as well."

Okay, so *not* just a shoe salesman. "Wow, that's pretty impressive. So you were a business major in college?"

Conall slid the box with her shoes into a bag and handed it to her. "No. I studied sports medicine with a specialty in injuries to the feet." Seeing her expression, he shrugged. "I love to run, so I decided to get out of the clinic and open a running store. I do gait analysis and make recommendations if I see issues."

A doctor.

"But you don't actually do surgeries or see patients?"

"Not anymore. I had a practice in Dublin for a couple of years, before I decided to get out of medicine. Now I partner with local clinics to provide patients with the footwear they need."

Rachel considered him for a moment, trying to wrap her head around the fact he had studied to become a sports doctor, only to give it all up to open a running store. She honestly didn't know whether to be impressed or alarmed.

"What did your family think about your decision?" she finally asked. She couldn't imagine her mother would have supported her if she'd suddenly decided to give up textile design and pursue something entirely different, not after investing so much in her education. But even as Rachel acknowledged she herself was very risk-averse, there was something undeniably enticing about the idea of following your heart's desire and not allowing the expectations of others to determine your path. "I only mean that it must have come as a shock to them."

Conall looked sharply at her, as if he suspected her of judging him, or perhaps thinking less of him for his drastic career change.

"Don't get me wrong—I admire what you did," Rachel said quickly. "I don't know many people—actually, I don't know anyone—brave enough to do what you did."

The tension in Conall's expression eased. "Sure, my parents were surprised, but they supported my decision. After all, there's no point in spending a lifetime doing something if it doesn't make you happy."

She thought of her cousin, Lori, who was desperately unhappy in her current job, but unwilling to look at other options for fear of offending her father.

"So . . . running makes you happy?" she ventured.

"It does, yeah. My spare time is spent organizing and supporting marathons and other running events around Ireland. Ballylahane is hosting a hill run at the end of the summer. There's still time to register, if you're interested."

Rachel wanted to ask him more about his unusual career choices, but she sensed he wouldn't welcome her interest. He had deliberately moved the conversation away from the topic, and while he seemed relaxed, there was something in the set of his jaw that discouraged her from asking additional questions. But she was curious. In her world, normal people did not walk away from a lucrative medical career to do something as ordinary as *run*. But while she sensed there was more to the story than he was telling, she restrained herself from probing further.

"A hill run?" Rachel repeated. "Thanks, but I could barely walk up that hill yesterday, never mind run. I think I'll pass."

Conall nodded. "I understand. What about a tiny wee walk? You did want to see the view from Ballylahane Head, right?"

"I did, but not if it means risking another boghole accident."

KISS ME UNDER THE IRISH SKY

"There's an access road on the backside of the hill," Conall explained. "We could drive most of the way, and the short walk to the top is actually very dry and safe. That's the way the lads and I had come when we saw you fall."

Rachel considered what she knew of him. He seemed like a genuinely nice guy and there was no doubt she found him attractive, but what did she really know about him? As she considered whether to accept, the bell over the door tinkled merrily and they both turned to see a young man enter the shop.

"Heya, boss," he said to Conall and disappeared into the back room.

"That's Michael, my assistant," Conall explained. "We could go now if you've a mind to."

"Now?"

"Sure. Unless you have other plans?"

"Er, no, I don't. But I don't even know your last name."

Conall grinned. "Sorry, I thought you did. It's McDermott. Seamus is my uncle, and you're here to learn the business of weaving tweed, yeah?"

Rachel smiled helplessly. "Yes, that's right. But how did you know that?"

"It's a small town. And I talked with my uncle last night."

"Of course you're related," Rachel said. "That's why he said to say hello to wee Conall."

He gave a huff of laughter. "I have almost six and a half

feet, and yet I'm still wee Conall to him."

"Well, he's a good character reference. Seeing as you're related, and since you did rescue me from certain death, I suppose I can safely go walking with you."

"Excellent. Hey, Michael, I have to run. Lock up for me, will you?"

The young man popped his head into the shop. "Sure thing, boss. I've got it covered."

"Good lad." Conall retrieved a jacket from the back room, and after taking Rachel's shopping bag, opened the door and indicated she should precede him outside. "After you."

They reached a small convertible parked near the corner of the street, and Rachel waited as Conall opened the passenger door for her. "I almost got in on the wrong side," she laughed. "I still can't get used to driving on the other side of the road."

"You're welcome to give it a try, if you'd like," Conall offered. "Are you familiar with a stick shift?"

"No, sorry," she said cheerfully, and climbed into the passenger seat. "It's probably safer if you do the driving—for the sake of everyone else on the road."

He was a good driver, negotiating the narrow roads and sharp turns with an easy expertise. When they rounded a bend and came across a stray sheep that had wandered directly into their path, he didn't seem at all fazed, simply negotiating the car around it while Rachel squeezed her eyes shut and tried not to scream. As the road wound upward, Rachel caught glimpses of the blue sea through the hedgerows on her left. A few minutes later, Conall pulled the car onto the shoulder and they both climbed out.

"We'll walk from here," he said. "It's only ten minutes. How do your runners feel?"

"They feel great. Are you going to put the top up on the car?"

Conall peered at the sky. "Nah, I don't think it will rain."

"I was thinking more of thieves who might want to go through your things."

"The car—and everything in it—will be safe," he said. "There's literally no crime in Ballylahane, unless you count Maggie Mallone's cooking." He gave her a conspiratorial wink. "She and her husband own the pub."

Rachel gave a surprised laugh. "Okay, well, I guess I won't eat there."

"Oh, you can eat there, just not on Thursday night, which is when she's in the kitchen. The rest of the time, her man does the cooking and it's grand."

After stashing her pocketbook and shoes into the small trunk—or boot, as Conall called it—they crossed the road to where a path led into the trees. Rachel followed Conall, aware he had shortened his longer stride to accommodate hers.

"Have you lived in Ballylahane your whole life?" Rachel asked.

"Yeah, except for my college years, which I spent in Galway and Dublin, followed by a short stint in Melbourne. They're fantastic cities, mind you, but they're not Ballylahane."

"You lived in Melbourne? As in Australia?" She looked at him with renewed interest. "When was this?"

"Right after college." He shrugged and Rachel had the distinct sense he regretted having said anything. "I was there for such a short time that it's hardly worth mentioning."

"Well, Ballylahane is beautiful," Rachel agreed. "But don't you ever want a little more excitement?"

Conall grinned. "You've not been here when Donegal's county football teams compete. It can get downright murderous."

"Sounds about the same as our American football." Rachel smiled.

"Seriously, though, the village is small, but it has everything I need. I've known the people here my whole life and after being away for so long, I was happy to come back. Besides, there are no better trails for running than here in the northwest of Ireland."

As if to support his statement, four runners appeared through the trees in front of them, and Conall pulled her to one side of the trail to give them room. Recognizing Conall, they shouted greetings as they ran past.

"Friends of yours?" Rachel asked as they resumed walking.

"Members of my running club."

"Just how often do you run?"

"Every day, sometimes twice a day." Seeing her surprise, he shrugged. "It's how I relax."

Rachel laughed. "Okay, well, normal people do things like read a book or take a nap."

"And miss out on all this?" The trees fell away and before them stretched a high, grassy hill. To her left was the glittering blue ocean and the low rise of green mountains in the distance.

"Oh, look at that," she breathed.

Before she knew what he intended, Conall caught her hand in his. "C'mon, let's run a bit."

The unexpected contact startled Rachel and made her feel flustered, even as it gave her a thrill of girlish excitement. His hand was large and warm, his fingers closing securely around hers with an easy confidence.

"Oh, no! Conall, I can't run!" she protested, laughing, but he was already tugging her along behind him.

To Rachel's surprise, she found she could run. With her hand tucked warmly into Conall's, he pulled her along the path until finally, laughing and breathless, they reached the top. Conall collapsed onto the grassy knoll and pulled her down beside him. There, spread out before them, was the most magnificent vista Rachel had ever seen. They were sitting on a headland and the ocean crashed onto the rocks far below. Curving out to either side were more cliffs, topped with emerald-green fields. In the distance, the coastline curved back toward the sea in a series of majestic cliffs and rolling hills.

"How beautiful," Rachel said with a sigh of contentment.

"Yeah, it is." Something in his tone made Rachel look at him, only to find him watching her. Before she could wonder about it, he pointed to a distant island floating in the blueness of the water. "That's the island of Roan Inish."

"Does anyone live there?"

"No, not anymore. It's not much more than a barren rock, really, surrounded by skerries, or smaller rocky islands."

"Have you been out there?"

"Yeah, I took a kayak out there once." Bracing his arms on his bent knees, he angled his head to look at her, his irises startlingly blue in the sunlight. "The place had a haunted, lonely feel to it."

"Is it really home to selkies?"

Conall laughed. "You know the story, eh? Well, I don't know if it's true, but I didn't see any half-human, half-seal people the day I was there." He considered her for a moment. "If I did see a selkie, I'd leave her be. I wouldn't steal her sealskin and hide it from her."

"Why not?" Rachel pulled at a stalk of grass and smiled at him. "Legend has it, selkies make wonderful wives and mothers."

"Yeah, but if she finds her sealskin, she abandons her

family for the lure of the sea." Conall turned his gaze back to the island. "That's not a heartbreak I'd risk."

Rachel was silent for a moment. "No. You'd need to find a really good hiding spot."

Conall laughed and pushed himself to his feet. Extending a hand to her, he pulled her up. "Well, that would never work in my case." He smiled down at her, but his blue eyes were serious. "I've never been good at hiding anything."

Chapter Three

RACHEL CAST A sideward glance at the man in the driver's seat. His profile showed a strong, square jaw and a nose that might have been called prominent on another man, but looked proud on Conall McDermott.

"Thank you for driving," she said as he maneuvered the car along the winding road that led beyond the village and toward the bay. He had put the top up on the convertible and the interior of the car seemed small and intimate. She balanced a brightly colored gift bag and a bunch of cut flowers wrapped in paper on her lap. "I probably wouldn't have had much luck calling an Uber."

"Probably not," Conall agreed. "It's not that far to his house, but I'd not have you walking after dark."

"I thought Ballylahane has no crime."

"It doesn't. But there are no streetlamps, and I'd hate to see you fall into a pothole or take a wrong turn and end up in a field." He flashed her a swift smile to let her know he was teasing, but she was already grinning back at him.

"You're a quick study, Conall McDermott. You already have me figured out."

"I'm not sure that's true," he said with a rueful laugh. "But you're here for what—three months? I've still got loads of time."

"We'll see," she said, unable to resist teasing him a little. She found she was looking forward to getting to know him better.

Near the bay, he turned onto a narrow road that wound upward, until finally, he pulled into a small parking area in front of a large stone house. Ivy rambled over the walls and enormous rhododendrons edged the lawn.

"Wow, this is incredible," Rachel said, peering through the windshield. The house where Seamus McDermott lived with his family commanded a view of the village and the small bay below. The paned windows glowed a warm pink and yellow from the reflection of the setting sun.

"It is nice," Conall agreed. "McDermotts have lived here for almost two hundred years. It was built for the mill owner when the tweed factory first opened."

"One of your great-great-grandfathers?" Rachel guessed.

"A great-great-great-uncle, actually."

Climbing out of the car, he rounded the hood and opened Rachel's door, lending her a hand as she juggled the flowers and gift bag.

"So your father and Seamus are brothers?"

"Yes. Seamus is the oldest of the four siblings, which includes my father and my two aunts, Isla and Nora."

"Where does your father live now?" she asked as they

crossed the driveway to the house.

"He and my mum have a house in town," he said, knocking on the door. "Dad manages the export sales for McDermott Mills. You'll meet him before too long."

Before she could reply, the door opened and Seamus and his wife were there, welcoming them both inside.

"I'm Rose. It's lovely to meet you, Rachel," his wife enthused. "Imagine you meeting our Conall on your first day here! Seamus told me what happened, but I really want to hear your version."

Rachel laughed, her gaze finding Conall's and sliding away again. "Well, there's not much to tell except that he literally saved my life. If he hadn't come along when he did, nobody would have ever known what happened to me."

Catching the playful gleam in her eyes, Conall gave an exaggerated stretch, flexing his fingers. "Yeah, it was a tough job, but someone had to do it."

Rachel gave a mock gasp of outrage, but couldn't help laughing when he gave her a cheeky wink and bumped his arm against hers, letting her know he was teasing.

Rose made a tsking sound and drew Rachel deeper into the house. "What a terrifying experience, and not a very good first impression of our little town. Come on in and let me get you something to drink."

"Here, these are for you and Seamus," she said, handing Rose the flowers and the small gift bag. "Thank you so much for having me over tonight."

"Oh, how lovely! And the pleasure is all mine. I've been looking forward to meeting you," Rose said.

Rachel followed her into a sitting room with comfortable furniture pulled up in front of a massive stone fireplace. In spite of the high ceilings and deep casement windows, the stone manor felt both warm and welcoming.

As they entered the room, two women rose from their chairs and Rose quickly introduced her daughters, Fiona and Mary-Kate. Fiona looked to be several years older than Rachel, while Mary-Kate looked to be barely out of high school. They each had what Rachel was coming to recognize as the McDermott coloring, with dark-red hair and blue eyes. After the introductions were made and a glass of wine was pressed into Rachel's hand, she took a seat next to Conall on the wide sofa.

"You and Fiona should have plenty to talk about," he said. "She studied textile design in Paris before she came home to drag McDermott Mills kicking and screaming into the twenty-first century."

Fiona laughed and reached down to pat a small pug who lay by her feet. "Conall exaggerates. I simply persuaded my father to install some more modern equipment, and we updated our computers and our sales department." She gave a modest shrug. "And I may have had some influence with certain fashion designers in the industry."

"Mr. McDermott said I'm to spend tomorrow with you in the design studio," Rachel confirmed, smiling at the other woman. "I hope you have a lot of patience. My experience is more with home textiles and not apparel."

"I'm looking forward to it," Fiona assured her. "It will be nice to have a set of fresh eyes. Sometimes I think I'm just using the same patterns over and over and only changing up the yarns."

"Don't let her fool you. Fiona is the backbone of the business," Seamus said, pride in his voice. "And you're to call me Seamus. We don't stand on formality, not around here. I've known most of the workers at the mill my whole life and we're like a family."

"Is it the same with your family business?" Rose asked.

Rachel hesitated. "My uncle owns the business and my grandfather ran it before him. But it's such a big operation and being in the city—well, I'm not sure it's as family-oriented as McDermott Mills. We have more than four hundred employees, and honestly, I think my uncle only knows a handful of them personally. He spends most of his time in meetings and leaves the day-to-day operations to his managers."

"Ah, I understand," Seamus said, but Rachel knew he didn't.

"So you'll go to work for your uncle when you return to Chicago?" Mary-Kate asked.

"Yes, that's the plan." She didn't tell them that she had worked at her family's factory every summer since she was a teenager, or that she'd won several prestigious awards for her designs during college and grad school. This internship would round out her wheelhouse of experience by enabling her to design tweed and also see the art of handweaving, which had all but disappeared in the United States, except for small cottage industries. "This internship is the last requirement I have in order to obtain my advanced degree in textile design. Once I graduate, I'll work for Lakeside Industries as a designer."

"I hope working for McDermott Mills is a positive experience for you, Rachel," Seamus said.

"I'm sure it will be."

Rose stood. "Dinner is ready, so let's sit down to eat while it's still warm."

Conall rose and walked with Rachel into the adjoining dining room, where the table had been elegantly set. He pulled a chair out for Rachel and sat down next to her. Leaning close, he spoke softly into her ear. "Doing okay?"

She nodded, but cast him a grateful smile. "I'm glad you're here."

"Me too."

She realized it was no less than the truth. She held his gaze for an instant before looking quickly away. She was beginning to understand what people meant when they talked about the charm of the Irish. But, as appealing as he was, she hadn't come to Ireland to get involved with someone, especially when there was absolutely no chance of it going anywhere. In three months, she would return to

Chicago, so no matter how handsome or charismatic Conall McDermott might be, there was no point in encouraging any kind of relationship with him. She had come to Ireland to learn about tweed—and maybe something about her father—and not to indulge in a spring fling.

Definitely no flings.

She glanced at Conall, who was laughing at something Fiona had said, his blue eyes bright with amusement, his smile infectious. Something loosened and slowly spread in the pit of her stomach, like warm honey. Something that felt suspiciously like longing.

No flings, no flings, no flings.

Okay, so she might need to put that in writing, keep it in her pocket, and pull it out to read whenever she felt tempted. She should probably have it laminated.

The meal passed quickly, with conversation and laughter flowing freely. The gathering reminded Rachel of dinners at her uncle's house in Chicago when her five cousins were present. After her own father had died, Uncle Jack had taken on the role of surrogate father, as involved with her life as if she'd been his own daughter. That had been particularly comforting after her mother had remarried. Rachel had always felt like an interloper in her mother's new life, but Uncle Jack had provided both stability and familiarity in a world turned suddenly upside down.

Rose brought out a sticky toffee pudding for dessert, along with tea, coffee, and an assortment of Irish whiskeys and after-dinner liqueurs. "Is there anything you're hoping to do while you're here, Rachel, that we can help with?" she asked, smiling across the table. "There are some lovely castle ruins not too far from here, and some caves as well."

"I would love to do some sightseeing," Rachel confirmed. "I don't have a car, but I thought maybe there were some tourist agencies or local guides I could hire for the weekends when I'm not working."

"Well, you'd need to go into Donegal town for that," Seamus mused. "But I'm certain we can find a way for you to see the sights without the need to hire a guide. Conall, what do you think?"

"I'd be happy to show you around," he said quickly.

"Oh, I couldn't bother you," Rachel protested. "You have a business of your own to run, and I'm sure you have better things to do than act as my tour guide."

"My shops are closed on Sundays and Mondays," Conall said. "Michael works Saturday afternoons, from noon to closing, so I have most of the weekend free. Why don't I pick you up at half one on Saturday?"

Looking at the smiling, expectant faces around her, Rachel could think of no good reason to refuse. Surely she could spend an afternoon in his company without turning it into something it wasn't—like a fling.

"Where would we go?"

"Wherever you'd like," Conall said. "Although I have a few ideas about places you might find interesting."

Rachel laughed, won over by his obvious enthusiasm. "Sure. Why not? If you're up for it, then count me in."

"There, that's settled then," Rose said, satisfied. "You're in good hands with Conall. He knows the places the tourists don't go to. You'll have a wonderful time."

"Conall, could you do me a favor? The next time you see Flynn, ask him if we could visit the farm?" Seamus asked. He looked at Rachel. "Flynn O'Rourke and his family own a working sheep farm. Before you return home, we'll make sure you experience the entire wool process, from hoof to cuff, so to speak. What do you think, Fiona?"

Fiona paused in the act of raising her teacup. "Don't include me in this, Dad. I've seen more than my share of sheep farms, the O'Rourkes' included. Besides, they don't raise sheep for the wool."

"No, but Flynn does his own shearing. I think Rachel would enjoy seeing that." He gave Rachel a conspiratorial wink. "You can't work in a woolen mill and not visit the source of the wool. Well, not the source for *our* wool, but you get my meaning."

"I'd like that," Rachel enthused. "I've never visited a sheep farm, and Mrs. O'Leary said it's lambing season right now."

"Oh, yeah, you're bound to see plenty of wee lambs," Rose said.

"I'll mention it to Flynn the next time I see him," Conall promised. "But I can drive Rachel out there if you've other commitments, Uncle Seamus. I know you're busy at the mill."

"I wouldn't mind if you did, as long as it's alright with Rachel," Seamus said.

"Of course, whatever is easiest for you," Rachel replied, but she didn't miss the look Seamus exchanged with his wife. Surely they didn't think Conall had volunteered to bring her himself because he was interested in *her*?

Did they?

"Great. It's a date," Conall said.

Rachel focused on her cup of tea, refusing to acknowledge the tiny spurt of alarm—and yes, pleasure—she felt, knowing she would spend more time with Conall.

No fling, she reminded herself sternly.

But as they drove back to the B&B after dinner, there was no denying the awkward tension in the small car, as if Conall realized he'd been completely transparent.

"You'll enjoy seeing the sheep farm," he said finally. "Flynn and I have been friends since we were lads. We're running a marathon up north in a few weeks. Normally we'd train together, but this is a particularly busy time of year for him, so he's been keeping close to the farm. It'll be good to see him."

"I'm looking forward to it," Rachel said. "I'm hoping to see as much as I can in the few months I'm here."

He shifted in his seat and cast her a sidelong look. "I'm headed into Galway next weekend. Would you like to come along?"

Rachel stared at him in dismay. Was he really inviting her to go away with him for a weekend?

"No, no, not with just me," he clarified, seeing her expression. "Mary-Kate and Fiona are coming along as well. Mary-Kate attends university in Galway and Fiona has a number of friends there. I need to look in on the shop, so we decided to make a weekend of it. We'll head down on Saturday and come back Sunday afternoon."

"Oh. I don't know." Rachel hesitated, tempted despite herself. "It sounds like a family thing, and I wouldn't want to intrude."

"No, you wouldn't be intruding. The more the merrier. Galway is great and there are loads of pubs and shops. We could listen to trad music, if you're interested."

"Trad music?"

"Traditional Irish music."

That appealed to Rachel. Galway had been on her list of places to visit, and going there with a group of people who were familiar with the city sounded infinitely better than going on her own.

"Next weekend?" That was still nearly two weeks away.

"Yeah, if you're free."

"Where would we stay?"

"I have a friend whose family owns a small hotel in town. I've already reserved a couple of rooms for myself and the girls. I'm sure they won't mind if you want to stay in their room, but I can book a third one, if you'd like. It's where I always stay when I'm there for more than a day."

"As long as I can pay my own way, I would love to go. I've heard so many great things about Galway, and it would be so much nicer to be there with other people than on my own."

"Definitely."

They pulled up in front of the B&B. Thrusting the small car into park, Conall jumped out and rounded the hood to open Rachel's door.

"Thanks for the ride," she said, smiling up at him. "I had a lot of fun tonight."

"Yeah, I did too. I'll see you later, then."

Neither of them moved, and Rachel had a sudden, overwhelming urge to reach up and kiss him, which was absolutely the worst idea ever. Before she could act on the impulse, she turned and fumbled with the latch on the gate.

"Okay. Good night, Conall."

He waited as she opened the gate and only when she was inside and closing the door did he climb back into his car. She listened as he drove away, until finally she couldn't hear the engine anymore, and only then did she make her way upstairs to her room. Flinging herself across her bed, she stared at the moon through the window and acknowledged she might be in a wee bit of trouble.

Chapter Four

WHEN RACHEL ARRIVED at McDermott Mills the following morning, it was to discover Fiona had been unexpectedly called to Dublin to meet with a client, and likely would not return until the following week. As a result, Rachel spent the next several days on the manufacturing floor, under the guidance of the mill manager, Timothy Connelly. An older man who had worked at the mill for nearly forty years, he was a patient and humorous instructor, demonstrating how the massive looms were warped and programmed to automatically weave an intended pattern, and how the finished fabrics were inspected, washed and dried, and then inspected again before being rolled onto large bolts.

Rachel had worked at her family textile factory every summer since she'd turned fifteen, but McDermott Mills was an entirely different experience, mostly because the scale of the operation was so much smaller. She truly had the sense of being involved in something very personal.

She hadn't expected to see Fiona at all until the following week, but when she arrived at the mill on Friday morning, it was to discover she had returned from Dublin early and had brought her small pug, Grace, to work with her. Now she and Rachel were in the design room on the second floor of the brick mill building. An enormous wooden worktable covered in black cloth dominated the room. Sunlight flooded through the tall windows and on a nearby wall hung a large vision board, also covered in black fabric, which featured a dozen or more swatches of different tweeds grouped together by color and design. The room was large and airy and yet, it felt curiously intimate as she and Fiona bent over the table and examined an assortment of yarns, fabric swatches, and photographs of nature, while Grace snored softly beneath the table. Fiona was in the beginning stages of designing a pattern for a luxury women's clothing line.

"We weave and design fabrics here for our own collections," she said. "But we also ship to international designers. Those patterns are, of course, proprietary. We're best known for our tweeds and suits, but we also have a full lifestyle collection for men and women."

Rachel knew McDermott Mills employed their own apparel designers, but she had not yet visited the retail shop located in the center of town, and made a mental note to stop there on her way home.

"How much of your sales is for just the fabric, and how much is for finished clothing?" she asked.

"Oh, you'd have to speak to the sales department for that information," Fiona said. "At a guess, I'd say it's a fifty-fifty split, but I'm honestly not sure. We produce fabrics two years in advance of when they'll actually be available to the public as garments."

Sorting through the dozens of photos strewn across the table, Rachel picked up a photograph of a field awash in pale-green and gold grasses, blooming with deep-pink and purple heather against a pine forest. Overhead, the sky was a vivid cerulean blue. "This is so beautiful. I absolutely love the colors."

"Yes, that's a nice one. I took it not too far from here," Fiona said. "Nature so often provides us with a beautiful palette of colors. My goal is to capture those hues in a gorgeous plaid pattern."

"That sounds lovely," Rachel commented. "The colors will really evoke the surrounding countryside. Is the next step to go through the yarns and select the shades that most closely match those in the photo?"

"There are a couple of ways to pull the colors from the photo," Fiona said. "I have this particular photo on my computer and I set the resolution to a really low number in order to see the individual pixels. I create my own palette by selecting colors from the pixel squares, then arrange them in shaded order."

She withdrew a second copy of the photo that had a series of colored blocks beneath it, perfectly capturing the hues found in the photo, ranging from the palest pink to deep forest green.

"What do you envision for a pattern?" Rachel asked.

"For these colors, I might choose a windowpane check pattern, using a combination of lambswool and cashmere. That will keep it light, but luxurious. I envision a fabric that would be perfect as a skirt or a spring jacket, or even a shawl."

"Lovely," Rachel murmured, fingering a skein of mauve lambswool. "It must be difficult to select the actual yarns, though. There are so many to choose from."

Fiona smiled. "Actually, that's the fun part. I bring my palette downstairs to where we store the yarns and make my selections from those that best match my photo." She indicated the assortment of skeins on the table. "These are the yarns I initially chose, but now I have to narrow them down to just five or six. More than that, and it might look a bit muddled."

"Seamus did show me the finished bolts of fabric, but I would love to see where the yarns are kept," Rachel said.

"Let's head down there," Fiona said, setting a swatch down on the table. "I'll show you the archives, too, where we keep a sample of every pattern that's ever been created here."

The yarn was stored in a large room adjacent to where the weaving looms were located, and entry to the room was allowed only after checking in with a woman at a nearby desk. Fiona had to raise her voice to be heard over the rhythmic pounding of the power looms.

"This is where we keep both our yarns and our archived

patterns. In order to retain control over our inventory and our proprietary patterns, this area is controlled," she explained. "We once hired a designer who was secretly working for a competitor, and several designs went missing before we realized what happened. Now, no one is allowed to remove any pattern sample from this room without authorization."

Rachel nodded. Lakeside Industries employed similar measures to protect their designs, so she understood. She looked around with interest. One wall of the room was fitted with a hundred or more wooden dowels and from each dowel hung a skein of yarn, identified by a tag.

"These are all the current yarns we have in stock," Fiona explained. "If I wanted to use a particular yarn, I would make note of the stock number on the tag. We also have a catalog, here, of the different yarns that are available to order from our suppliers, and we attend exhibitions several times a year to select new yarns and threads. Over here are the yarns that have already been loaded onto spindles and are ready to be moved into the weaving room."

She indicated a series of floor-to-ceiling steel shelves loaded with thick spindles of thread in every color imaginable. There were hundreds of spindles, each of them several feet long.

"Where does the yarn come from?" Rachel asked. "Is it all from Ireland?"

"Sadly, no. Most Irish wool is very rough and not suitable for clothing, although we do have a nice merino wool that we sell for handknitting. The bulk of our yarns are imported from New Zealand and Australia because it's longer and softer, and more suited to the luxury fabric we produce."

"I had no idea," Rachel said, surprised. "Most of my textile experience is with silks and satins and heavy cottons. I don't know as much about wool products or tweed. There are so many sheep in Ireland that I thought surely the wool was used to make the famous Irish sweaters and tweeds."

"Most Irish wool doesn't stay in Ireland, mainly because there are so few commercial wool processors in the country to clean the wool before spinning it into yarn. Our wool arrives cleaned and dyed and already spun, which allows us to concentrate on the weaving."

"But you also employ traditional handweavers, right?"

"We do, yeah. We have a dozen or so individuals located throughout Donegal who handweave the fabric in their homes."

"Do they dye the wool, as well?"

"No. The raw wool fiber is dyed at the source, before it arrives in Ireland," Fiona said. "The color is more consistent that way."

"So it's truly dyed-in-the-wool." Rachel indicated a door at the far end of the room. "What's through here?"

"Ah, that's our archives room." Fiona opened the door and ushered Rachel in. "This is where we store sample swatches of every fabric ever woven at McDermott Mills."

The room was long and narrow, and made even smaller by the tiered racks of fabric swatches that occupied either side of the room, from the floor to the ceiling. Each swatch was pinned to a hanger and identified with a numbered tag. Lifting one in her hand, Rachel saw the tag included the name of the pattern, the date it was created, the different yarns used in the weave, and the name of the designer.

"The swatches are organized by year," Fiona explained. "So the most recent fabrics are toward the front and they go back all the way to 1848."

Rachel made her way slowly through the room, running her fingers across the hanging swatches, marveling at the variety of colors and patterns. "How many designers have you had over the years?"

Fiona blew out a hard breath. "Oh, let me think. We have four designers here now, including myself, and I think that's been fairly standard for the past forty years or so."

"Do you think my father might have designed a pattern while he was here?"

"I'd say he likely did. Let's take a look, shall we? Do you know what year that was?"

"He was here in 1992, but I'm not sure which months."

Fiona moved through the racks, sifting through the swatches until she finally stopped, looking at the racks over her head. She pressed a button on the wall, and the racks of samples began to rotate downward.

"Here we are," she said. "This rack contains the swatches

from 1990 through 1995."

"Wonderful," Rachel said. "I don't want to take up any more of your time, but if you don't mind, maybe I could come down here on my own one day and look through the swatches."

"I'm sure that would be fine," Fiona said. "We create about one hundred new patterns in any given year, so you should be able to look through the entire year fairly quickly."

"My uncle Jack said my father had a natural talent for design," Rachel said. "His home textile patterns were very popular, and some of them are still in production."

"Can I ask how he died?"

"A heart attack," Rachel said, drawing in a deep breath. "He was only forty-one years old. He looked the picture of health, so nobody suspected his heart was a ticking time bomb, just waiting to go off."

"I'm so sorry. That must have been very hard for you and your mother."

Rachel gave a short laugh. "For me, certainly. I was just thirteen years old. For my mother? I'm not so sure. She remarried less than two years later and sent me off to boarding school so she could bond with her new husband."

"Oh," Fiona murmured. "I'm sorry."

Realizing she'd made Fiona uncomfortable, Rachel shook off the memories. "It was a long time ago. Well, thank you so much for showing this to me. I'll come back another day and look through the swatches. How wonderful if he did design something. I like to think there's something of my dad still here."

"I'm sure he would be very proud of you, following in his footsteps," Fiona said.

"I hope so. Did you always know you wanted to go into textile design?" Rachel asked as they made their way back to the design room.

"Not always," Fiona replied with a rueful smile. "As a teenager, I wanted to be a vet, but I can't bear to see an animal in distress, so that career was out. Then one day, my dad invited me along on a photo shoot at a castle, where these top models were wearing our clothes. The models were gorgeous, of course, but the clothing was even lovelier. Beautiful jackets and coats and skirts, and men's suits made of wool so fine and lightweight that you'd swear it was silk." She smiled. "I was hooked. I wanted to design fabrics that would be both beautiful and classic, that people would be proud to wear."

"Well, I would say you've more than succeeded," Rachel said. "Your designs are exquisite. I can't wait to see the whole design process. I'm looking forward to visiting the sheep farm as well."

Fiona paused, as if considering. "So you and Conall are going sightseeing tomorrow, are you?"

"Yes," Rachel said, caught off guard by the sudden change in topic. "Your father was the one who suggested it. I told Conall he didn't need to, but he insisted."

"Of course he did," Fiona said with a wry smile. "You're a pretty girl, and Ballylahane is a small, quiet town. Naturally, you'd catch his eye."

Okaaay. Rachel wasn't sure if she should be insulted or flattered.

"Conall has been nothing but kind to me. I'm not sure he's interested in me in the way you're implying." Rachel paused. "But even if he was, you sound as if you disapprove."

Fiona shook her head. "No, of course not. It's none of my business. I just don't want to see him get hurt."

Rachel didn't know how to respond. She was torn between indignation and embarrassment. "I'm here to learn about Donegal tweed," she finally said. "I'm not looking for a relationship."

"Good. Because Conall doesn't need to go through that again."

"Again?"

Fiona sighed. "Sorry. He wouldn't want me to tell you, but when he was studying at the university in Galway, he met a foreign exchange student and fell pretty hard for her. When the semester ended, she stayed on for the summer, presumably to see where the relationship might go. Everyone thought she and Conall would get engaged. She seemed keen on the idea of living in Ireland, but in the end, she went home. Back to Australia."

"Australia?" Rachel stared at Fiona with renewed interest. "He told me he once lived in Melbourne."

"Did he?" Fiona seemed surprised. "Interesting. He never talks about that time."

He hadn't wanted to talk about it that day in his shop, either, but now Rachel's curiosity was piqued. She wanted to know more. She wanted to know everything.

"So what happened? You said he was still in college. Did he do a semester in Australia in order to be with her?"

"No. He was in the middle of his last year of clinical training when she left. He couldn't have gone to Australia even if he wanted to." She paused. "He stayed and finished the program. He graduated with honors and the following day, he boarded a plane to Australia. He intended to work over there, since she didn't want to live in Ireland, but—" Fiona broke abruptly off, as if she'd said too much. "Anyway, I'd just hate to see him get hurt."

Rachel's smile was forced. "I understand. He's your cousin and you feel protective, and I get it. But you don't have to worry, because I'm not interested in Conall, except as a friend."

Even as the words left her mouth, something inside Rachel cringed, as if her subconscious knew she wasn't being truthful.

"I'm relieved to hear it." Fiona visibly relaxed. "I just— well, I thought you should know what he's been through."

"Of course. Thank you for telling me." She thought of a younger Conall, in love and filled with dreams for the future, and couldn't quite suppress a rush of something that felt very much like jealousy. Only that was crazy, because she barely knew Conall. She had no reason—and no right—to feel jealous about the mystery exchange student he'd once been involved with.

"Do you have a camera?" Fiona asked.

"I do. It's in my backpack, actually."

"Then take the afternoon off," Fiona suggested. She made a sweeping gesture toward the threads and fabric swatches on the table. "All of this will still be here on Monday. The weekend is here, it's a beautiful afternoon, and the sun is shining. Get outside and explore the area."

"Are you trying to get rid of me?" Rachel asked, narrowing her eyes in mock suspicion.

"Not at all, but what better way to find inspiration than in nature?"

"I don't have a car, and I wouldn't know where to begin," Rachel protested.

"Go out the back exit and you'll see a footbridge across the river. There's a walking path just on the other side," Fiona said encouragingly. "See where it takes you."

Rachel glanced at her watch. It was almost three o'clock, and she and Fiona had been at it since early that morning. "Okay, but only if you're sure."

"I'm sure!" Fiona laughed. "Go and enjoy yourself, but I want to see the photos on Monday."

"Okay, thanks." Grabbing her backpack, Rachel left the mill.

Outside, the sun was warm on her face and the breeze held the salty tang of the sea. Crossing the footbridge, she made her way along a paved bike path, stopping to snap pictures of the delicate pink flowers that grew in thick clusters along the hedgerow. The trail wound along the river behind town and meandered through a dense forest before it changed to packed earth and began to climb a low hill. Rachel caught occasional views of the bay and the ocean, shimmering blue and green in the sunlight. She took some pictures, framing the sea in the dark-green leafiness of the surrounding foliage. She snapped pictures of a fairy-tale thicket of ancient trees that seemed to float on a carpet of purple bluebells, of sheep grazing in the fields, and a white-washed cottage, clearly abandoned and overgrown with rhododendrons.

Eventually, the trail led back to town and into a small parking lot. From where she stood, Rachel could see the street where Conall's shop was located, as well as the sign for the McDermott Mills' retail shop and café. She began walking toward it when her phone vibrated in her pocket. Glancing at the display screen, she smiled and answered.

"Hey, Lori!" she said happily. "Miss me already?"

Her roommate for the past four years, Lori Woods was also Rachel's cousin and her best friend.

"I *do* miss you!" Lori wailed. "Please tell me you're miserable over there, surrounded by nothing but gorgeous green hills, fluffy sheep, and rainbows around every corner."

Rachel laughed, made her way to a bench outside the woolen shop, and sat down. "Well, I wouldn't say there's a rainbow around every bend, but it is pretty spectacular. Lori, there are these amazing cliffs that overlook the ocean, and my landlady has sheep in her front yard. And I fell down a boghole and probably would have died, except I was rescued by this really cute guy."

"Wait. What?" Lori exclaimed. "You've already met someone?"

Rachel rolled her eyes. "I'm fine, by the way, thanks for asking."

Lori laughed. "I'm glad, but more on the cute guy, please?"

Rachel described the incident, the walk she and Conall had taken to the clifftops, and Conall's invitation to join him for a weekend in Galway.

"I am so envious!" Lori enthused, but there was no animosity in her voice. "Leave it to you to find a tall, handsome ginger the first day you're there."

"Oh, come on," Rachel teased. "You have Seth Bieler."

Seth was a rising star at Lakeside Industries. He and Lori had been dating for several months, although she always denied there was anything serious between them.

"Oh, please," Lori said, and Rachel could almost see the eye roll. "He's handsome and he's smart, but he's probably just using me to get closer to my dad. You know how much he wants a promotion."

"Not the commodities manager position?" Rachel asked in disbelief. "No way. Your dad knows how much you want that job, and how perfect you would be for it. He'd never even consider Seth."

"Yes, well, my father won't even give me an official job title," Lori complained. "I'm just his assistant—his go-to girl when he needs something done."

"And you've done everything perfectly," Rachel assured her. "You've proven your worth over and over again, so don't even worry."

"Well, I do have some exciting news," Lori said. "Guess where I am right now!"

At that moment, the door to the woolen shop opened and Conall McDermott stepped onto the sidewalk, the sunlight picking out the highlights in his bright hair. Seeing her on the bench, a smile creased his handsome face.

"Lori, I'm sorry, but I need to go," Rachel said, lowering her voice. "You-know-who just showed up."

"Mr. Red-Hot?" Lori squeaked. "Okay, but call me as soon as you're done talking with him."

"I will," she promised, and disconnected the call.

Looking up, she gave Conall a wide smile. "Fancy meeting you here!"

"I thought you'd still be working."

"I am. Sort of. Fiona gave me the afternoon off to take some work-related, inspirational photos." She lifted her camera from where it still hung around her neck. "I've just walked the entire path from the mill to that parking lot over there."

"That's a good five kilometers," Conall observed. "Did you get anything good?"

"Tons of photos, actually. Lots of beautiful flowers."

"Yeah, it's a gorgeous time of year. Right now, the pink sea thrift is just beginning to bloom along the cliffs. It's spectacular."

"That sounds lovely." She stood up. "Well, I won't keep you. Are we still on for tomorrow?"

"Of course. What are you doing now?"

She indicated the door to the woolen shop. "I was just going to check out the store."

"Are you thirsty after your walk?"

"I am, actually."

"Great." He looked at his phone. "I don't have to be back at the shop right away. Come with me."

"Where?"

"You'll see."

Chapter Five

RACHEL FOLLOWED CONALL into the shop, wondering what he was up to. The interior was cozy, with wide-plank wooden floors, whitewashed stone walls, and tempting stacks of soft woolen scarves and wraps. The walls were lined with racks of tweed jackets and skirts and outerwear in every hue and pattern imaginable. Sales clerks greeted them cheerfully, but Rachel had no time to stop and admire anything, as Conall was already bounding up a wide staircase at the back of the shop. A sign above the stairwell read The Yarn Spinner's Café, and Rachel caught whiffs of coffee and baked goods.

The café was an intimate, sun-drenched oasis of wooden tables and chairs. Along one wall was a long counter with a multitiered display case stuffed with cakes, muffins, scones, and a variety of other delicious-looking baked goods. Chalk-board menus listed salads, sandwiches, and hot meals with ingredients like baby prawns and Donegal rooster potatoes. The café was doing a brisk business, with most of the small tables occupied, but Conall found them a spot near the tall windows that overlooked the river.

"I had no idea this was here," Rachel said as she slid out of her backpack and sat down, laying her camera on the surface of the table.

"I come here just about every day for lunch," Conall admitted with a grin. "I love the vegetable soup, and the flatbreads are good too. What will you have?"

"Have you already eaten?"

"I have, yeah, but no worries. I don't mind keeping you company while you have something."

Rachel perused the menu. "In that case, I'll have the blueberry scone with lemon glaze, and a side of raspberry jam and clotted cream. And a cappuccino."

"Right. Let me get that for you."

"Wait." She rummaged through her backpack and found her wallet. "Here," she said, handing him a ten-euro bill. "Take this, no arguing."

She was glad when he didn't object, but took her money and stepped away to place her order. While he did that, she scrolled through the pictures she had taken. Some of them had come out quite well, including the sweet little abandoned cottage and the carpet of bluebells in the forest.

"Here you are," Conall said as he set a tray down on the edge of the table and proceeded to place her scone and coffee in front of her. He had ordered a cappuccino for himself, and as he stowed the tray and sat down across from her, he placed a small pile of money next to her plate. "There's your change. I did pay for my own coffee."

"I wish you had let me pay for it," Rachel said, giving him a stern look. "After everything you've done for me, a cup of coffee is the very least I could do in return."

"If you really want to do something," he said, slanting her a speculative glance as he stirred his cappuccino, "then have dinner with me one night next week."

Rachel hadn't expected that and took a moment to round up her startled thoughts, focusing instead on splitting the scone and spreading one half with clotted cream and thick jam.

"Really?" she finally said, looking at him. "We already have plans to go sightseeing tomorrow."

"And your point is?" He leaned back in his chair, cradling his cup in his big hands as he watched her. A smile lurked in one corner of his mouth and the expression in his blue eyes sent her heart into a happy skip. Rachel felt her reservations slide off the table. But recalling her earlier conversation with Fiona, she felt she had to say something.

"You might be tired of my company after dragging me around for an afternoon. You might be happy to drop me off at Mrs. O'Leary's once our sightseeing is over. You might decide you never want to spend another minute in my company, but because you're too polite to cancel a dinner date, you'll be trapped."

Conall laughed, and his blue eyes crinkled in the nicest way. "Okay, I somehow don't think I'm going to feel trapped." He sobered and studied her face for a moment.

"It's just dinner, Rachel."

"I just don't want you to think—"

Conall leaned forward. "You don't have to say it. *I know.* In three months, you'll return to Chicago. I get it. But for now, at least, you're here, and I'd like to spend time with you. Do you really enjoy having dinner by yourself?"

"Honestly? No, but I've traveled on my own before, and I don't mind my own company." Impulsively, she reached out and put a hand on his arm, but he'd pushed his shirt-sleeves back and the contact with his warm skin was electric enough that she swiftly pulled her fingers back. "I just don't want you to think you need to entertain me."

Conall looked amused, as if he'd guessed the reason for her abrupt withdrawal. "I don't do anything unless I want to, but if you'd rather not—"

"No," Rachel interrupted. "I want to, I do!"

She wanted to spend time with Conall. She really did. But she also knew she was in danger of liking him too much. Even now, there was no mistaking the satisfaction in his blue eyes and Rachel felt a small thrill of awareness shoot through her.

"Good," he murmured, and lifted his coffee. "Then it's settled."

RACHEL WOKE TO the sound of rain drumming against the

windows of her room at the B&B and, looking outside, was disheartened to see sullen gray skies and a steady downpour. Certain her outing with Conall would be canceled, she was marginally heartened when the rain slowly subsided over the course of the morning, leaving behind a moody, leaden sky and drifts of fog that wafted over the hills like ghostly vapors.

"He'll not cancel your plans on account of a bit of rain," Mrs. O'Leary assured her over breakfast. "This is a soft day."

Seeing Rachel's confused expression, she'd gone on to explain. "A soft day is when the rain is misty to the point of being invisible, yet the air feels wet. There's a hazy sort of cloud, but the temperature isn't too cold. This is fine weather for the west of Ireland."

So Rachel had pulled on a pair of waterproof boots she'd purchased during a college trip she'd made with Lori to the Maine coast, and a lightweight anorak over a warm sweater. She pulled her dark hair into a simple ponytail and stuffed a small backpack with a few snacks, bottled water, her good digital camera, and a zoom lens. As an afterthought, she added a pair of sunglasses. She was nothing if not an optimist.

To her surprise, Conall arrived in a rugged, white Range Rover with meaty tires. "I switched vehicles with my dad this morning. This one will do better on the back roads than my car, especially in this weather," he explained. He took one look at her boots and turned quickly away, but not before Rachel saw the grin he tried to hide.

"What?"

"Nothing," he said, his voice rich with amusement. He glanced back at her feet. "What on earth are you wearing?"

Rachel stuck out one foot. "These are my duck boots. You don't like them? They're very popular in the States."

"I'll take your word for it," he said, and his mouth curved into a smile.

That smile did something to Rachel—made her feel as if someone had switched on a heat lamp inside her chest, because despite the raw, chilly day, she suddenly felt warm all over. She ran a swift eye over him, looking for something—anything—to tease him about in return, but could find nothing. In fact, he looked heart-stoppingly handsome in a charcoal cable-knit sweater and a pair of well-worn blue jeans that hugged his backside and muscular thighs in all the right ways. He wore a pair of lace-up hiking boots with a lug-sole and looked deliciously outdoorsy and masculine. Rachel could easily picture him steering a fishing vessel on the stormy Irish Sea, or walking the windswept cliffs that overlooked the Wild Atlantic Way. With his bright hair and blue eyes and a scrub of coppery stubble on his square jaw, he could easily have been a model for the Donegal tweed his family produced in their mill. Rachel felt suddenly, unexpectedly shy.

"You look . . . nice," she finally said.

"Thanks, you do as well."

"Except for the boots, of course."

"Except for the boots," he agreed cheerfully. "But if any-one can pull those off, you can."

Rachel laughed as he opened the passenger door for her. "I'm not sure if that was a compliment or not."

She climbed into the Range Rover, but before Conall closed the door, he leaned in and grabbed her gaze. "With you, Rachel Woods, it's always a compliment. Never doubt it."

Then he closed the car door, leaving Rachel to feel both absurdly pleased and more than a little alarmed. Despite her resolve to keep their relationship firmly in the friend zone, she couldn't deny the pull of attraction, like the tug of an outgoing tide, eroding the firm ground beneath her feet. If she wasn't careful, she would lose her footing and get sucked in.

"Where are we going?" she asked as he started the engine and steered the vehicle through town and then onto a narrow road that wound its way deeper into the countryside.

"Well, I initially thought I'd take you to see the caves at Maghera Strand, with a stop along the way to see the Kilclooney Dolmen, but I think we'll save that for another day. The caves are best viewed when the weather is a bit warmer." He glanced at his watch. "We should arrive in under an hour."

"Arrive where?"

Conall glanced at her and waggled his eyebrows. "The most spectacular spot in all of Ireland, in my opinion. And on a day like today, there won't be many tourists. If the mists clear, you won't be disappointed."

Rachel suppressed a smile. "But you're not going to tell me the name of where we're going?"

"Have you heard of Slieve League?"

Rachel shook her head. "I don't think so."

"How about the Cliffs of Moher?"

"Of course. They're iconic."

"Slieve League has some of the highest sea cliffs in Ireland, three times higher than the Cliffs of Moher. Don't get me wrong, the Cliffs of Moher are fantastic, but Slieve League is truly a natural wonder."

"Why haven't I heard of them?"

Conall shrugged. "Most tourists don't come this far north. They tend to focus on the southern part of the country and rarely travel much beyond Galway. The Ring of Kerry is gorgeous and the weather tends to be more cooperative in the south, but in my opinion, the northwestern part of Ireland is where you'll find the most stunning scenery."

Looking out the window, Rachel had to agree with him. They passed rough, rolling bogland dotted with sheep, while low, craggy mountains loomed in the distance. Patches of sun occasionally broke through the cloud cover, illuminating the countryside in patches of sunlight.

"Look," Conall said, pointing through the windshield.

A rainbow arched over the roadway ahead of them, high and bright. "Fluffy sheep and rainbows around every corner," Rachel murmured.

"Beg your pardon?" Conall slanted her a questioning look.

"Oh, it's something Lori said to me on the phone the other day. She said I must be miserable over here, surrounded by nothing but gorgeous green hills, fluffy sheep, and rainbows."

"Who is Lori?"

"She's my cousin and also my roommate in Chicago. We're probably closer than most sisters, actually."

"It's great when your best friends are also family," Conall said. "Do you have brothers or sisters?"

"No. After my dad died, my mother remarried pretty quickly, but they didn't have any kids. I think they prefer it that way."

Which was an understatement. Her mother had focused all her energy and attention on her new husband in the months following their wedding, and Rachel had felt like an outsider. Her stepfather, Mike, had taken a hands-off approach to parenting, saying he didn't want to replace her father. He hadn't been unkind, just uninvolved. When they'd decided to move to Arizona just six months after the wedding, Rachel had begged them to let her stay in Chicago. Her mother had initially refused, but her objections had seemed half-hearted. Mike, not surprisingly, had supported Rachel's request, and her mother had finally relented and enrolled her in a girls' boarding school not far from where her uncle lived with his family. After boarding school, she'd lived with Lori while she went to college, and the arrangement had worked out so well that neither of them had ever considered getting their own place.

"What about you?" she asked. "Do you have siblings?"

"I do, yeah. A younger brother and sister, both at university."

"What are they studying?"

"Shane is in the marine biology program at the university in Galway, and my sister, Breena, is studying literature and creative writing in Dublin."

"Wow, very impressive," Rachel said. "What about your mom?"

"She teaches Irish language at a local primary school."

"Do you speak Irish?"

He gave her a chagrined look. "A bit, but not as well as I should, as my mum is quick to remind me. I can understand it better than I can speak it."

"Say something for me."

He gave a huff of self-conscious laughter. "What would you have me say?"

Rachel shrugged. "I don't know—anything."

He seemed to consider for a moment. "Alright. *Táim sásta go bhfuil tú anseo.*"

To Rachel, the strange, lilting words seemed to fall easily from his lips. "That sounded beautiful. What does it mean?"

He glanced at her. "It means, *I'm happy you're here.*"

"Oh." Rachel smiled. "I'm happy too."

She realized it was no less than the truth. Despite the melancholy weather and the iron-gray clouds that skittered across the horizon, she was happy in Conall's company. When eventually they turned onto a narrow road with tall hedgerows on either side, she sat up a little straighter in her seat. She couldn't see over the hedges, and the road was barely wide enough for the Range Rover to pass. Several times, branches brushed against the side mirrors.

"What happens if we meet a car coming in the other direction?" she asked.

"No worries," Conall assured her. "There are occasional pull-offs, and one or the other car simply backs up until there's room to pass."

As if to prove his words, they came to a break in the hedgerow, where the road widened just enough for a car to pull off to the side. But they didn't see another vehicle for the next mile or so, when the hedges suddenly gave way to low stone walls bordering wide open fields filled with yet more sheep. In the distance, Rachel saw a dark-blue strip of ocean. The road was still narrow, and Rachel found herself clutching the door handle as it grew ever more steep and winding, climbing upward at seemingly impossible angles. As Conall maneuvered the Range Rover around one hairpin bend, Rachel realized they were approaching the sea cliffs he had spoken of. Between craggy outcroppings of rock, she could see flashes of the ocean. Then the road widened unexpectedly to reveal large parking lots on either side and a small stone building at the center of it all. Beyond the parking lots, a paved road climbed steeply into the hills. Conall glanced at his watch.

"We're still early. The visitor's center hasn't opened yet."

As they approached the building, an elderly man with a bright orange vest came out to greet them. He and Conall exchanged a few words, and the man waved them through.

"They just built the visitor's center a few years ago, but with COVID, this is the first year it's been open," Conall explained as he thrust the Range Rover into gear. "Before that, the road was just gravel and anyone could drive to the top. Now everyone is required to park down here and hike up, unless you have a disabled badge on your vehicle."

"Oh, well I can hike up," Rachel protested. "He shouldn't give us special treatment."

"It's no problem," Conall assured her. "They aren't likely to get many visitors this early in the morning and you'll be glad for the car if the rain doesn't let up."

Rachel was thankful they were driving, as they negotiated the first steep incline. Rounding a curve, she saw the road continued to wind upward until it disappeared around a bend in the distance.

"How far is it to the cliffs?"

"Nearly three kilometers." He glanced at her. "Still wished we had hiked up?"

"No," she admitted. "My ears are popping from the altitude."

Her first distant view nearly took her breath away. Soaring majestically out of the churning sea and topped with verdant green, they were an awe-inspiring sight.

"Look at that!" she exclaimed in delight, then, "No, don't look! Keep your eyes on the road!"

"I see it," Conall replied, laughing. "And as long as you don't make any unexpected movements, I'll try not to drive off a cliff."

Realizing she had grabbed his arm in her excitement, she quickly pulled her hand back. "Sorry!"

"No, don't be. I'm just teasing you. You're safe with me."

Rachel realized it was true; she did feel safe with Conall. They reached a fork in the narrow road with a sign that pointed one way toward a cliff walk, and another way toward a viewing point. "Which way?"

Peering through the windshield, Conall seemed to consider for a moment. "The weather is still a bit damp, and the ground is likely to be slick. I'd rather not risk the cliff walk, as the wind gusts can be tricky on a day like today. We'll have a great view from the parking lot."

He turned left toward the viewing point and they drove until they reached a livestock gate that was closed, blocking any access to the road beyond. Conall thrust the vehicle into park.

"I'll just be a second," he said, and jumped out.

Rachel watched as he opened the gate, before returning to drive the Range Rover through, and then climbing out again to close the gate behind them.

"That's to keep the sheep away from the cliffs," he explained. In another minute, they reached a second parking lot that seemed to sit literally on the cliffs' edge. Conall pulled into a spot. There were several food trucks parked along the perimeter of the lot, all of them closed.

"Looks like we have the place to ourselves for now," he remarked, glancing around.

"You were right," Rachel breathed in awe, staring out at the cliffs. "This is unbelievable."

Grabbing her backpack, she pulled her camera out and changed the lens before climbing out of the vehicle. The wind nearly knocked her over, and she leaned against the Range Rover for support as she pulled her hood up and slipped the camera strap over her head.

"Here, hold on to me," Conall said. "There's a walking path over there, and you'll get some great shots."

Leading her onto the path, he put himself closest to the cliffs' edge and kept her on the inside, where it was safer. Billowing bunches of pink sea thrift carpeted the grass on either side of the path and grew in thick clumps on the rocky ledges. A gusty blast of wind caused her to stumble and Conall quickly reached out to steady her. For a moment, she simply clung to him, spellbound by the expression in his blue eyes. When his gaze dropped to her mouth, Rachel thought he might actually kiss her, but he seemed to recollect himself and released her.

"These trails can be tricky when the wind is gusting," he said. "You should hold on to me."

Rachel did, grateful for the solid support of his arm. They picked their way along the trail until they came to viewing platform with a sturdy railing, where they had unobstructed views of the bluffs in either direction. The cliffs themselves were ragged and rocky, jutting in and out of the surf. There were several coves with pebbled beaches far below them, but Rachel could see no way to get down to them. Seagulls wheeled and cried on the air currents while the gusty wind carried the salty tang of the sea, and far below, she could hear the roar of the surf as it battered the rocks. All in all, the experience was overwhelming and wonderful, and Rachel knew it was something she would never forget.

"Thank you, Conall!"

He looked at her in surprise. "For what?"

"For this." She gestured expansively with her free arm. "It's amazing!"

He smiled warmly at her. "I'm glad you're enjoying it. Here, there's a picnic table where you can sit and safely take photos."

The wooden table was perched close enough to the edge that Rachel could sit on top and snap pictures to her heart's content. As she switched out her lens, Conall moved away from her to stand near the edge, his hands pushed deep into his pockets. The wind buffeted him and ruffled through his hair, and he turned his face into the gusty blasts. Wearing only his Irish knit sweater, he seemed impervious to the elements. Quickly, before he noticed, Rachel snapped several pictures of him with the cliffs and the blue-green sea providing a dramatic backdrop. Just as she was about to turn her camera away, the clouds parted and a shaft of sunlight turned Conall's hair to flame. He turned his head and looked at her.

Click, click, click.

She turned the lens reluctantly away and instead snapped pictures of the cliffs, the seabirds in flight, the sheep grazing in the distance, and the pink flowers that grew in abundance everywhere she looked. She wanted it all. She wanted to bottle the memory and tuck it away so that when she was back in the concrete city of Chicago, she could pull it out and remember what this day had been like, and how she had felt perched on the edge of the world.

She felt as if she had finally come home.

Chapter Six

A S THEY RETURNED to the Range Rover, Rachel felt numb with cold. The unrelenting wind seemed to have penetrated both her jacket and her sweater and settled into her bones. Climbing into the driver's seat, Conall turned on the engine as Rachel briskly rubbed her hands together.

"It'll be warm in no time. Here, this might help." He leaned toward her and for one wild, crazy second, Rachel actually thought he might embrace her—or kiss her—and her heart leaped in anticipation. She actually leaned forward to meet him halfway, but instead, he reached behind her seat and produced a small, soft-sided lunch container. After unzipping it, he withdrew a thermos and two travel mugs. "I brought along some hot coffee, thinking we might need something to warm us up. Interested?"

"Yes, please." Feeling foolish, and hoping he hadn't noticed how she'd practically welcomed an advance, she watched as he poured steaming coffee into one of the mugs before he covered it with a lid and handed it to her. "Thank you. That was very thoughtful of you."

"Of course." He smiled and poured another mug for

himself. "Cheers, or *slainte*."

"*Slainte*."

Wind buffeted the Range Rover as heat blasted from the air vents. They sipped their coffee in silence as they contemplated the ocean and the cliffs.

"Oh!" Rachel set her mug in the center coffee holder. "I almost forgot. I have snacks if you're hungry."

"I'm always hungry."

Grateful for something to do, Rachel opened her backpack and withdrew the candy bars and snack-sized bags of crackers and chips she had packed that morning. "Sorry it's not something healthier."

"How about we find somewhere to grab some real food?" He gave her a meaningful look. "And this does not count as the dinner date I asked for yesterday."

Rachel felt her cheeks go pink beneath his regard. "Fine. Maybe somewhere with a fireplace." Feeling warmer, Rachel shrugged out of her windbreaker and placed it on the back seat. "Do you have somewhere in mind?"

"I do, yeah," Conall said, unzipping his own jacket and following her example. "It's about an hour or so from here. Can you hold out that long?"

Unwrapping a candy bar, Rachel held it up and then took a bite. "I believe I can."

Conall chuckled and thrust the Range Rover into gear. After passing through the livestock gate and maneuvering along the cliff road, Conall turned on the radio and Rachel

KAREN FOLEY

hummed along to a familiar song as they drove through the country. The weather had partially cleared and she enjoyed the views of the sheep in the fields, along with the occasional horse and donkey.

They'd been driving for less than thirty minutes when Conall pulled the Range Rover to the side of the road and switched off the engine. Looking out, Rachel caught her breath at the sheer beauty of the scenery. They were parked at the entrance to a long, deep valley, where lushly green hills rose steeply on either of side of a narrow, winding road. Patchy sunlight illuminated the peaks in some places while wisps of fog rolled across others.

Rachel climbed out of the car and stood beside a low stone wall, just taking it all in. Tiny cottages dotted the hillsides and she could just make out a small village several miles away, at the far end of the valley.

"This is incredible," she said as Conall came to stand beside her. "I feel like we're in the Scottish Highlands."

"This is Glengesh Pass, also known as Glen of the Swans." At her inquiring look, he shrugged. "I've no idea why. All I know is the valley was carved out during the Ice Age."

"Can we drive through?"

"Yeah, that's the plan," he assured her with a smile. "We're headed to the town of Ardara on the far side of the valley."

He pronounced the town as *Ard-RA*, rolling the r's in the

way Rachel had come to love. "Is that where we're having dinner?"

"There's a pub that's quite good," he said. "Nothing fancy, but if my memory is correct, there is a fireplace and they serve the best seafood chowder in County Donegal."

"Sounds perfect." Rachel retrieved her camera and snapped some pictures of the valley, admiring the contrast and variation of the deep-green hills against the pewter skies. "Look at those colors! I'm hoping I can use some of these photos as inspiration."

"For what?"

Rachel lowered the camera and smiled at him. "I'm going to design my own Donegal tweed pattern."

"Ah. Well, that's something special, isn't it? Maybe the start of something big. Just think—I'll be able to say I knew you when."

Rachel fiddled with the cap on the camera lens, uncertain how to respond. Even if her tweed pattern was a hit, it would be just one of hundreds of McDermott tweeds, and it wasn't as if she was going to create more than two or three patterns in the short time she was here. She had a career waiting for her in Chicago, and she enjoyed designing upholstery and drapery fabrics. Even if the photographs she took didn't lend themselves to creating a tweed design, she would always have them to remind her of this day. She would take this experience—this amazing, awe-inspiring day—and tuck it away in her memory bank to treasure when she was back home.

"Yes," she finally said, looking at him. "It's pretty special."

THE TOWN OF Ardara was more than twice the size of Ballylahane, the main road crowded with brightly painted shops and pubs, and dominated by the four-story Nesbitt Arms Hotel.

"Ardara is where most of the wool coming into the country from New Zealand and Australia is processed," Conall informed her, as he parked the Range Rover. "The town is known as the Tweed Capital of Donegal. You'll want to come back one day and visit the Ardara Heritage Center, a museum dedicated to the production of Irish tweed."

"You've obviously been there," Rachel observed.

"Oh, yeah. It's practically a required day trip during primary school, but very interesting."

"I'd love to see that."

As they made their way along the sidewalk, past woolen shops and pubs, Rachel found herself transfixed by the colorful little town. Festive banners in the Irish colors of green and orange had been strung over the streets and flapped gaily in the wind, while large flags fluttered from the storefronts and over the entry of the hotel.

"Are they getting ready for a festival?"

"Funny you should ask, because Ardara is also called the

Festival Capital of Donegal," Conall said, steering her deftly out of the way of a group of teenagers who were excitedly talking into their smartphones. "You just missed the Ardara Walking Festival last week, and I think the next one is the Cup of Tae festival, which is actually a music festival and not much to do with tea."

"Wow, the tweed capital *and* the festival capital?" Rachel laughed. "Sounds like a perfect combination. When is the Cup of Tae festival?"

"I'll check the dates, but I think you may already have returned to the States by then."

They were both silent for a moment.

"Bad timing on my part," she said, her tone regretful.

They reached a door front and even before Conall pushed it open, Rachel could hear lively music and voices from inside. The pub was cozy and dark and had an old-world feel. The main room was filled with noisy conversation and laughter, and a small group of musicians sat at a corner table playing an Irish tune on three fiddles and an accordion. The pub smelled deliciously of savory food and smoky wood.

"Over here," Conall said, indicating a snug booth near the fireplace, where the current occupants were just leaving. He gave Rachel a conspiratorial wink. "Now that's what I call perfect timing."

He exchanged some friendly words with the other party, and then helped Rachel remove her jacket before she slid into the booth, eyeing the fire with appreciation. Conall sat

KAREN FOLEY

down across from her and pushed the empty beer glasses to
the edge of the table.

"Absolutely perfect," Rachel agreed, beaming at him.

He pulled a menu from the stand and perused it. "What
would you like to drink?"

"A pint of Guinness, of course, and I'll try the seafood
chowder since you recommended it."

"That's my girl."

Something hot and bright radiated through Rachel at his
words, warming her in a way the nearby fire never could.

My girl.

He hadn't meant it literally, of course, but she suddenly
wondered what it would be like to be his girl, his love, the
one he would do anything for. She felt a stab of envy toward
the unknown exchange student he had once fallen in love
with and wondered what had happened to make their
relationship fall apart.

A waitress appeared, interrupting her musings. As she
cleared their table, Conall chatted with her before giving her
their request for drinks and food. After she left, he pushed
the sleeves of his sweater up, revealing strong forearms
liberally dusted with cinnamon hair. He wore a braided
leather band around one wrist. His hands were big and
square, with long fingers and neatly trimmed nails. Rachel
had always had a thing for a man's hands—they were one of
the first things she noticed when she met someone new—
and Conall's hands surpassed her standards. She watched as

he picked up the salt shaker and turned it over in his fingers. She had noticed his tendency toward touching things—herself included—that made her think he was a tactile person. Was that part of his reason for becoming a doctor? The ability to work with his hands to do something good and meaningful? For a brief instant, she imagined his hands on her.

"What are you thinking about?" he asked. "You seem lost in thought."

Rachel flushed, very glad he couldn't read her thoughts. "I was just thinking what a perfect afternoon this has been. Thank you for showing me the cliffs, and for—for this. I know you don't have a lot of free time, so it means a lot that you'd spend your afternoon taking me around."

His blue eyes warmed as he gave her an indulgent smile. "Yeah, it was a real hardship for me. I would much rather have been out running in the cold and wet, or sitting by myself in my house, bored out of my mind."

"Have you always liked running?"

Conall's mouth quirked. "My mum says I was born with runners on my feet."

Rachel laughed, picturing a high-energy little boy with bright hair and an irrepressible grin. "I can almost believe that."

"If there was a sport that involved running, I did it. Rugby, hurling, football—I loved them all. Then, when I was fourteen, I ran my first marathon and I was hooked." He shrugged. "Never thought I'd carve a career out of it, but here I am."

They were interrupted by the waitress, who returned with two tall pints of foaming Guinness, two bowls of steaming chowder, and a plate heaped with homemade brown bread and whipped butter.

"There you go," she said, her smile including both of them. "Will you be needing anything else?"

"No, we're perfect," Conall assured her.

Rachel suppressed a smile at his choice of words and reached for her beer instead. "To a perfect day."

"Absolutely." Conall clinked his pint against hers.

Rachel took a sip of the rich, creamy stout. "Oh, wow, this is delicious."

But the beer paled in comparison to the chowder, which was rich and savory and loaded with fresh seafood. As they ate, they chatted easily about a variety of things. Rachel found Conall to be an entertaining and well-informed companion, relating humorous anecdotes from his own life and interspersing their conversation with interesting tidbits of Irish history. She couldn't remember the last time she had laughed so much.

"I spent several summers working on a fishing trawler," he said as he finished his chowder and slid the bowl to one side.

"Did you enjoy it?"

"On good days, yeah, it was great. But we'd go out even

when the weather was foul and the seas were rough, and then it could be really brutal."

Rachel had a vivid image of Conall at sea, looking rugged and manly in his foul weather gear as he hauled in the catch. "What did you fish for?"

"Mackerel, mostly. Some herring and blue whiting. I'll take you to Killybegs one day. It's not far. It's the largest fishing port in Ireland and is quite impressive. But it's a tough way to make a living. I have a massive amount of respect for fishermen."

"Well, I'm glad you decided to choose a different career path."

Conall laughed. "I had no choice about it, really. Every time the sea turned rough, I'd go green around the gills. Not much use for a crew member who's always hanging over the rails."

"Oh, no!" Rachel stared at him, and then burst out laughing herself. "That's terrible!"

"It was, yeah." He grinned. "It was years before I could eat mackerel again. Just the smell made me queasy."

"You said you did it for two summers. Why did you go back if you knew you were prone to seasickness?"

Conall shrugged. "I guess I had something to prove. But there was no getting over it, and I had to finally admit I wasn't cut out for the work." He chuckled. "If I hadn't left on my own, I likely would have been fired."

There was no bitterness or regret in his tone, only a wry

humor that Rachel found infinitely appealing. "So what made you go into podiatry? That seems an unusual career path for someone who doesn't actually want to perform foot surgeries."

"I suppose it is. I've played football and rugby since I was a kid, and I've always followed the professional teams. I began to realize how many foot injuries athletes sustain, and—" He broke off, looking a little sheepish. "I had this idea that I could be a team doctor or sports therapist on one of the national teams. My grades were good, so I went through the program, but I needed clinical experience if I wanted to work for a sports team. I opened a practice in Dublin, but it wasn't long before I knew my real passion was long-distance running."

"But couldn't you do both?"

"I could, yeah, but after working in a clinic, I knew foot care wasn't what I wanted to do. Opening a running shop just seemed to make sense." He gave a rueful laugh. "My family thought I was mad and maybe I was, but luckily it all worked out."

"Weren't you scared to make such a drastic change?" Rachel asked. "I mean, you'd put so much time and effort into your medical degree."

Conall shrugged. "I was nervous, I won't lie. But I couldn't see myself doing something that didn't fulfill me. Life's too short not to chase your dreams. There was a learning curve involved, but luckily I'm a quick study and I met some great people in the industry who helped me get started." He gestured with his hands. "And here I am."

Rachel felt a surge of admiration for this man who had chosen to pursue his dream rather than conform to the expectations of others.

"What about you?" he asked. "Did you always know you wanted to go into textile design?"

Rachel considered his question. "Not always. In fact, I don't think I really considered it until after my dad died. He loved it so much, and he was always designing something. I loved to just sit and watch him sketch out his ideas. I think I initially went into the business because it made me feel closer to him, but then I fell in love with it too. I did several trips to India and Pakistan to watch raw materials like silk and cotton being produced, which was an amazing experience." She smiled at him. "And now here I am in Ireland, learning about Donegal tweed."

To her surprise, Conall didn't seem all that enthralled with her story. A rueful half smile lifted one corner of his mouth and he gave her a resigned look. "Yeah, here you are."

For three months, and then you'll leave.

He didn't have to say the words out loud for her to know he was thinking them. At the end of three months, she would return to Chicago and they would likely never see each other again. She found the thought oddly depressing.

"About tomorrow," she ventured, hoping to ease some of the tension in the air. She was wading into treacherous waters and she knew it, but she didn't care for this somber side of him. She'd rather throw caution to the wind and accept whatever he chose to offer, and deal with the consequences later. They still had three months, after all.

"Ah, right," Conall said, visibly brightening. "I offered to collect some bolts of cloth from the local handweavers and thought you might be interested in riding along. Seamus mentioned that you wanted to see the handweaving process, and the scenery isn't too bad, either."

If the scenery only included Conall McDermott, Rachel thought she would be completely satisfied. "I would love to join you."

"Great. I'll come round about half eleven if that works."

"I'll be ready."

When the waitress brought their tab, Conall picked it up before she could see the amount.

"Please, let me pay my share," Rachel insisted, reaching for her wallet.

"No, this one is on me." The look he gave her brooked no argument, and Rachel sank back in her chair and watched as he counted out several bills and laid them on top of the tab. He peered out the window to where the clouds had once more begun to gather and thicken. "Looks like rain; we should probably head back."

The drive to Ballylahane took no more than thirty minutes, but by the time he drew the Range Rover to a stop in front of the B&B, rain had begun to fall in earnest.

"Hang on," he said. "I'll grab an umbrella from the back and see you to the door."

"No, please," Rachel protested. "I don't need an umbrella." To prove her point, she opened the door and prepared to climb out, pausing to look at Conall. "Thanks. I had a really nice day."

"Yeah. Me too." He leaned across the center console and looked at her with such intensity that Rachel felt her heart stutter. "Rachel—"

Whatever words he might have said were lost as the door to the B&B was thrown open and a woman ran out into the pelting downpour with an umbrella over her head.

"Finally!" she cried. "You're back."

Rachel stared in stunned disbelief at her cousin, Lori Woods. How was it possible that her best friend was standing there in the rain, grinning at her like a fool?

"Lori?" she finally managed. "What are you doing here?"

In answer, Lori threw an arm wide and laughed. "Surprise! I'm your new roommate."

For a moment, Rachel was too surprised to speak, but as Lori stood beneath her umbrella, looking expectantly between her and Conall, she managed to pull herself together.

"Conall, this is my cousin, Lori Woods. Lori, this is Conall McDermott."

Stepping into the open passenger door, Lori thrust one hand toward Conall. "It's such a pleasure to meet you." She beamed, her eyes sparkling with interest. "I've heard so much about you and how you rescued Rachel."

"*Lori*," Rachel protested softly.

But Conall only laughed and leaning across Rachel, he shook Lori's hand. "It's great to meet you. How long are you here for?"

"I'm not sure." Lori shrugged. "A few weeks maybe?"

"Then I'm sure we'll see each other again." Conall turned to Rachel. "We can take a raincheck for tomorrow."

Disappointment, fierce and sharp, stabbed through her. She wanted to argue, but knew that would look bad when her cousin had only just arrived. But before she could reply, Lori intervened.

"A raincheck for what?"

"Nothing," Rachel assured her.

"We were planning to visit some handweavers in the country tomorrow," Conall said.

"Oh, well, don't cancel on my account," Lori replied. "Honestly, I can entertain myself and I'll probably be too jet-lagged to do anything besides sleep. Rachel, you should definitely go."

"Are you sure?" Rachel knew she should feel guilty about leaving Lori on her own, but she really wanted to spend the day with Conall. Besides which, she hadn't known Lori would show up unannounced.

"I absolutely insist," Lori said.

Conall laughed. "Okay, then, but it's no problem if you

change your mind. I'll come by at half eleven."

"I won't, but thank you just the same. It was nice meeting you, Conall."

Rachel climbed out of the vehicle and joined Lori beneath the umbrella. "Thank you," she breathed, before turning back to wave goodbye to Conall.

"Wow," Lori said as they watched the Range Rover rumble away. "If I fall into a boghole, do I get one of those too?"

"Sorry," Rachel said cheerfully. "I'm beginning to think he's one of a kind."

Chapter Seven

"I JUST TALKED to you yesterday. Why didn't you tell me you were coming here?" Rachel demanded as she sat on the bed with her legs tucked beneath her and watched Lori rummage through her small suitcase.

Lori threw her a tolerant look. "Okay, well, you cut me off and hung up before I could tell you that I was at O'Hare Airport and on my way to see you. And you never called me back." A teasing smile curved her lips. "You were so anxious to talk to Mr. Red-Hot that I never had a chance. By the way . . ." She fanned herself with her hand. "He really is pretty hunky. I've always said gingers don't get nearly enough credit, and those blue eyes—whew!"

It was on the tip of Rachel's tongue to say *Hands off; he's mine*, but she bit the words back. They weren't true and they would never be true because she and Conall were worlds apart, literally. And even if they were true, she and Lori had an unspoken agreement to never encroach on the other's romantic interests, past, present, or future. Just the fact that she found Conall attractive would be enough for Lori to keep her distance.

"Well, I did call you back, but it went to voice mail, so you were probably already on your flight. But why are you here?" she persisted. "I thought you were trying to prove to your father that you were ready for the commodities manager position."

A guarded look came into Lori's eyes and to Rachel's surprise, she turned away and made a show of shaking out a blouse and putting it on a hanger. "I am, but I needed a vacation," she said over her shoulder. "I haven't had any time off in over a year, and since you were in such raptures about how beautiful this place was, I thought I'd come over and see for myself."

"On the spur of the moment." Rachel couldn't keep the wry disbelief out of her voice.

"Yes." Turning around, Lori gave her a bright smile and bounced onto the bed beside her. "Just think. It will be like the old days, just you and me and the whole, wide world at our feet. We can hit the clubs and go dancing, or spend the days biking through the countryside, looking for our next adventure." She bumped shoulders with Rachel. "C'mon, it's going to be great. Aren't you even a tiny bit happy to see me?"

With a huff of laughter, Rachel hugged her cousin, reluctant to tell her that in Ballylahane, at least, there weren't many clubs to hit, and opportunities for dancing might be limited. "Of course I am. I'm very happy." Pulling away, she searched Lori's face. "I just can't believe Uncle Jack let you come over by yourself. He's always so protective of you."

Lori pulled a face. "I know. I keep reminding him that I'm twenty-five, but he insists on acting as if I'm incapable of taking care of myself. He didn't put up too much of a fight about my coming over, since he knows you're here to keep me out of trouble."

"He worries about you, that's all." Rachel felt a pang of envy. The only girl among five children, Lori had been pampered her entire life. Treasured, really, by both her parents and her brothers. While her uncle Jack had been like a second father to Rachel, she was painfully aware that she would never be cherished in the same way that Lori was.

"Well," she said brightly, "we'll have to find you somewhere to stay. There's barely enough space for me in this room, never mind both of us."

Lori gave a dramatic sigh. "Fine. Mrs. O'Leary said she has no other rooms available or I wouldn't have imposed. Let me stay tonight, and I'll check in at the hotel tomorrow."

"Do you have a car?"

Lori's blue eyes rounded in surprise. "Absolutely not! For one thing, they only had manual shifts available at the rental desk and I am not going to drive a stick shift with my left hand. Secondly, I'd be terrified to drive on the opposite side of the road. My taxi ride here was terrifying enough."

Rachel gaped at her. "You took a taxi? All the way from Dublin?"

"Of course. How else was I going to get here?"

Rachel had taken a six-hour train ride from Dublin to Donegal and then caught a public bus to Ballylahane, but she had had several months in which to plan her trip. Lori had come here on a whim, which meant she'd likely had no idea how far the small village was from the Dublin airport.

"But that's a four-hour car drive. The taxi fare must have cost you a fortune."

Lori shrugged. "I was happy to pay it, and the taxi driver was great. We chatted the whole way and he gave me all kinds of tips on places to go."

"I'll check with Seamus tomorrow and see if we can rent a car somewhere—maybe they have an automatic shift available. Otherwise, you're going to be stuck here in Ballylahane with no opportunity to get out and see anything." Seeing Lori's horrified expression, she laughed. "I spent all day riding around with Conall and it wasn't that bad. If you just drive slowly, you'll be fine. Have you eaten?"

"Mrs. O'Leary fed me, and I explored a little bit of the town while I was waiting for you to come back. There are some cute pubs, and I can't wait to check out the shops."

"What will you do while I'm working?"

Lori made a dismissive gesture. "Don't worry about me. I can find plenty to keep myself busy, but I'm actually looking forward to just relaxing."

Rachel gave her a dubious look, but didn't argue. Lori had never been one to just relax. With her endless energy and enthusiasm, she'd never been happy to stay put for very long, which was why the position of commodities manager would be perfect for her. She'd get to travel, see the world, and meet new people. Knowing Lori as she did, she would find Ballylahane cute and charming for about three days, and then she'd be ready to move on.

"How long are you staying?"

Lori's glance slid away from hers. "Ten days, maybe more."

"That's great." Rachel hesitated. "Listen, you know, I really don't have to go with Conall tomorrow to meet some of the local handweavers. That can wait."

"No, you should go. Please don't change your plans for me."

"Come with us then," Rachel urged. "You'll get to see the countryside, and Conall is a great tour guide."

Lori shook her head. "No, thanks. I'd just be a third wheel."

"That's not true," Rachel protested, pushing down the relief she felt. "Come with us. It will be fun."

"Maybe. We'll see. I have a feeling I might be too jet-lagged. In fact, if you don't mind, I think I'm going to crash now. I'm exhausted."

"Okay, you don't need to decide right now."

After Lori climbed into bed and fell asleep, Rachel moved to the deep armchair and tried to read, but found she couldn't focus on the pages. Her thoughts kept drifting back to Conall and the events of the day. He'd invited Lori to come with them tomorrow, but what if he'd only done it out of courtesy? What if he had no interest in carting them both around? Worse, what if he was attracted to Lori?

Her gaze lingered for a moment on her cousin. She lay sprawled under the blankets, snoring softly, taking up more than her share of the bed, as she did everything. Many people mistook Rachel and Lori for sisters. While they both had dark-brown hair and hazel eyes, that's where any similarity ended. Rachel was tall and slender, and her long hair was thick and straight, whereas Lori was shorter and curvy, and her chin-length bob was naturally wavy. Rachel had always been the serious one, while Lori had been a little on the wild side, wanting to experience everything life had to offer, without the restrictions of her family. With her sweetly innocent face and lushly curved figure, Lori drew male attention wherever she went. There had been times when Rachel had actively disliked going out with her, since she became all but invisible in Lori's company. But her cousin's effervescent personality and generous nature made it impossible not to like her.

Rachel knew Lori would be hurt and bewildered if she thought other women envied her. She truly believed all women were sisters who should build each other up, not tear each other down. Just thinking about Lori as a potential rival for Conall's attention made Rachel feel guilty. She should be happy that Lori was here to share part of this adventure with her, but instead she felt troubled and even a little resentful.

Setting her book aside, she slid into bed beside Lori and turned out the light, hugging the edge of the mattress, but it was hours before she found sleep.

"So, WHERE EXACTLY are we headed?"

The day was clear and bright, and the only remnant of the prior day's bad weather was a gusty breeze that sent the white clouds skittering across a blue sky. Rachel wore a pair of black leggings paired with ankle boots and a soft merino wool sweater in a shade of deep, hunter green. She'd left her hair loose around her shoulders and had applied only the barest amount of makeup, just enough to erase the evidence of a restless night's sleep. Conall, on the other hand, looked well-rested and ruggedly handsome in a light-blue button-down shirt under a dark-blue nubby tweed vest. He'd rolled his shirtsleeves up and his hair was attractively messy from the wind.

"We'll visit Kieran Cullen first; he lives in a little village called Cleendra, near the sea. After that, we'll drive on to Kerrytown, and you'll meet Tom Gillespie. He's been weaving tweed in his home for nearly fifty years. After that, we can catch the motorway and make good time getting back." He glanced over at her. "Having second thoughts?"

"No, of course not. I want to meet the handweavers and see their workspace, if they'll let me. This is what I came over here to do." She gave him an apologetic smile. "I just feel a little guilty leaving Lori behind."

"But we did invite her to join us."

"She claimed she was too tired."

"We won't be away long," Conall assured her. "I'll have you back in time for supper. Dierdre runs the front desk at the hotel and she'll keep an eye on your cousin."

Rachel nodded. "Of course. I don't know why I'm even worried. It's just that it's so strange for her to show up here the way she did without any prior warning." She shrugged. "Anyway, she said she needed a vacation and since I was already here, she decided to visit Ireland."

"Makes sense."

On the surface, Rachel couldn't find any reason to doubt Lori's word, but there was something about her unexpected arrival that nagged at her. Lori rarely did anything on the spur of the moment, and almost never without consulting with her first. But she'd made it clear to her father and anyone who would listen that she wanted to travel, and hoped for a career that would enable her to satisfy her wanderlust. So perhaps this was exactly what she'd claimed—an opportunity to visit Ireland while Rachel was here to share the experience with her. Determinedly, she pushed thoughts of Lori aside and instead focused on the scenery and the man sitting beside her.

The road followed the coastline, along fields filled with sheep and cattle, through small villages and past the silhouettes of ruined churches and ancient castles, until Conall turned at a sign for Crohy Head. Rachel stared out the window, enchanted by the sight of lush green fields edged with stone walls and shimmering blue ocean against a backdrop of distant mountains.

"Does Mr. Cullen live in the village?"

"He lives near Crohy Head, a bit beyond Cleendra. There is no village, so to speak," Conall answered. "Not in the sense that Ballylahane has a town center and a main road. This area is mostly vacation homes. The nearest shopping is just north of here, in Dungloe."

They turned down a small dirt lane edged with stone walls and a profusion of wildflowers. To her right, the land swooped down to the ocean in a series of green, terraced fields. Small whitewashed houses dotted the rural landscape.

"Here we are," Conall said.

They had arrived at one of the small cottages Rachel had admired. This one had windowsills and a door painted a cheery shade of red, and was perched on a hillside facing the ocean. Daffodils bloomed in a colorful burst of yellow along the driveway. Behind the house were a small outbuilding and a paddock constructed of stone walls overgrown with creeping ivy, sporting a bright-red gate. A small, shaggy donkey stood inside the perimeter, watching them with cocked ears.

"Oh, my goodness, look how cute he is!" Rachel exclaimed, and immediately began rummaging in her backpack for her camera and a treat. "Think he would like an apple?"

"I think he'd take anything you offered him," Conall said. Rachel wasn't sure, but he added something under his breath that sounded like, *I know I would.*

As they climbed out of the car, the back door of the house opened and an older man with a shock of white hair and a neatly trimmed beard appeared. He lifted a hand to Conall.

"Hello! Good to see you, lad." His bright eyes turned to Rachel. "And you've brought your lovely girlfriend."

Rachel couldn't bring herself to look at Conall to gauge his response.

"Ah, no." Conall drew her forward and made introductions. "This is Rachel Woods, from Chicago. She's doing an internship at the mill and learning about handweaving. I thought, if you don't mind, she might see your setup."

Kieran smiled. "No, I don't mind at all. A pleasure to meet you. All the way from Chicago, you say? And how are you liking County Donegal?"

"I love it," Rachel assured him. "Your property is lovely. Would it be alright if I gave your donkey an apple?"

"Oh, sure, he'll love that. Will you come in for tea after? Claire just put the kettle on."

Rachel made her way over to the paddock, gratified when the little donkey gobbled the apple from her palm and then allowed her to take some pictures of him, even pulling his lip back to show a gummy smile. Rachel laughed and rubbed his nose and scratched along his jaw. An older woman appeared in the doorway to the small house, wearing an apron over her sweater and slacks. She smiled broadly when she saw Conall. "Hullo, Conall, and who do you have with you?"

"I'm Rachel." She smiled at the older woman. "I wanted to see the handweaving process, so Conall brought me along."

"Oh, very good. Excellent. First, come in and have some tea," she invited.

"Oh, thank you, no, we don't want to intrude," Conall replied.

"It's no bother," Kieran insisted. "We don't mind at all."

"Really, we only stopped by to collect the tweed and maybe have a quick look at your workshop, if you don't mind."

Rachel watched the exchange with interest, sensing the back-and-forth negotiation of tea was completely normal, and even expected.

"I'll show you the workshop, but I insist you stay for a spot of tea afterward," Kieran said, emphatic.

Conall grinned. "Sure. We'd love to, wouldn't we, Rachel?"

"Absolutely." Rachel gave the donkey a last pat and smiled at the couple. "It sounds wonderful."

Kieran looked satisfied. "Excellent. Come along, this is where I do my weaving."

They followed him to the outbuilding, and he opened

the door to reveal a tidy workshop with curtained windows, a cozy peat stove, and shelving that held dozens of spools of wool and weaving accessories. Dominating the space was a large handloom. Constructed of wood and iron, the frame was almost as big as the room itself.

Rachel moved around the loom, studying the construction and admiring the intricate pattern being worked on the warp. "This fabric is gorgeous. Does it have a name?"

"It's called undulating twill," Kieran said. "Very popular, I'm told."

"You must have spent hours preparing and threading the loom."

"Yeah, it takes about five hours to set her up, but then it goes fairly quick. I can weave three meters in an hour, more if I really set my mind to it."

Rachel heard the pride in his voice and tried to envision a time when hundreds of such handlooms were employed by weavers in their homes all over the country. The craftsmanship and quality of the fabric was undeniable.

"Kieran is a master weaver," Conall told her. "He's been weaving cloth for McDermott Mills for almost forty years. He's the best there is."

"Comes from years of practice," Kieran said, giving Rachel a conspiratorial wink. "I've been weaving since I was a small, wee lad."

"Would you show me how it works?"

"Of course." Kieran seemed pleased by her request.

"Would you mind if I take some pictures?"

"No, not at all."

Rachel stepped back as he climbed onto the bench behind the loom and made some adjustments to the hundreds of fine threads that made up the warp. A rope with a wooden handle hung from an overhead bar, and as he began to manipulate the shuttle, he simultaneously worked a series of wooden pedals with his feet, which raised and lowered eight threaded shafts in a specific order, determining the pattern. Rachel watched, transfixed by the intricate coordination of hand and foot. The wooden clack of the shuttles and treadles was both familiar and soothing, and she thought she could easily watch Kieran work the loom for hours. She snapped a few pictures and watched as the pattern began to evolve beneath his swift hands until soon he'd added another foot to the finished fabric. All too soon, however, he stopped and stepped down.

"That's it. That's how it works." He indicated six neatly folded bundles of finished tweed, tied with a cord. "You can bring these back with you, Conall. Do you have new warp and wool for me?"

"I do, yeah," Conall said. "It's in the truck. Let me just go and get it."

After Conall left, Rachel bent to inspect the finished fabric, in differing shades of blues and greens. The wool was sumptuously soft and flecked with bright color. "This is lovely work, Mr. Cullen. How many hours a day do you weave?"

"Oh, I dunno," he replied. "It depends on the day. Some days, I can easily spend ten or twelve hours out here. Other days, I may only work in the morning."

"I'll bet you're a very good step-dancer," Rachel said, smiling at him. "You're extremely coordinated."

Kieran grinned. "I am, actually. You should come to the festival in Ardara this summer, when the local weavers display and sell their products. There's music and dancing, and plenty of good food. It's a grand day."

"If I'm still here, I won't miss it," she assured him, stepping aside as Conall entered, carrying two large bins filled with spools of thread and assorted accoutrements.

"Here you are," he said, setting the bins down. "You're all set for supplies, then?"

"I am," Kieran assured him. "Now, come in and have some tea."

They sat at a small kitchen table, watching as Claire prepared tea and busied herself setting out cups and plates, sugar and cream. The kitchen itself was cozy, with a white wood-burning stove and oven on one wall, and two small armchairs drawn up on either side. The window over the sink faced the paddock and the green fields and, beyond that, the ocean and distant mountains.

"You're in luck. I made a tea cake this morning," Kieran said. "You can tell me if you like it, Miss Woods."

"Oh, please call me Rachel," she said, watching as Claire

placed a large golden bread on the table, studded with dark currents. "You made this yourself?"

"He did," Claire assured her, pulling out a chair and sitting down. "We married later in life, so Kieran was a bachelor for many years. Learned to make do for himself, all the better luck for me. He does most of the baking." She covered one of Kieran's work-roughened hands with her own. "Spoils me silly, he does. I keep telling him he's going to make me fatter than Humphrey—that's our donkey."

Rachel laughed and couldn't help sliding a glance at Conall. He seemed comfortable and relaxed, enjoying the easy banter. Catching her eye, his mouth curved in a small smile. As Claire poured the tea, Rachel cut a slice of cake for each of them, and then watched as Kieran applied a generous helping of creamy butter to his. Following his example, she liberally slathered her own slice and then bit into it, relishing the flavor.

"Oh, this is delicious!" she exclaimed. "I may need to ask you for the recipe."

Kieran chuckled. "Don't know that I have a recipe. I could make it with my eyes closed. I'm willing to bet young Conall here knows how to make a good tea cake as well."

Rachel gave Conall an expectant look, amused when he shifted uncomfortably in his seat. "Well, don't tell my mum, but I never really got the hang of cooking. I do alright, but I haven't ventured into baking."

"What gives it such a unique flavor?" Rachel asked, coming to his rescue.

"The secret is to soak the currants in tea overnight, and then add the dry ingredients to the tea mixture. Keeps it moist and flavorful."

"It's wonderful," Rachel enthused. "Does it matter what kind of tea?"

"No, I don't think so," Kieran said. "I occasionally use a chai tea, which adds a note of cinnamon. That's quite nice too."

Rachel took another generous bite, enjoying the rich flavor, when Conall reached over and made a careful swipe of her chin with his napkin. "Butter," he murmured, holding her gaze. "It's gone now."

Rachel felt her cheeks go warm beneath his steady regard. "Thank you. At least it's not mud." She dragged her gaze away to find Claire watching them both with an indulgent smile.

"You make a lovely couple," she said. "And if I know young Conall, he spoils you the way my Kieran does me."

"Oh!" Heat washed into Rachel's face and for a moment, she was too embarrassed to speak. "No, you're mistaken. We're not a couple. That is, we only just met each other last week."

"Oh, so it's early days yet," Claire said with delight, unabashed by her mistake. "Still getting to know each other, then."

Rachel couldn't bring herself to look at Conall.

"I came across Rachel trapped in a boghole," he said. Amusement laced his voice. "I decided she was too pretty not to rescue."

Kieran chuckled softly. "I agree. She has a rare smile."

Rachel murmured her thanks and risked a glance at Conall. He watched her with a warm expression in his eyes that caused her heart to thump hard in her chest and make her wish for things that couldn't possibly come true. Like staying in Ireland and allowing Conall to spoil her.

Chapter Eight

THEY LEFT AFTER tea and visited another handweaver named Tom Gillespie, before finally turning back toward Ballylahane. The cargo area of the Range Rover was stuffed full with bins of finished tweed in hues of blue, brown, gray, and purple heather, and the interior of the vehicle carried the pungent, earthy scent of the wool. If Conall thought at all about the awkward exchange in Kieran's kitchen, he didn't mention it and outwardly didn't seem at all fazed by the assumption they were a couple.

"So you've had a glimpse into the life of a handweaver," he said. "What did you think?"

"I think there's something to be said for slowing down and enjoying the simpler things in life. I'm a little bit in love with the Cullens' cottage. Imagine waking up to that view every day."

"Yeah, it's pretty special." He slanted her a speculative look. "You wouldn't be bored living in the country?"

Rachel considered his words carefully, sensing there was more behind the simple question than he let on. "A few weeks ago, I might have said yes, but now I'm not so sure.

I've never really considered myself a nature person, but I've loved getting outside and seeing the countryside. Everything is so beautiful and . . . peaceful. Magical, even. I wouldn't want to live too far away from civilization, though," she continued. "I like to go to dinner at restaurants and occasionally catch a movie. But I could see myself owning a donkey and a couple of sheep, and making tea cake for visitors."

"Could you really?"

"You sound surprised."

Conall glanced at her, his eyes warm. "I'll admit, you do continue to surprise me, Rachel Woods. In a good way."

Rachel looked quickly away, but his words seeped into her like sunshine.

"Do you think Mr. Gillespie minds living by himself? He didn't seem overly enthusiastic to see us," she said after a moment, changing the subject.

Tom Gillespie had been older than Kieran Cullen and lived alone on the outskirts of the small village of Kerrytown. He had been friendly enough, but Rachel sensed he was a man who enjoyed his solitude. Like Kieran, he had converted a backyard shed into a workshop and did his handweaving there, in the company of his three dogs. Rachel had not dared to ask him for a weaving demonstration.

"I hear he was married, a long time ago," Conall said.

"Really?" Rachel had a difficult time imagining the crusty old man with a wife. "What happened?"

"I only know she died very young and he never remarried."

"Oh." She glanced at Conall. "How sad. He must have loved her very much."

She understood the grief of losing someone too early, especially when there was every reason to believe they still had many years ahead in which to live and love. Knowing Mr. Gillespie had suffered such a tragic loss, his isolated lifestyle and aloof manner made more sense to her.

"Yeah, I'd say so," Conall agreed. "That, or she made him so miserable he swore he'd never get married again."

"That's a terrible thing to say!" Rachel exclaimed, and gave him a light punch on his arm.

"Okay." Conall laughed. "I take it back."

"I am curious, though," Rachel mused. "How much do handweavers earn?"

Conall shrugged. "I couldn't say, but enough to make a decent living. The handwoven fabric is the most expensive, because it's so labor-intensive. Seamus is a fair man, and I think he pays his handweavers a respectable salary. Of course, it's based on experience, as well as the quality and the quantity they can produce."

"It's a little sad to think that when Kieran eventually retires, there isn't a son or grandson to take over the work for him."

She thought of her own determination to follow in her father's footsteps. She would ensure his legacy lived on.

"I think companies like McDermott Mills are sparking a renewed interest in handweaving," Conall said, correctly interpreting her mood. "More young people are learning the art, and there's a studio in Donegal that only uses handlooms for their products."

"So there's hope," Rachel said. "I wonder if Kieran would be interested in being a teacher. He's so talented."

"He is," Conall agreed. "You have a kind heart, Rachel, and I think you made Kieran feel appreciated. Like his work mattered. Even Mr. Gillespie seemed to brighten up a bit with your visit. You have a way of making people feel comfortable around you. I like that about you." He glanced at her and grinned. "That, and your rare smile."

"That's nice of you to say," Rachel murmured. Did he feel comfortable around her too? Because she realized *comfortable* was not how Conall made her feel. Alive, yes, and a little self-conscious, she was all too aware of him as a gorgeous, smart, intensely driven man who did things to her equilibrium simply by touching her. "I hope they both know their work does matter. I hate to think of handweaving disappearing."

"I don't think that will happen."

They had left the village of Kerrytown behind and were driving through the rural countryside. Unlike the dramatic hills near Cleendra, the landscape was flat with only the occasional rise of hills in the distance. The road was unevenly paved and potholed, and they had been bouncing along for about fifteen minutes when the Range Rover suddenly pulled to the left, and a strange *thump-thump-thump* sound came from beneath the vehicle.

"Did we hit something?" she asked in alarm. She hadn't seen anything in the road, but worried that maybe they had struck an animal.

Conall pulled over as much as he could on the narrow road. "Either a rock or a pothole. I think we have a flat."

"Oh, thank goodness."

Conall cast her an amused glance. "You enjoy changing tires?"

"No, of course not. But for a moment, I worried we might have hit a sheep."

He looked affronted. "I'm a better driver than that."

"Sorry. Can you fix it?"

"Yeah, no worries."

He climbed out of the Range Rover, and Rachel scrambled after him. The front tire on the driver's side was completely flat.

"I'll just grab the jack and the spare, and we'll be back on the road in no time," Conall assured her. Unbuttoning his tweed vest, he removed it and laid it across the driver's seat before rolling his sleeves up. Together, they unloaded the bins of fabric from the cargo area onto the side of the road, until Conall could access the storage compartment where the jack and lug wrench were located.

"Where is the spare tire?" Rachel asked, seeing none.

"It hangs from the undercarriage," Conall said. Removing a small cap, he revealed a lug nut and began turning it with a wrench. "Look underneath and tell me what you see, if you don't mind."

Rachel bent down and peeked beneath the rear of the vehicle and watched as the spare tire began to descend on a cable from where it was attached to the bottom of the vehicle. "I see it. It's almost on the ground."

"Right." Crouching beside her, he released the tire from the cable and dragged it out from beneath the vehicle, grunting with effort.

"What can I do to help?" she asked.

Conall glanced up at her, and a smile tilted one corner of his mouth. "Just give me lots of praise and moral support. We men thrive on female admiration."

Rachel laughed. "Done."

She watched as he rolled the tire toward the front of the car and then used the wrench to loosen the lug nuts.

"Here, hold these for me." He dropped the heavy bolts into her hands, his fingers brushing hers.

"You're doing an amazing job," Rachel enthused, crouching next to him. She said it partly to tease him and partly to hide her own reaction to the brief contact. "I've never seen such a manly display of strength and agility, and you manage to look so handsome."

Conall grinned. "Now you're getting the hang of it."

How would he react if he knew she wasn't just teasing?

She enjoyed watching him. His forearms were roped with sinew and veins, and his wrists were thick and strong. After raising the vehicle with the car jack, he deftly changed the tire, secured the lug nuts, and lowered the Range Rover again. Then he rolled the flat tire to the back of the car and secured it beneath the chassis.

"That should do it," he said, dusting his hands together as he half sat on the open tailgate.

"Nicely done," Rachel praised. Rummaging through her backpack, she withdrew two bottles of water and handed him one. "You deserve a reward."

"That's it?" he complained, taking the water. "A measly bottle of water for all my efforts?"

"What did you expect?"

"I've learned never to expect anything," he answered, setting the bottle down. "But I've learned it can't hurt to ask for what you want." He pressed a finger to his lean jaw. "A kiss."

Rachel's heart stuttered for an instant. Was he serious? She looked from his jaw to his eyes and saw the gleam of challenge there. He didn't think she'd do it, and although her instincts screamed this was a bad idea, she couldn't help but be tempted. It would only be a quick peck on the cheek. A harmless, totally platonic, friend-zone, unexciting kiss where only *her* lips would be involved, not his.

Setting her own water bottle down beside his, she stepped closer. They were on eye level and he watched her through lowered lashes, his expression inscrutable. Her pulse still skittered erratically, and she hoped he couldn't sense the sudden giddy thrill she felt at being so close to him. Leaning forward, she quickly pressed her mouth against his cheek. He radiated heat, and the light stubble of his whiskers was scratchy beneath her lips. She heard his swiftly indrawn breath, and then he seemed to stop breathing altogether.

She pulled back just enough to meet his eyes, which had turned a dark, turbulent blue. Then she made the mistake of dropping her gaze to his mouth. She stared, transfixed. His square jaw framed a mouth that was wide and generous. A tiny scar bisected his lower lip and, without conscious thought, Rachel moistened her own lips. Lifting her hand, she traced one finger across the small disfigurement.

"Here?" she asked, her voice barely above a whisper.

He gave a grunt, which Rachel took for assent. He still watched her, unnerving her with the heat and intensity of his gaze.

"Close your eyes," she commanded softly. She would lose what little courage remained if he watched her.

He did, his lashes a sweep of burnished gold against his cheeks. Slowly, taking her time, she covered his mouth with hers. His lips were warm and firm, and for a moment, Rachel thought he wouldn't kiss her back. Then he made a small sound of approval and slanted his mouth across hers. Gentle, yet insistent, exploring the shape of her and then parting her lips to press his tongue against hers, his kiss was slow and searching. Rachel couldn't prevent a small sigh of pleasure. With each pass, he explored deeper, and Rachel welcomed the intrusion, stepping into the splayed vee of his legs and sliding her hands over his broad shoulders. He tasted faintly of sweet tea and he smelled like warm wool and soap. She moved closer, wanting to consume him, her senses alive with awareness. He cupped her face with one hand while the other slid slowly down her back. There was nothing tentative about the kiss or the way he touched her, one hand warm against her cheek, while the other splayed across her hip.

Rachel was so absorbed in his kiss that she never heard the rumbling of the car on the road until it drew alongside them and the driver merrily honked his horn. They broke apart with a startled laugh, but Conall didn't release her, keeping his arms loosely around her.

"Sorry," she said, dropping her head against his shoulder.

"For what?" He stroked a thumb along her jaw. "I've been wanting to kiss you since I first pulled you out of that boghole. Call me crazy, but when I'm not with you, I'm thinking about you, and when I am with you, all I can think about is how much I want to kiss you."

Biting back a smile, Rachel smoothed the front of his shirt with her fingertips, momentarily at a loss for words. What would he say if she told him she felt the same way? His kiss had undone her, made her momentarily forget where she was. More than that, it made her forget her resolve to keep things platonic. Beneath her fingertips, she could feel the heavy thud of his heart. The top buttons of his shirt were open and his pulse beat strongly along the side of his throat. Knowing she was wading into dangerous waters but unable to resist, she pressed her mouth against the small throb. His skin was hot and smooth. She touched the tip of her tongue to him.

"Rachel," he said on a half groan. "You're killing me."

"Sorry." *Not sorry.* Reluctantly, she stepped back, moistening her lips. She could still taste him, clean and just a little bit salty from his exertions. Without meeting his gaze, she turned away. "We should probably get going."

Conall caught her arm. "Wait."

Before she could guess his intent, he slid one hand along her jaw and pressed a brief, hard kiss against her mouth. Pulling back, he searched her eyes. Rachel averted her own gaze, not wanting him to see how much the kiss had unsettled her, or how much she wanted him to continue kissing her.

"Right," he finally said. "I'll just load these bins, and then we can be on our way."

"Can I help?"

"No. You've done enough. I've got it from here."

Rachel stood uncertainly for a moment as he began lifting the bins of tweed and stowing them in the cargo area. After a moment, she took the water bottles and climbed into the passenger seat to wait. Several minutes later, Conall joined her, pulling his vest back on but leaving it unbuttoned. He turned the engine on but made no immediate move to pull back onto the road.

"I like you, Rachel Woods," he said, slanting her a rueful look. "I like you a lot. I'm not going to apologize for it any more than I'm going to apologize for kissing you. In fact, I should probably warn you it's likely to happen again. Are you okay with that?"

"Yes." The single word came out on a breathless sigh.

"Good." With a last, meaningful look, he thrust the vehicle into gear and they lurched back onto the road. Rachel turned to look out the passenger window, unable to hide her smile or the bright burst of happiness his words induced.

"YOU *KISSED* HIM?"

"Shh!" Rachel cast an uneasy glance around. "You don't need to broadcast it!"

She and Lori were having supper in the dining room of the Grand Arms Hotel, at a table overlooking the main street. The room shared space with a cozy pub, and both the bar and the dining room itself were nearly full.

Lori leaned over the table. "On a scale of one to ten, how was it?"

Rachel felt her face go warm. "It wasn't bad. Possibly on the high end of the scale."

Lori gave a small laugh and sat back in her seat. "In other words, it was great."

"Okay, it was great, but it didn't mean anything. It *can't* mean anything because in three months I'm going home." She gave Lori a helpless look. "I don't want to hurt him."

I don't want to get hurt.

"Listen," Lori said, her voice earnest. "He's a big boy. He knows you're only here for a few months. If you like spending time together, then you should. Just enjoy yourselves."

"Easy for you to say," Rachel grumbled. "It's not your heart at risk."

There was a momentary silence. "Wow. You really like him, don't you?"

"Yes. *No.* I don't know." Rachel made a groaning sound. "What should I do?"

"Nothing." Lori leaned forward. "It was a kiss, Rachel. It's not like he proposed. Just . . . go with it. Enjoy yourself. The rest will sort itself out, you'll see."

Rachel nodded. "Right."

Maybe she was making too much out of it. But she did like Conall—she liked him a lot. She liked his enthusiasm and his sense of humor, and the way he made people feel comfortable in his company. Most of all, she liked the way he made her feel, as if she was the most beautiful woman in the world. As if he'd rather be with her than anywhere else. Just the memory of his kiss made her feel hot and shivery all over, and the thought of his hands on her body stirred something restless and achy inside her.

"So, you're working tomorrow," Lori said brightly, changing the subject. "Would it be alright if I came by to see you?"

"Sure. I break for lunch at one o'clock if you want to come by then. I can show you the pattern I'm working on."

"Will I get to meet the famous Seamus McDermott?"

"Maybe. I don't know," Rachel replied. "I don't actually see too much of him, since he's always in meetings or traveling. But you can meet his daughter, Fiona. She's the lead designer."

"Great! I'll bring lunch."

Rachel laughed. "Sounds good. What will you do until then?"

Lori shrugged. "Don't worry about me. I'm going to check out the shops and do some exploring."

"Okay. Seamus asked Conall to arrange a visit to a local sheep farm. I'm not sure when that will be, but would you like to come along?"

Lori wrinkled her nose. "A sheep farm? I don't know. It sounds a little too earthy for me."

Rachel laughed. "Well, I'm not exactly the outdoorsy type, either, but I'm looking forward to it. C'mon, you can't come to Ireland and not visit a sheep farm. It'll be fun, and maybe you'll even get to bottle-feed a lamb."

"Yeah, somehow I'm not seeing that as a highlight of my trip." Lori laughed, but the sparkle in her blue eyes belied her words. "Will it be just you and Conall? You know, third wheel and all."

"It'll just be the three of us," Rachel confirmed. "And the guy who owns the farm. He's a friend of Conall's. I think they run marathons together."

"Ah," Lori said, grinning. "A *fast* sheep farmer. How can I refuse?"

Chapter Nine

THREE DAYS LATER, Rachel and Fiona were in the design room when Seamus poked his head in. "Conall's just arrived," he said, quickly assessing Rachel's attire. "Glad you dressed sensibly. It's likely to be a bit mucky out there."

"Is it that time already?" Fiona asked, glancing at her watch.

Rachel felt a little bemused herself. It was only midmorning, but time had a way of slipping past unnoticed whenever she was working at the woolen mill. She'd become so engrossed in what she was doing, the morning had passed in a blur.

"I told my cousin we would pick her up at the hotel," Rachel said, closing her laptop. "Is that okay?"

"No need, as Conall already collected her," Seamus replied. "They're waiting in the parking lot. Should be a fine day. No rain in the forecast."

"Lucky for you." Fiona smiled when her father had left. "Trust me when I say there is nothing worse than tramping through a sheep field in the rain. Except maybe tramping through a peat bog."

Rachel laughed. "Well, thank goodness that's not on the agenda."

Fiona arched an eyebrow. "Don't be so sure. Flynn likes to get as much physical labor as he can out of visitors. He invites them to try their hand at cutting peat and, for some strange reason, they all want to do it."

"Sounds like a smart man."

Fiona laughed. "He is very persuasive, I'll give you that."

"You're sure you don't want to join us?" Rachel asked, taking her backpack and jacket from the hook.

"Absolutely." Fiona indicated her skirt and heels. "I'm not exactly dressed for a sheep farm. But you have fun. I can't wait to hear all about it tomorrow."

As Rachel stepped outside, Lori waved to her from the passenger seat of the Range Rover as Conall came around the rear of the vehicle. She hadn't seen him since the day they had kissed, and found herself feeling inexplicably shy.

"Good morning," he said, his gaze warm.

"Hi." She indicated her backpack. "I'll just throw this in the back."

Glancing toward Lori, he lowered his voice. "It's good to see you."

"You too," she murmured. "It should be a fun day."

"I hope so. Just—" He broke off and rubbed a hand across the back of his neck.

"What?" She hadn't seen him at a loss for words before.

"My pal, Flynn, is—well, he's a real charmer. At least,

the ladies seem to think so."

"And your point is?"

"Well, I'd appreciate it if you didn't encourage him. If Lori wants to have at him, great. But not you. Not right in front of me. Not sure I could stand by and watch that. Sorry, but there it is."

Rachel stared at him, open-mouthed. He was all but telling her he'd be jealous if his friend hit on her, or if she flirted with him. For a moment, she didn't know how to react, feeling equal parts dismay, indignation, and—yes—a girlish thrill of pleasure at his possessiveness.

"Okay," she finally managed, handing him her backpack. "I'm not sure what that says about me, that you think I'm the kind of girl who would kiss someone and then turn around and flirt with his friend, but you don't need to worry." She gave him a pointed look. "I've been warned."

A dark flush stained his cheekbones. "That's not what I meant."

"What did you mean?"

Conall's lips twisted in a rueful smile, and Rachel could see frustration in his expression. "Forget it. I shouldn't have said anything. You'll understand once you meet him."

Without waiting for a reply, he strode to the front of the Range Rover and climbed into the driver's seat, leaving Rachel to climb into the back seat.

"Everything okay?" Lori asked, turning to look at Rachel.

Rachel gave her cousin a bright smile. "Yes. Conall was

just telling me that we're in for a real treat. Apparently, the sheep farm has all kinds of, er, *attractions*."

In the rearview mirror, Rachel met Conall's eyes and she arched an eyebrow, daring him to contradict her. He narrowed his own eyes, silently promising retribution.

"Oh, well, I can hardly wait," enthused Lori.

The drive to the farm took them out of the village of Ballylahane and along the coast to where the sea traveled inland through a long, narrow inlet. Here, the green hills rose majestically on either side of the turquoise water. They turned onto a narrow road that wound its way upward, bordered on either side by stone walls and wire fencing. The views from the top were stunning. The steep hills swept down to the narrow expanse of water, and then rose sharply upward again on the other side. Clouds scudded overhead and cast intriguing shadows across the mountainous landscape.

"I've never seen anything so dramatic," Lori breathed. "I am blown away by the beauty of it all."

"That's a saltwater fjord below us," Conall said. "One of the few in Ireland, and nearly one hundred fifty feet deep."

Several boats navigated the waters of the fjord and Rachel could only imagine how spectacular the view must be from a boat.

"Do they offer boat tours on the fjord?" Lori asked, as if reading her thoughts. "I'd love to do that."

"Nothing official," Conall said. "But Flynn has several

boats. I'm sure he'd be willing to take you out, if you were to ask."

They turned off the road onto a rutted lane, where long-haired sheep with black faces and curling horns grazed on either side, barely lifting their heads as the Range Rover rumbled past. Up ahead, a whitewashed stone barn and several cottages perched on the edge of the bluff. Paddocks and outbuildings rambled across the property and the view down toward the water was almost dizzying.

"And who, exactly, is Flynn?" Lori asked.

As Conall drew the vehicle to a stop beside the barn, a man appeared in the entry, wiping his hands on a rag. Rachel heard Lori's swift intake of breath and had to admit, the guy almost took her own breath away as well. Tall and broad-shouldered, he had thick black hair that fell over his forehead and a square jaw that might have been chiseled out of the same rock as the seaside cliffs. He wore a pair of jeans stuffed into tall rubber boots, and a thick, cabled sweater that emphasized the muscular planes of his chest and shoulders. Three border collies swarmed around his legs, each of them gazing up at him in adoration. Seeing Conall, he lifted a hand in greeting and his face broke into a grin.

"That," said Conall ruefully, "is Flynn O'Rourke."

"He looks like a movie star," Lori said, her eyes round.

Rachel silently agreed, and now she could appreciate Conall's apprehension. Flynn O'Rourke looked as if he had come straight from Hollywood central casting to play the role of a rugged, hunky Irish fisherman. He was tall, dark, and devastatingly handsome. She wondered that women weren't lined up along the country lane just to get a peek at Flynn. In the rearview mirror, Conall's gaze met Rachel's in a clear message: *Now do you understand?*

Rachel did understand. The guy looked like Henry Cavill and Matt Bomer rolled up into one delicious, manly treat for the eyes. But while she could appreciate Flynn's masculine beauty, Rachel didn't feel the same irresistible pull of attraction she felt whenever she looked at Conall. If someone had told her just a month ago that she was a sucker for gingers, she wouldn't have believed them, but watching Conall give the other man a swift, one-armed embrace, she knew it was true. In her opinion, Flynn O'Rourke was no match for Conall McDermott.

"Thanks for having us," Conall said. "This is Rachel Woods. She's here from Chicago to learn about Irish weaving."

Rachel found her hand engulfed in Flynn's big, warm hand and she felt certain the smile he gave her would have immolated most women. Up close, his eyes were a striking shade of silver-gray, fringed by the thickest lashes Rachel had ever seen on a man. His teeth were strong and white and he had dimples you could drive a truck into. Honestly, the guy should come with a fire extinguisher and a warning label.

"Rachel," he said. "My pleasure. Welcome to O'Rourke Farm. How long are you planning to be here?"

"Er, about three months." He didn't release her hand, and it wasn't until Conall directed his attention toward Lori that Rachel finally tugged her hand free. "And this is my cousin, Lori."

"So wonderful to meet you," Lori gushed, all but pushing Rachel aside. She placed her hand in Flynn's larger one and smiled up at him in a way that Rachel knew all too well. "I've only just arrived and I'm dying to see your, er, farm."

Flynn's eyes glowed with humor. "Well, then, let me show you around. I hope you won't be disappointed."

Lori laughed, and Rachel could have sworn her eyelashes actually fluttered. "Trust me, I don't think that's possible."

Rachel barely resisted an eye roll at her cousin's blatant flirting. She risked a glance at Conall, surprised to find him watching her. He gave her a small shrug as if to say, *I told you so.*

"Don't mind the dogs," Flynn said, reaching down to pat the nearest one. "This is Rob, and that one is Brody. And that smaller one there is Quinn. He's in training."

"Is he still a puppy?" Rachel asked, bending down to scratch behind Quinn's ears. He leaned into the caress and his tongue lolled happily.

"Yeah, I think he's about a year old. We found him abandoned or lost on a country road about three months ago. We spread the word, but no one has claimed him. I don't normally take on dogs that haven't been raised around livestock, but there was something about him that just sort of grabbed me." Flynn shrugged. "So far, he's not much of a herding dog, but he has a good personality. I don't want to send him to the shelter, but I might not have a choice if he doesn't start to mind."

"I thought border collies had a natural instinct to herd," Rachel said, glancing up at Flynn.

"They do, but Quinn here just likes to run. He'll chase the sheep all day, but he's not much interested in heeding commands." Flynn made a tsking sound. "He'll just confuse the other dogs if he doesn't learn to obey."

"I would take him if I could," Rachel said, and crouched down to kiss the dog's nose. "Wouldn't I, Quinn, you sweetie?"

Quinn apparently agreed, as he covered her chin and lips with a wet slurp of his tongue, setting Rachel back on her heels with a startled laugh, so that she almost lost her balance.

"Careful," Conall said, catching her arm before she went over backward. Quinn, apparently thinking this was a fun game, went down on his front paws and barked at her, even as his tail furiously wagged. "Down, Quinn."

To Rachel's surprise, the dog immediately dropped on his haunches and barked again, looking ready to play.

"Thanks," she said as Conall pulled her to her feet. "You always seem to be right there when I need you."

"I do my best," he replied, clearly amused. "Wouldn't say much for my heroics if I saved you from a boghole only to let you fall into a puddle."

Rachel glanced at the ground where she'd been crouching, realizing there was a sizeable mud puddle directly behind her.

"Maybe you should take him," Flynn suggested, his eyes dancing. "He seems to mind you better than he does me."

"That's a great idea," Rachel enthused, cheerfully ignoring Conall's warning look. "He'd make a good running partner for you."

"I'll think about it," Conall said.

Just inside the barn door, Flynn indicated a shelf lined with rubber boots in varying sizes. "They may not be fashionable," he said, looking at Lori's delicate heeled shoes. "But you'll be glad for them when we get into the muck out there."

When they had each swapped out their shoes for a pair of boots, Flynn led them outside to a small pen, where a dozen sheep crowded together against the gate. They had black faces and long, coarse wool, and each of them had a splash of bright blue paint across their back.

"What kind of sheep are they?" Lori asked. "And why have they been painted?"

"These are Mayo blackface sheep," Flynn replied. "We prefer them because they're hardy and can withstand the tougher conditions here in the northwest. The blue paint is used to keep track of which sheep belong to which farmer and which field. The bright-green paint you see on those sheep in the field over there helps us with breeding. We hang a bag of paint under the neck of a ram before it's released into a field of ewes for tupping. When the ram mounts a ewe, the bag of paint leaves a mark on her back and then I know to move that ewe to another field."

Lori's eyebrows rose. "That's, uh, ingenious." She turned to Rachel and lowered her voice. "Let's hope that practice doesn't catch on with humans. And did he really say *tupping?*"

Flynn gave her an impassive look, clearly not amused. "It's just how it's done, and it's a real term. Look it up."

"Do you sell the wool?" Lori asked, unabashed.

"We can do, but it's not very profitable. The wool is too coarse for clothing, but it makes for good carpets and can be used in knitting."

"Do you use sheep milk to make soaps or body lotions?" she persisted.

"Er, no."

"What about cheese? Yogurt?"

Rachel exchanged a look with Conall and fought to suppress a laugh at Flynn's aggrieved expression.

"This is a working sheep farm," he said with exaggerated patience, as if speaking to a child. "We don't make soaps, lotions, cheese, or yogurt. We make mutton and lamb chops."

Lori's expression turned to one of horror. "No! Please tell me these sweet little sheep won't end up on someone's dinner plate."

Flynn blew out a hard breath. "Fine. I won't tell you. We simply raise sheep for the sheer pleasure of it, and because sheep farming is so good for the environment."

"Really?" Lori looked hopeful.

"*No.* Now if you're ready, I'll demonstrate how the dogs work to move the sheep from one location to another."

"Oh!" Lori cast a furious look at Flynn as he deliberately turned his back to her.

"Well, what did you expect?" Rachel asked her when she was sure Flynn couldn't hear them.

"I don't know," Lori hissed, leveling a mutinous glare at Flynn's broad back. "But I'll never order lamb chops again, that's for sure. What an annoying man."

Rachel suppressed a smile. They watched as the three dogs moved restlessly back and forth between the gate and Flynn, obviously waiting for him to issue a command.

"Conall, hang on to Quinn's collar. I'm going to release these sheep and I don't want him mucking up the works." He turned to Rachel and Lori. "They'll instinctively head down the incline toward the water. I'll have Rob and Brody bring them up to that shed you see on the far hill, and then back here to the paddock."

Shading her eyes, Rachel spotted a small outbuilding, at least a half mile away. "How will they know to bring the sheep there?"

"Watch and see," Flynn replied, and opened the gate.

Rachel watched as the small group of sheep bolted through the opening and made a beeline for the lower ground, rapidly disappearing down the steep incline. To Rachel's surprise, neither of the dogs moved, but simply lay on the ground near Flynn's feet, their sharp eyes never leaving the herd. Then, at a soft command from Flynn, they bolted. Quinn gave a fitful whine, but with a word from Conall, he sat down, pressing his haunches against Conall's leg as he watched the flock. The speed and agility of the dogs as they pursued the sheep was amazing to watch. The two dogs moved to either side, running back and forth along the perimeter of the herd, forcing the sheep into a tight group.

Flynn alternately issued commands like *away* and *come-bye* and *steady*, and the dogs immediately responded. They ran with their heads low, anticipating the movement of the sheep, working in unison to move the flock back up the hill toward the outbuilding.

"How can they hear you?" Lori asked in astonishment. "You're not even raising your voice, but they obey you."

"Their hearing is exceptional," Flynn said. "They have no trouble understanding me, and they want to please me."

"Really?" Lori asked, sending Flynn a sidelong look of interest. "Why?"

"It's just the way they're bred," Flynn replied, issuing another soft command. "They live to work. They're happiest when they know they've done a job well."

"Except for Quinn," Conall said drily, giving the dog a

pat.

"Yeah, except for Quinn," Flynn agreed.

When the sheep had been successfully returned to the paddock, everyone applauded and cheered while Flynn rewarded each of the dogs with praise and a pat.

"That's all the reward they get?" Lori asked in disbelief.

"That's all the reward they need," he said, intercepting Lori's doubtful look. "My praise is what they want."

"You don't give them a treat?"

"Nah. They wouldn't be interested, at any rate."

"Do you shear your own sheep?" Rachel asked, curious. The sheep in the paddock had long, coarse wool that looked as if it had been growing for years. Moreover, it was dingy and matted with dirt and dung in spots. Whoever thought sheep were fluffy and white and soft would be surprised if they could see these sheep, she thought.

"We do, yeah," Flynn said. "Would you care to see?"

"Yes!" Rachel and Lori exclaimed in unison.

"Ah, bloodthirsty are you?" Flynn laughed. "Very well. Let me grab a pair of shears."

He returned moments later, and they watched as he separated a sheep from the herd and pulled her by the horns to an open spot in the paddock. In one deft movement, he turned her onto her rump, using his legs to support her body.

"You're going to use scissors?" Lori asked in horror, eyeing the long, wicked-looking blades.

"I am, yeah. Don't worry—she's done this before, so she's not afraid." He pushed his fingers deep into the fleece and separated it. "You can see how thick her fleece is. We typically don't shear until early summer, but we've been having an unusually warm spring. She'll be happy to get rid of this now for the warmer months."

"Is it hard work to shear a sheep?" Rachel asked.

"No. Once you get the hang of it, it's quite easy, actually. I've shorn hundreds of sheep and it takes only a few minutes."

They watched as he began at the sheep's exposed belly, using one hand to pull the fleece up and then quickly working the shears with the other. As fast as he worked, Rachel could see how gentle and careful he was. As the blades clicked, the fleece began to fall away from the sheep's body in thick, soft piles. Flynn never slowed down, pushing the shears beneath the fleece and swiftly cutting away the wool, exposing smooth, white skin beneath. Rachel found she could scarcely breathe, certain he would inadvertently cut or stab the tender flesh beneath the wool. But as the pile of fleece grew, there was no evidence of any injury to the sheep. Finally, when the last bit of wool fell away, Flynn stepped to one side and the sheep sprang up, looking relieved but unharmed as she returned to the flock.

"And there you have it," Flynn said, wiping a sleeve across his forehead.

"Won't she get cold?" Rachel asked, eyeing the shorn

animal.

"If she does, she'll seek warmth in one of the lean-tos or the barn, but like I said—we're having a warm spring. She'll be fine."

"What about the wool?" Lori asked.

"We do have buyers for the wool," he acknowledged. "It doesn't bring in much money, but every bit helps."

"But it's so dirty!" Lori gave a delicate shudder, as if she couldn't imagine anyone wanting to buy the fleece.

"Yeah, well, it has spent the past year on an animal that lives outdoors," Flynn said. "But once it's washed and properly processed, even you wouldn't turn your nose up at it."

"I'm not turning my nose up—" Lori broke off as she caught the laughter in Flynn's eyes. "Oh, you're *teasing* me!"

"Yeah, and why not when you make it so easy?" he asked, grinning.

"Mrs. McDermott said we might see some lambs," Rachel said hopefully, steering the conversation away from the wool, when it seemed Lori might argue with Flynn about the merits of teasing her.

"Oh, sure," Flynn said. "We have several lambs in the barn that need bottle-feeding, if you'd like to give it a go."

"Yes, please!" Rachel enthused.

"Yes, let's fatten them up for the slaughter," Lori muttered beneath her breath.

"Stop it," Rachel hissed. "You act as if you have no idea

where your food comes from."

"Not from baby sheep," she declared. "Maybe I'll buy them all and set them free."

Rachel gave her a sympathetic smile and linked her arm through Lori's. "I think you have a very big heart, but you should definitely live in the city. I don't think country life is for you."

"That doesn't break my heart." Lori laughed.

Inside the barn was an enclosure with four tiny lambs. Heat lamps kept them warm, and piles of straw bedding had been laid down for them. Unlike the adult sheep, the lambs were clean and white and their short fleece looked invitingly soft.

"Oh, how adorable!" Lori gushed, bending down to scoop one into her arms. "Why aren't they with their mothers?"

"Various reasons," Flynn said. "But mostly because the mother wasn't successful in nursing them, in which case we bring them in here and take care of them until they can be returned to the flock."

"Take my picture, Rachel!" Lori begged. "They won't believe this back in Chicago!"

Laughing, Rachel snapped several photos of Lori cuddling the lamb, and when she reached out and dragged Flynn into the picture, took some of him as well. Rachel didn't miss how pleased he seemed by Lori's attention, his earlier annoyance apparently forgotten. Glancing at Conall, she found him watching the other couple with amusement. As if he sensed her looking at him, he turned and their eyes met.

"Hey," he said softly, coming to stand beside her. "Having fun?"

"I am, actually."

"Those two seem to have hit it off," he observed, indicating Flynn and Lori, who were still playing with the lambs. "Sorry if I came across a bit strong this morning, but you must see why I had concerns."

"He's very good-looking," Rachel acknowledged quietly, raising her gaze to his. "But he's not my type at all."

Whatever he saw in her expression must have reassured him, because his features softened and he leaned in toward her. "That's good to hear. But now I'm curious—what is your type?"

You.

Before she could say as much, Flynn broke the spell.

"I've made up some bottles of formula," he said, extricating himself from Lori's grasp. "Just show them the bottle and they'll come to you. If you give me the camera, I'll take some pictures."

He handed each of them a bottle, and they spent the next few minutes laughing as the lambs greedily guzzled the warm formula.

"They're so sweet," Rachel said, reluctantly setting one of the lambs down. "Thank you so much for letting us do this."

"Of course, it's my pleasure," Flynn said, but his smile

was for Lori.

"Don't be fooled," Conall said drily. "He'll get his pound of flesh out of each of you. Or should I say pound of peat?"

"Ah, yes," Flynn said, rubbing his hands together. "Which of you would like to try your hand at cutting peat?"

"Is it dirty work?" Lori asked, looking doubtful.

"You've got your wellies on," he said, indicating her rubber boots. "You'll be fine, and I'll be there to prevent you from falling in."

Rachel cast a glance at Conall and suppressed a smile as he gave her a conspiratorial wink.

"Sure," Conall said. "We can't let the girls go back to Chicago without trying their hand at cutting turf."

Lori narrowed her eyes. "What makes me think I'm not going to enjoy this?"

Flynn took two long-handled peat-cutters, similar to a spade, down from the wall and handed one to Conall. "Come along then. It's a bit of a walk."

They followed him along a gravel road that led away from the farm and into the hills that overlooked the fjord. The dogs ran ahead of them, clearly happy to be part of the excursion. Eventually, they came to an open field where a long, black channel had been dug into the earth. All around were neatly stacked piles of rectangular-shaped peat logs, drying in the sun.

"Here we are then," Flynn said, leading them to the edge of the pit. He bounced up and down on the balls of his feet.

"You can feel the ground is spongy here and quite wet. We're standing on a peat bog, which takes thousands of years to develop. It's actually an accumulation of decayed vegetation. Because there's so much water content, we cut the turf into bricks and let it dry before we bring it indoors to burn. I'll show you how it's done, and then you can give it a try."

Rachel watched as he stepped into the ditch where the earth had been dug away in a series of steps. Using his foot, he pushed the spade into the rich, black earth and in one easy movement, created a neat, rectangular block which he pitched up onto higher ground. He dug out a dozen more turf blocks before handing the tool to Lori.

"Come down here beside me," he said, extending his hand to help her climb down the earthen steps. "Let's see how you do."

Rachel watched as he showed Lori how to hold the spade and dig out the wet turf, lending his help when she didn't have the strength to throw it onto higher ground. "Well done," he praised her, after she had successfully cut four or five bricks. "You've done a fine job. We'll make a turf-cutter out of you yet."

"Not if I can help it," Lori retorted cheerfully, but nonetheless looked pleased by Flynn's approval.

Rachel took her turn, surprised at how much work it was to cut and throw the peat blocks. "Don't I get any extra assistance?" she asked crossly when Flynn made no effort to help her.

"You're doing fine on your own," he assured her, standing back with his arms crossed over his chest. He gave her a wink. "Keep going."

"Never mind. You've proven yourself," Conall said, taking the peat-cutter from her and extending his hand to help her out of the ditch.

"What about you two?" Rachel demanded, looking between the two men. "We've done our work, and now it's your turn."

Conall gave Flynn an assessing look. "Nah, I don't think so. I'd be playing right into Flynn's hands by falling for his 'Tom Sawyer' tricks. Besides which, I wouldn't want to make him feel bad about himself."

Flynn's astonished expression was almost comical. "And why would I do that?"

"Because I can easily beat you in a turf-cutting competition, and you know it."

Lori laughed and clapped her hands. "Yes! This I have to see."

"Let's have a contest," Rachel urged. "Let's see which one of you can cut more peat."

"Why not?" With a good-natured shrug, Flynn took a peat-cutter and stepped down into the ditch. "Get down here, McDermott, and let me show you how it's done."

With a satisfied grin, Conall peeled off his windbreaker and grabbed the second turf-cutter, before he stepped into the ditch. A light breeze rippled his tee shirt, briefly outlining the muscles of his chest and shoulders. "Ready when you are."

Flynn's expression was determined. Setting his spade aside, he reached behind his head and grabbed a fistful of sweater, dragging it off and nearly taking the underlying tee shirt with it. For a brief instant, Rachel had a glimpse of his impressive six-pack and the light furring of dark hair on his chest. She glanced at Lori, whose mouth had fallen open and whose gaze was riveted on Flynn.

"On my mark," Rachel called, suppressing a grin. "Gentlemen, grab your turf-cutters! Ready, set . . . go!"

They watched as each man dug into the rich, black earth, cutting and tossing bricks of peat so fast that Rachel and Lori were forced to jump back from the edge of the pit or risk getting hit by a flying clod. Within seconds, two piles of turf began to grow as each man continued to bend, cut, and throw. Flynn's face turned ruddy and Rachel could see Conall's shirt darkening with sweat as he kept up a furious pace. Soon it was obvious that, while Flynn's pile was higher than Conall's, the big man was losing steam.

"Had enough?" Conall asked, his teeth flashing.

Flynn flung the turf-cutter away and heaved himself out of the pit. He flung himself onto his back on the damp bog, arms outstretched. "I'm done for," he gasped.

"We have a winner!" Lori cried, triumphantly gesturing toward Conall.

"I'm dying," Flynn moaned, cracking one eyelid to look

at Lori. "I may need oral resuscitation."

For just a second, Rachel thought the other woman might actually do it.

Laughing, Conall set his own spade aside and climbed out, reaching his hand down to his friend. "Not a chance, mate. C'mon, on your feet."

Flynn rose to his feet and dragged the hem of his shirt upward to wipe his face, giving them another glimpse of his cobbled stomach. "Well done, McDermott. But it's only because you're a marathon runner that you have better endurance."

"What are you talking about? You run marathons too."

"Yeah, but I only do it for the free beer at the finish line." He grinned, dropping his shirt back into place.

Reaching out, Conall grasped Flynn's hand in a firm handshake and then pulled him in for a brief bro-hug. "Good job, mate."

Rachel suspected that Flynn could have gone on cutting peat indefinitely, but she appreciated how he'd ended the friendly competition while both men still had some energy left. Lori seemed impressed, too, but Rachel suspected that had more to do with Flynn's abs than the size of his peat pile.

"Congratulations," Rachel said, smiling at both men. "That was impressive, and now you have enough peat to last you an entire winter."

"Well, I don't know about that," Flynn said. "But it'll

get me through a few cold nights at any rate. Well, that's about it as far as what happens here on the farm. Is there anything else you'd like to see?"

"I can't think of anything," Rachel said.

"Thank you so much for showing us the farm," Lori added.

"Of course, it's been my pleasure. I hope you come back again."

Rachel didn't miss how his gaze lingered on Lori, or how she turned pink and pretended to brush some invisible dirt from the hem of her sweater and refused to look at him.

"What about Quinn?" Rachel asked, looking at Conall. "Will you take him home?"

Flynn bent down to rub the dog around his neck. "He's a good boy, just not cut out for herding." He glanced at Conall. "If you'd like to take him, you'd be doing me a favor."

Conall didn't look entirely convinced, but Rachel could see how his expression softened when he looked at the dog.

"Oh, please take him," Rachel pleaded. "He really likes you, and he obeys you."

"Says the woman who isn't responsible for his care and feeding," Conall grumbled good-naturedly. "What am I to do with him during the day when I'm at the shop?"

"Can't you bring him with you?" Rachel asked. "Fiona brings her dog, Gracie, to work sometimes. He'd enjoy it, and I think your customers would as well. He could be the mascot of Heart and Sole, and you could feature him in your running videos."

As if he understood the discussion was centered around him, Quinn padded over to Conall, pushed his head beneath Conall's hand, and looked up at him adoringly.

"How can I say no when you look at me like that?" he demanded, stroking the dog's ears. "Very well. I'll take him, but you owe me."

"I owe you?" Flynn said in astonishment.

"Yes. With Rachel working at the mill most days, Lori is on her own and without a car. Maybe you can take some time out of your busy schedule to show her around?"

"That's a great idea!" Rachel enthused. She wanted to hug Conall for his quick thinking. She'd been feeling guilty about leaving Lori on her own so much while she worked at the mill, and it was obvious to her that there was some sort of attraction between the two, even if Lori liked to pretend otherwise. She acknowledged she also had a more personal reason for encouraging a relationship between the two— Conall might be more willing to spend time with her if Lori and Flynn came along, than if it was just herself and Lori.

"Oh, no," Lori protested, looking horrified. "Please, that's absolutely not necessary. I'm completely capable of entertaining myself."

"Yeah, sure," Flynn said, as if she hadn't spoken. "I can do. How about tomorrow I pick you up at eleven?"

Lori looked less than thrilled with the prospect. "I don't

want to be the favor you owe someone because they agreed to take your dog."

Flynn laughed. "Is that what you think? That I'm only doing it because Conall agreed to take the dog?"

"Well, aren't you?"

"You don't know me very well," Flynn said, looking amused. "If you did, you'd know I never do anything unless it pleases me."

Chapter Ten

"I CAN'T BELIEVE Conall had the nerve to set me up with a sheep farmer!" Lori grumbled as she prowled around the design room at McDermott Mills, picking up fabric swatches and photographs and peeking at the design Fiona was working on. Fiona was in a meeting with Seamus and several of the company directors, so Rachel and Lori were alone.

"Oh, come on," Rachel said with a smile. "I think you like him. And he could hardly keep his eyes off you yesterday. He's very handsome. Besides which, he practically runs the operation by himself, so he obviously has some business savvy."

Lori gave a noncommittal shrug. "I guess so."

"Where is he taking you?"

"I'm not sure. A waterfall, I think, and then a bite to eat somewhere." She paused. "What about you?"

Rachel had made plans to have dinner that night with Conall, since Lori would be out with Flynn. They'd agreed he would pick her up at the B&B at six o'clock.

"I'm not sure where we're going for dinner," she said.

"The pub, probably, or maybe the hotel restaurant. I don't mind where we go, to be honest."

Lori gave her a sly smile. "So I probably shouldn't suggest to Flynn that we meet up with you and have dinner together?"

"If I knew where we were going, I would tell you," Rachel assured her. "Is Flynn picking you up here?"

"No. I'll walk back to the hotel and meet him there."

Rachel put down the colorful array of yarns she was sorting through. "Why are you here, anyway? You could be enjoying a leisurely breakfast at the hotel or taking a walk along the river. Why come visit me? Not that I mind, of course." She smiled at her cousin. "I like seeing you."

"I was bored," Lori said. "Besides, I didn't get a chance to see the mill when I brought you lunch the other day."

That was true. Eager to get outside and enjoy the weather, Rachel had met her cousin in the parking lot of the mill and they had walked to the river and eaten their lunch on a nearby bench.

"Was there something particular you wanted to see?"

Lori shrugged, picked up a sheaf of papers near Fiona's workstation, and studied them absently before setting them down again. "I've never been to a tweed factory and I wanted to see how it compares to Lakeside Industries."

"And? What's the consensus?"

"Well, it's not even in the same league. I peeked into the weaving room as I came up and, honestly, the power looms are ancient."

"They do the job," Rachel assured her. "So, maybe McDermott Mills isn't as big or technologically advanced as your father's company, but I think they do just fine."

"Define *just fine*. How much revenue do they bring in each year?"

Rachel shrugged. "I have no idea. I know they sell custom fabrics to some of the big fashion houses, and they also have their own line of men's and women's clothing, both casual and bespoke. If you're interested in seeing the quality of the clothing, you should visit the retail shop in town."

"I did," Lori admitted. "And you're right—the clothing is very nice. Very pricey too. Do they manufacture any home textiles?"

"Aside from some woolen throws, I don't think so." Rachel studied her cousin, perplexed by her sudden interest in McDermott Mills. "Are you sure this is just you satisfying your curiosity? Did Uncle Jack ask you to check up on me?" A sudden thought occurred to her. "Did he ask you to spy on McDermott Mills?"

Lori gave a bright laugh, but to Rachel's ears, it sounded forced and artificial. "No! Why would you even think that? They're not even in the same league as Lakeside Industries and anyway, why would my father be interested in *tweed*?"

The question was valid, and Rachel could think of no good reason why her uncle would have any interest in the McDermott Mills operations. Still, something seemed off.

She narrowed her eyes. "You can't fool me, Lori Woods. I know you too well. You're up to something and I may not know what it is right now, but I will find out."

"What will you find out?" Fiona breezed into the room with a stack of folders in her arms and looked expectantly between Rachel and Lori.

"Oh, nothing," Lori said airily. "Rachel always thinks I have ulterior motives."

"Oh." Fiona looked puzzled. "Is this about your date with Flynn?"

Lori threw her arms up in exasperation. "It's not a *date*. I didn't even want to go with him, but Conall made it a little difficult for me to refuse. Talk about awkward! Flynn O'Rock is probably just as annoyed as I am by the whole thing."

"It's O'Rourke, not O'Rock," Fiona said, amused. "Although the name would suit him."

"Because he's as hard and dumb as a—"

"Oh, jeez, look at the time!" Rachel exclaimed. "You should probably get going, Lori."

Lori frowned. "Why? I still have plenty of time."

Rachel gave her a deliberate, meaningful look. "But you'll want to change your clothes, maybe put on some makeup. You're actually looking a little washed out."

"Am I?" Lori frowned, and then her face cleared. "Oh, yes, I am! Must be the anticipation of my *date*! Okay, ladies, I'll leave you to your work. Rachel, let's have lunch tomorrow and compare notes."

With a cheeky grin and a wave, she left the room. Rachel gave Fiona an apologetic glance. "Sorry. I had no idea she was coming here this morning."

"It's fine," Fiona said, waving her concerns away. "We're very family-oriented here, and if your cousin wants to come visit, she's more than welcome. After all, it's not like you're on a time clock. You're not even getting paid for your work."

"I signed an agreement with both the university and your father, and I'd hate for him to think I'm not taking this internship seriously. But Lori isn't going to be here for very long, and I do want her to have fun."

Fiona laughed. "Somehow, with Flynn as her tour guide, I don't think that's going to be an issue. He's very popular with the ladies."

"I hope they have a good time or I'll never hear the end of it."

"Well, it's only one day, after all. It's not like she ever has to see him again if it goes badly. Right?"

"I suppose so," Rachel replied. Privately, she doubted if Lori could avoid seeing Flynn again during her stay, especially since Conall had invited them both to the upcoming marathon on the Causeway Coast, in which he and Flynn were both running.

Closing her laptop, Fiona scooped it up along with her paperwork from where it lay scattered across the design desk. "I'm sorry to desert you, but I have a meeting with one of our wool suppliers in Ardara this afternoon, so I should get going." She paused. "I would bring you along, but I'm having dinner afterward with some friends, and you probably have plans with Lori."

Rachel gave the other woman a bright smile. "I do, yes," she fibbed. She hadn't wanted Fiona to know about her dinner date with Conall, not after she'd warned Rachel about getting involved with him. "Enjoy yourself."

"Thanks." Fiona paused in the doorway. "Don't work too late. Get outdoors and take advantage of the nice weather. Days like these are rare!"

After she left, Rachel continued to work on her own design, which was still in the very early stages. She hadn't yet settled on a color scheme but knew she wanted to weave a plaid pattern that incorporated the vibrant hues she had come to love in the Irish landscape, specifically, varying shades of green, gray, violet and pink. She wondered which tweed pattern her father had selected, if indeed he had created a pattern during his days at McDermott Mills. On impulse, Rachel made her way down to the archives room, and signed in at the check-in desk.

"Looking for inspiration, are you?" Miriam asked. "Well, you've come to the right place. Nearly two hundred years of designs in that room."

"I'm hoping to learn if my father designed a pattern while he was here."

"Wouldn't that be grand?" The older woman smiled at

her. "Give a shout if you need any help."

Inside the archives room, Rachel was assailed by the familiar smell of fusty wool. The racks closest to the bottom were the most current designs, so Rachel pressed the button and waited as the upper racks slowly descended, checking the dates as they rotated past. Finally, when she found the patterns from the 1990s, she stopped the machine and began to carefully sort through the hanging swatches until she reached those from 1992.

There were dozens and dozens of tweed samples, each bearing an identification tag. Most of the designs were traditional herringbone, salt and pepper, or checked tweeds in conventional color schemes of blue, brown, and gray. But then her fingers skimmed over a swatch that made her breath catch, it was so beautiful. She knew, even before she read the tag, that this was the one. This was the pattern her father had created more than thirty years earlier. With trembling fingers, she lifted the tag and read the information. Along with the serial number were written the names of both the pattern and the designer.

"Eileen" Designer—Roger Woods, May 1992

Removing the swatch from the rack, she opened it to its full size and quickly snapped some photos with her camera. The pattern, woven in a lusciously soft merino wool, was a plaid tweed in misty shades of blush rose, pale green and bluish gray, with an overlaid windowpane check in deep magenta and forest green, evoking images of the green hedgerows and wild sea thrift against the backdrop of the Atlantic. The pattern was lovely and feminine and Rachel wondered if her father had designed it with someone particular in mind. Had Eileen been a real person, or had he just liked the name?

"What are you doing in here, all by yourself?"

Startled, Rachel looked up to see Seamus in the door-frame, looking at her with a quizzical expression.

"I found a pattern that my father designed," she said, holding out the swatch.

"Did you now?" Stepping into the narrow room, Seamus took the fabric from her and studied the tag. "Ah, yes. A lovely pattern it is too. Quite contemporary for the time, when most weaves were traditional, masculine tweeds."

"I wonder how many yards were produced and if it was popular?" Rachel mused. "What do you suppose was made from this cloth? Maybe a ladies' jacket or skirt?"

"I can check the records, if you'd like."

"You don't mind?"

"Of course not. It's all electronic now, so it wouldn't take more than a few minutes." Seamus smiled at her. "I'm happy to do it."

"Do you know if he named the pattern after an actual person? Was there someone he knew whose name was Eileen?"

"It's possible," Seamus acknowledged. "But it was a long

time ago, and if he had a sweetheart while he was here, I no longer recall."

"Of course," Rachel murmured. She wouldn't dream of contradicting him, but something in his expression told her he wasn't being entirely truthful. She smiled and handed him the swatch. "I appreciate any information you can find about the weave and what it was used for. Personally, I think it's gorgeous, but—" She smiled. "I could be biased."

Seamus took the fabric sample and stepped aside, so she could exit the archive room. She waited as he paused at Miriam's desk and dutifully signed the swatch out.

"Even I must follow the rules," he said, tucking the swatch under his arm. "Well, is there anything else I can help with?"

Rachel shook her head. "No, but thanks very much for checking on that pattern for me. I should get back to work."

"How are you managing? Are you settling in and finding your way?"

"I think so. Fiona has been a great mentor, and I've started working on a pattern of my own." She indicated the room where the yarn samples were kept. "It's just a matter of selecting which yarns to use. There are so many beautiful ones to choose from that it hasn't been easy!"

"Very well, I'll let you get on with it," he said. "I'll let you know about the weave as soon as I can."

After he'd gone, Rachel turned to Miriam, who gave her an indulgent smile. "You found what you were looking for, did you?"

"Yes. The fabric that Seamus just signed out was designed by my father, who did a college internship here about thirty years ago," she said proudly.

"Imagine that! And here you are, following in his footsteps. What a pretty pattern that was too! Lovely pinks and greens."

"He called it 'Eileen,'" Rachel offered. "I wonder if he might have named the design after someone he knew, maybe here in Ballylahane?"

"Oh, now, that's a thought. There are several Eileens hereabouts, I should think."

"Do you know someone by that name?"

At that moment, Miriam's desk phone began to shrill loudly. "That would be the boss," she explained. "Sorry, love, but I need to take this call."

Rachel nodded. "Of course." Leaving the archives, she made her way back up to the design room and sat looking at the assorted yarns on the table. How was it that her own preferences for color so closely matched those of her father? She recalled again the lovely blush rose that had anchored his design, complemented by misty greens and blues. Her father had chosen to weave his design with merino wool, but Rachel wanted something even more luxurious for her own creation. She lifted a skein of cashmere in a pale blue-green hue that reminded her of lichen. Thoughtfully, she held it against another rose-colored skein, and then added a third skein in a deep forest green.

Great.

She had basically selected the same colors that her father had chosen. With a sigh, she dropped the yarn back onto the table. It was no use. She couldn't get her father's design out of her head. As much as she admired the pattern, she didn't want to replicate what he had done. Glancing at her watch, she saw it was nearly four o'clock. Maybe a walk before she met Conall would help. She needed to get outside, clear her head, and come back in the morning refreshed and ready to create something that was uniquely her own.

After cleaning up her workstation, she stashed her camera in her backpack, closed the door to the design room, and made her way outside. The afternoon was clear and sunny, and a light breeze lifted her hair. She would take the long way back to the B&B, along the walking path that followed the river. But as she crossed the parking lot toward the bridge, someone called her name. Turning, she saw Conall leaning against the side of the building, his newly adopted dog, Quinn, sitting on the ground beside him.

"Hi," she said, unable to keep the pleasure out of her voice. She glanced at her watch. "What brings you here? It's only four thirty."

He straightened and walked toward her. He wore a pair of faded jeans that fit loosely through his hips but did nothing to hide the strong muscles of his legs, and a pristine white tee shirt sporting the logo of his shop on the front. A leash dangled from one hand.

"I was waiting on you, actually."

"Oh!" Disconcerted by his sudden appearance and the impact of his smile, Rachel turned her attention to Quinn. Crouching down, she stroked the ruff of his neck and his velvet ears, laughing as he covered her chin with a wet kiss. "Well, I'm very glad to see you too!"

"I'm not sure if that was meant for me or Quinn," Conall said drily when she rose to her feet. "But I'm going to pretend it was me, so don't say anything and crush my hopes."

Rachel blushed. "Of course it was meant for both of you. Why were you waiting for me?"

"I thought you might like to go for a walk along the beach and maybe have a glass of wine before dinner."

"Now?"

"Yes, now." The expression in his eyes was warmly amused. "Unless you've made other plans."

"No," she admitted. "But I had planned to change my clothes and freshen up a bit."

His gaze traveled over her, and there was no mistaking the male appreciation in his eyes. "Trust me, you look great."

"Thanks. Where are we going for dinner, anyway?"

"There's a little place on the water that makes a decent fish pie."

Rachel had never heard of fish pie. "Is that similar to a seafood casserole?"

"I would say so, yeah. Fresh fish and herbs cooked in a cream sauce and baked with smashed potatoes on top. Trust me, it's delicious."

"It sounds good," she agreed.

He reached for her backpack. "Here, I can carry that for you."

"Oh, thank you. Just let me get my camera out first." After retrieving the camera, Rachel allowed him to take her pack, watching as he shrugged it over one shoulder. Together, they left the mill and turned in the direction of town, Quinn padding obediently beside them.

"How is Quinn settling in?"

"Very well, I think," Conall said. "We go for a run in the morning, which he quite enjoys, and then I bring him to the shop for the day. We go for a quick run at lunch, and then again after I close the shop. By the time we get home, he's exhausted most of his energy."

"I'm exhausted just thinking about it. Did you close the shop early today?"

"I took the afternoon off. Michael is there and he'll close up for me. I don't have your phone number and I wanted to catch you before you left."

"Ah," she said, her tone teasing. "So you used me as an excuse to duck out of work?"

"I did, absolutely." He laughed. "How was your day, speaking of work?"

Sunlight dappled the sidewalk and glinted off the storefronts and, to Rachel's eyes, everything seemed to sparkle.

"Fine. Fiona had to leave early for a meeting in Ardara, so I was on my own for most of the afternoon. But I did have one exciting thing happen today."

He looked at her with interest. "What was that?"

"I found a pattern that my father designed while he was here, a beautiful plaid in shades of pink, green, and gray. Honestly, Conall, it's gorgeous, and I'm not just saying that because my father created it. Here, let me show you."

They stopped walking while Rachel opened her camera and quickly scrolled through the photos she had taken. They bent their heads together as they studied the display screen. Rachel got intoxicating whiffs of clean laundry and sun-warmed cedar. When his hands came up to hold the camera, his fingers brushed against hers, sending pleasurable zings of awareness through her.

"Hey, that's fantastic," Conall said, studying the images. "It's quite feminine, isn't it?"

"It is," Rachel agreed. "Even Seamus said it was a very unique pattern for the time, when they mostly sold gray or brown tweeds."

Their eyes met, and being so close, Rachel could see the amazing striations of color in his irises, everything from silver and green to deep, swimming-pool blue. For a moment, she forgot to breathe.

"Just the one design, then?" he asked, looking back at the camera and breaking the spell.

"Ah, yes," she said, collecting herself. "So far, anyway. Seamus came in while I was looking at the swatch and I got distracted. I never got back to looking through the rest of the samples. He's going to check his records and let me know how many meters of the fabric were woven and what it was used for."

"That's wonderful, really," Conall enthused. "I'm happy for you."

"Thank you. It felt a little surreal." She turned the camera off and they resumed walking. "He called the pattern 'Eileen,' and I can't help but wonder if there was someone special that he named it after." She glanced at Conall. "I asked your uncle, but he didn't seem to know and just sort of shrugged it off."

"Well, that's odd, considering his own sister—my aunt—is named Eileen, but everyone calls her Isla. Hardly anyone calls her Eileen."

"Do you think she knew my father? She would be about the same age, wouldn't she? If my dad were alive, he'd be fifty-three years old."

"Yeah, that's about right. I think my aunt is about fifty years old."

"Does she live around here?"

"She lives just outside of Galway," Conall said. "She owns a small art studio where she sells her work."

"Would it be presumptuous of me to ask if I could meet her while we're there? To find out if she knew my father?"

"No, not at all. But don't get your hopes up. As far as I know, my aunt has never had any romantic relationships. She's never married, and she's never had kids."

"Well, maybe she did know my father and he ruined her for all other men," Rachel said, only partly teasing. "He was very handsome and he was single when he came over to Ireland."

"Could be," Conall acknowledged.

"I wonder if my father would approve of my coming over here," she mused. "I hope he would."

Conall stopped walking, turned toward Rachel, and put his hands on her shoulders.

"Obviously, I didn't know your father," he said. "But I think if he could see you now, he would be bursting with pride. Look at you, finishing your advanced degree, coming all the way to Ireland to learn about tweed and handweaving, and honoring his memory in the process." He tipped his head down to look directly into her eyes. "I think he would be very proud of you."

His words were so heartfelt and his expression was so kind that Rachel felt the sting of tears behind her eyes. Even her own family had never expressed the kind of positive affirmation of her career choices that Conall just had, and she found herself falling a little bit in love with him for it.

"Thank you."

"Come here," he said gruffly, and pulled her into an embrace, his arms warm and strong around her. Impulsively, she hugged him back, until Quinn jumped against them and began barking. Laughing, they broke apart, but Conall didn't let her go entirely. He kept one arm loosely around her shoulders as they walked, and it seemed only natural to put her own arm around his waist, noting how well they fit together.

"Quinn seems to have no problem obeying you," she observed, as the dog loped happily ahead of them, then circled back around them.

"Yeah, he's doing great. I bring the leash just in case, but he hasn't seemed interested in straying too far. We're still working on voice commands, but he's learning. He just needs a lot of positive reinforcement."

"I'm so glad you agreed to take him."

"I am, too, actually. It's nice to have him around the house in the evenings."

"I would love to have a dog, but they're not allowed in the building where I live."

"So you're right in the city, are you?"

"Yes," Rachel said. "Our building is actually pretty old, built in 1899, and only three stories tall. We're completely surrounded by high-rise buildings. I'm not sure how long we'll be able to stay there since a developer wants to purchase the building, tear it down, and build something modern."

"Where would you go?"

Rachel shrugged. "I'm not sure. Rent is expensive in the city, so we'd probably have to look farther out, in the suburbs. We got this place pretty cheap because it's so old, and because the train runs directly behind the building, which makes for a noisy apartment. Have you been to the States?"

"I have, yeah. I have friends in Boston and I've run the marathon there a couple of times." He shrugged. "I didn't win, of course, but I represented myself well."

"I'm sure you did."

They had reached the small harbor and they walked along the seawall, past the boats that were tied up and bobbing on the water, and past the small shacks used by the local fishermen to store equipment. At the end of the seawall was a pebbled beach that stretched for a mile or so until it reached the cliffs. Jumping down, Conall reached up and lifted Rachel down beside him.

"Thank you," she murmured, a little flustered by the ease and familiarity with which he handled her. "I can't help but think you grew up in a very close-knit family."

Conall gave her an inquiring look. "What makes you think so?"

"Well, don't take this the wrong way, but you're a very hands-on kind of guy." She felt her face go a little warm as she explained. "Maybe you don't even realize how often you touch me."

"Not nearly as often as I'd like." He raised his hands. "Sorry, just the truth."

He looked so unapologetic that a smile tugged at Rachel's mouth, even as tiny bursts of pleasure detonated inside her, like fireworks on a summer night. "No, it's fine. I just wondered."

He pushed his hands into his front pockets, as if he didn't trust himself not to reach for her again. "I'm a physical guy," he admitted. "I like working with my hands and I like people. That's part of what drew me to medicine in the first place."

"You probably did really well in school."

"I did, actually. I just couldn't see myself correcting ingrown toenails and bunions for the rest of my life."

Rachel gave a surprised burst of laughter and pulled a face. "Ew, no! I think you made the right choice in switching careers."

"Do you?" He slanted her a sideways look. "You don't think less of me for throwing away a lucrative medical career to become a shoe salesman?"

"I would hardly call you a shoe salesman," she protested, recalling how she had thought exactly that when she first saw him in his shop. "And I would never think less of someone who chose to follow their dream, as you have, and made a success of it."

"I do okay," he said. "I've never regretted the move."

They continued to walk along the pebbled beach while Quinn splashed happily through the shallow waves that broke against the shore. They had reached the edge of town, where small cottages and B&Bs overlooked the water, which sparkled beneath the late afternoon sun.

"This is so beautiful," Rachel commented. "Where are we eating? I had no idea there was a restaurant down here. What's it called?"

"Er, Conall's Kitchen?"

Rachel stopped walking. "What?"

To her astonishment, a flush crept up his neck. "It's not exactly a restaurant, Rachel. It's just my house."

"Your house?" She gaped at him. "You're cooking dinner for me at your house?"

"I am, yeah. Do you mind?" He looked sheepish. "It was that or Mallone's Pub and Maggie is in the kitchen tonight so . . . I figured I couldn't do any worse than her, and the view from my place is a bit better."

Rachel laughed. "No, I don't mind at all." They resumed walking. "Can you really cook fish pie?"

"I can, yeah. I learned from my dad, but I never did get the hang of baking, so I didn't make a tea cake for dessert. I picked up a lemon pound cake at the Yarn Spinner's Café instead."

Rachel peered along the shore at the houses that over-looked the beach. "So, which one is yours?"

"It's just there," he said, and pointed to a whitewashed cottage with a thick thatched roof and a bright-blue door. As they drew closer, Rachel saw there was a small patio enclosed by a low wall, with a table and chairs that overlooked the beach. A modern sunroom had been added to one side of the cottage, providing clear views of the ocean.

"You live here?" she asked in disbelief.

"I do. The house belonged to my grandparents, and after they passed, my parents lived here for a short time, but found it too small for a family with three kids. They moved to a larger house on the other side of the harbor, but they kept the cottage. When I made the decision to come back to Ballylahane, I bought it from them."

Quinn bolted ahead of them, leaping up the embankment toward the house, where he stood with his tail wagging furiously. Taking Conall's hand, Rachel allowed him to help her climb the sandy dunes to the grassy area behind the cottage. Opening a small gate in the stone wall, he ushered her onto the patio. A metal firepit and two teakwood chairs had been placed at the edge of the patio closest to the dunes and outdoor lighting had been strung over the table.

"This is incredible," she said, looking around in disbelief. With its sweeping views of the coastline and the ocean, the little cottage was like something straight out of a travel magazine. When she had first begun to make plans to travel to Ireland, she had envisioned staying in a sweet little cottage exactly like this one, but had quickly learned they were beyond her modest budget. Now she imagined what it would be like waking up to the sound of the surf each day and sitting on the patio to watch the sun sink over the horizon each night. She imagined cozy peat fires in the winter while the wind whistled around the house, knowing you were safe within its solid walls. "Conall McDermott, you are without a doubt the luckiest man in Ireland."

"Yeah," he said with a grin. "Right now, I believe I am."

Chapter Eleven

RACHEL FOLLOWED CONALL and Quinn into a small kitchen at the back of the house, not knowing what to make of his comment. He didn't elaborate, and she couldn't bring herself to ask, because she had a sudden certainty that it had everything to do with her. Maybe it wasn't intentional, but he was slowly weaving an irresistible picture of a life in Ireland, one that she could never be a part of because her own path led back to Chicago. Pushing the unsettling thoughts aside, she focused instead on her surroundings.

"This is so charming!" she exclaimed, taking in the old-fashioned enameled stove and red fridge, and a sink and counter that overlooked both the patio and the ocean beyond. In one corner of the kitchen was a table and two chairs, and Rachel could picture Conall eating a hurried breakfast there in the morning before going for a run.

"Well, I can't take credit for the modern upgrades," Conall said. "That was done by my mum when she thought they might sell the place or rent it as a vacation home."

"But you bought it instead?"

"I did. It's been in our family for generations and I

couldn't stand the thought of letting it go." Opening a low cupboard, he pulled out a bag of dry dog food and measured a cup into a bowl on the floor. Quinn began to noisily scarf the food, causing them both to laugh. Conall opened the refrigerator, pulled out a bottle of white wine, and retrieved two glasses from a cupboard. "Shall we sit outside?"

Rachel gave him her best pleading look. "Could I maybe have a peek at the rest of your house first? I mean, only if you don't mind. Aside from Mr. Cullen's house, I've never been inside an authentic Irish cottage and even then, I only saw the kitchen."

"No, not at all," he said. "It didn't even occur to me that you might be interested."

"Are you kidding? I think most Americans with Irish roots dream of moving to Ireland and living in a cottage exactly like this."

Conall set the glasses and wine down on the counter. "Does that include yourself?"

The question was asked lightly, but the expression in his blue eyes was serious enough that Rachel suddenly felt flustered.

"Well, yes, but it's just a dream," she said, stumbling over her words. "I mean, I have a life and a career waiting for me in Chicago. Everything I've done has been with the goal of working at Lakeside Industries."

"Of course. It was more of a theoretical question." There was an awkward silence, and then Conall gestured to the next room. "Well, let me show you the rest of the house. It's not much, but it's enough for me."

The cottage was compact, but still felt spacious, partly because Conall had a minimal amount of furniture and clutter. There was a small fireplace in the cozy living room and next to it, a wicker basket filled with peat logs. Overhead, hand-hewn beams supported the ceiling. The room was dominated by a comfortable-looking sofa and a large flat-screen television. A small home office occupied one corner of the room. Through the deep casement windows at the front of the house was a view of the church spire and the rooftop of the hotel, as well as the chimneys of the buildings in town. Beyond the living room, a set of glass doors opened into the sunroom, which was filled with fitness equipment, including a treadmill, a Peloton bike, and a weight bench.

"Your own home gym," she observed. "Very nice."

"Yeah, it made sense when the fitness centers were closed, and now I like the convenience of being able to work out whenever I like. Plus, I can open the windows and get a great breeze." He shrugged. "My mum would prefer I turn it into a family room or a dining area, but this works better for me."

"I can see why," Rachel acknowledged. "Look at that view."

Behind the kitchen was a bedroom, obviously Conall's, with a large bed pushed beneath the windows. The sheets and blankets were invitingly rumpled and one pillow still bore the imprint of his head. All kinds of steamy visuals swam through Rachel's imagination as she pictured him lying there. Dragging her fascinated gaze away, she focused instead on the graphic art on the walls, mostly large framed posters of marathon events from around the world.

"Sorry," Conall muttered as he moved quickly through the room, picking up discarded clothing and running shoes and tossing them into a closet. "I didn't think you'd be interested in my bedroom—" He stopped and stared at her, his expression appalled. "I mean—that is—I didn't know you'd actually be in my bedroom . . . you know what? Never mind. I'm going to stop talking. Sorry."

Rachel laughed. She couldn't help herself. He was actually flustered by her presence in his bedroom and she found it both adorable and infinitely appealing, because it meant he hadn't had any ulterior motives in inviting her to dinner at his house. She didn't know whether to feel flattered or disappointed.

"You don't need to apologize—or pick up—on my account. This is your home and I'm the one who should apologize for insisting on a tour when, obviously, you had no intention . . . that is, you had no plans . . ."

Before she could finish the thought, Conall was standing in front of her, his hands on her upper arms. "If you think I haven't thought about you in that bed with me, you'd be wrong," he said, his voice low. "And maybe I'm an idiot for telling you, but I've thought about it more than I want to admit."

"Oh." Rachel stared at him, mesmerized by what she saw in his eyes.

Heat.

Desire.

Something raw and urgent that caused her breath to hitch and warmth to bloom and spread everywhere in her body.

"I want you every way a man can want a woman, Rachel, and if that's not clear enough, maybe this will convince you."

Before she could guess his intent, he lowered his head and kissed her. But unlike the slow, searching kiss from before, this one was lush and deep, his mouth opening hers, and his tongue exploring in ways that drew excited shivers from her and made her cling to him. One hand traveled up her spine, his fingers splaying over her back until he cupped the nape of her neck and tilted her head to one side. His kiss gentled and traveled over her cheek to the fragile skin of her throat, where he nibbled and sucked the tender flesh until Rachel felt boneless and drenched with excitement. Their bodies were pressed together and she could feel the solid planes of his chest against her breasts, the way his hips nudged into her own, and his muscled thighs, honed to hardness through years of running, pressed against hers, which had suddenly lost any ability to support her. Her fingers clutched his back and only the sound of her own voice making small, needy sounds brought her back to her senses.

"Conall . . ."

He lifted his head and looked at her, his eyes a hot, soft blue. "Yes, sweetheart?"

The way he said *sweetheart*, the t's sharp and precise, turned the endearment into something that felt like a physical caress. Dazed, she stared up at him. "What are we doing?"

"Do you want to stop?" His voice was low and smoky-rough, his accent more pronounced. He was still holding her loosely, one hand rubbing slow circles between her shoulder blades.

It was all Rachel could do to prevent her gaze from sliding toward the bed. Did she want him to stop? *No.* But, unfortunately, she still retained enough sense to know they would be making a huge mistake if they continued. *She* would be making a mistake, because she was already falling hard for Conall, and getting physically involved with him would only make leaving him more difficult.

"I can't do this. *We* can't do this."

Releasing her, Conall stepped back and the sudden space between them seemed vast. His expression, so tender just seconds earlier, became shuttered. "Sure."

"No, you don't understand." She hastened to explain, reaching a hand out to touch the front of his shirt, needing contact with him. "I'm no good at this. I can't be casual, not about this. Not with you."

"Is that what you think this is? How I feel?" His brows drew together. "Rachel, there's absolutely nothing casual or superficial about my feelings for you. When I first met you in that field, I thought you were gorgeous and funny, and I hoped we might run into each other again. But then—"

"What?" Rachel could hardly breathe. She wanted—needed—him to finish his thought. The expression in his eyes caused heat to gather like hot liquid beneath her clothing until she felt steeped in awareness.

"But then I got to know you better, and I realized I'm attracted to everything about you. You're smart and you're sweet, and you literally light up when you smile. You have a way of making people feel comfortable, even when they don't know you. And the way you look at me sometimes—I think I could actually move mountains for you. Even when we're not together, I think about you." He paused, his gaze lingering on her. "You make me want to be the kind of man you could fall in love with . . . the kind of man you could spend your life with."

His words both thrilled and terrified her. Things were moving too fast. If she didn't slow down, she would find herself ditching all her carefully laid plans for her future. She swallowed hard. "We've known each other for such a short time."

To her dismay, he seemed almost amused. "That's true." He stroked a thumb over her cheek and then gently grazed the side of her throat with the backs of his fingers. "So let's have dinner and get to know each other better, and I promise not to overstep—unless you want me to."

A reluctant smile tugged at Rachel's mouth. She felt both relieved and disappointed by his apparent willingness to slow down. Her body still thrummed where they had been pressed together and his words repeated in her head like a promise.

You make me want to be the kind of man you could fall in love with.

She pulled in an unsteady breath because part of her knew it was too late—she was already half in love with him. Conall watched her carefully, as if he half expected her to object.

"Okay," she finally agreed. "As long as you understand that whatever happens, eventually I'm going back to Chicago. I have to."

"I know. I do." A roguish grin tilted his mouth. "But I still have more than two months to try to change your mind, yeah?"

Rachel couldn't help laughing at his brashly optimistic tone. "You can try."

They returned to the kitchen, where Conall turned on the oven and removed a covered dish from the refrigerator. Quinn roused himself from where he had been lying on a dog bed near the table and sniffed the air, hoping for a handout. After placing the dish in the oven and setting the timer, Conall uncorked the wine and handed Rachel a glass.

"Did you really make that yourself?" she asked, indicating the oven.

"I did," he said, looking affronted. "I put it together just before I came to meet you at the mill. I even purchased the fish at the dock in town." He narrowed his eyes. "There are some things I might tease about, but my fish pie isn't one of them."

Rachel laughed. "Okay, sorry. It's just that I've never met a guy who could actually cook something that didn't involve a slab of meat and an outdoor grill."

They stepped onto the patio and Quinn bolted through the door behind them and over the low wall, toward the dunes. Conall ruefully indicated a gas grill in one corner. "I'm more comfortable barbecuing, but I can use the oven in a pinch."

He pulled out a chair for her at the table and waited for her to sit down before joining her, scooting his chair close enough to hers that their knees brushed. A breeze stirred the tall beach grass behind the patio, and seagulls dipped and swooped over the waves. Rachel could see Quinn sniffing his way along the beach, occasionally looking back in their direction, as if expecting Conall to call him back.

"He won't go far," Conall said, following her gaze. "I think he knows if he wants to be fed, he needs to stick around."

"I think he just likes you," Rachel said, glancing at him. The sun was low in the sky, as round and orange as an apricot, turning his hair to burnished gold and catching the extraordinary blueness of his eyes as he looked out over the ocean. A dull ache had developed in her chest, and she recognized it as longing. She wanted to hold on to this moment forever. She'd told Conall she would eventually return to Chicago, but right now, she couldn't imagine ever leaving this spot. The tall dune grasses swaying on either side of the patio blocked her view of neighboring cottages, and with nothing but the wide expanse of the sea in front of them, they might have been alone in the whole world.

"This really is amazing," Rachel said, leaning back in her chair as she admired the view and let the rhythmic sound of the waves lull her. "Such a peaceful, beautiful spot."

"It is," Conall agreed. Reaching out, he captured her free hand in his and held it loosely, playing with her fingers. "I'm fortunate my parents agreed to let me have it. Not that I got a deal on it, but they likely could have gotten more if they'd sold it through a Realtor or rented it as a vacation house."

"I'm sure they're happy to keep it in the family," Rachel said, watching as he toyed with her hand. "Do you think you'll make Ballylahane your permanent home?"

"For now," he said, releasing her. "I'd like to open another shop in Wexford or Cork, but it would require my being on-site full-time, at least until I've hired a reliable manager. But regardless of where my shops are located, I'd like to make my home here in Ballylahane. I've belonged to the local running club for almost fifteen years and if you understand anything about Ireland, it's that we're fiercely loyal to our local sports clubs."

He said this with a grin, but Rachel recognized the ring of truth in his words.

"How many members does it have?"

"The Inishkeel Athletic Club includes Ballylahane and the surrounding area. It has about three hundred members. That's almost double what it had before I opened the shop, so I like to think I had something to do with growing the membership. I enjoy giving back to the community, and if I can encourage people to get outside, even better. In my opinion, there's no substitute for fresh air and exercise. It sharpens your focus and relieves stress, to name just a few benefits."

"It sounds like you've certainly made a difference," Rachel said.

He slanted her a grateful look. "I hope so. I need to be successful if only to show—"

"What?" Rachel prompted.

"To show my family that I'm not a failure. They've never said so, but I know they were disappointed when I gave up the clinic."

On impulse, Rachel reached out and caught his hand. "I'm sure they're very proud of what you've accomplished, Conall. I can't imagine why they wouldn't be."

He squeezed her hand gently. "Thanks. I appreciate that."

Their gazes met and held for several long seconds. For all

his confidence, there was a stark vulnerability about him that pulled at Rachel's heart and made her want to give him all kinds of assurances and promises—promises she had no idea if she could keep. Instead, she said nothing. They were silent for several moments as they sipped their wine and watched the waves, but Rachel's mind was working overtime. The thought of returning to Chicago and never seeing Conall again made her feel unaccountably depressed.

"Have you ever considered going international with your business?"

Conall looked at her sharply. "Do you mean America?"

Rachel nodded. "Yes, why not?"

Conall blew out a hard breath. "For starters, I think it could be difficult to break into the market over there, especially with so many established chain stores. Beyond the logistical challenges of obtaining visas and permits, I don't want to leave Ireland. I'm happy here, and my business is thriving."

"I understand." Rachel did understand. She wasn't sure she wanted to leave Ireland, either, and she'd only been here for a few weeks.

"You could always pursue a career in textile design here, in Ireland," he countered quietly. "Seamus would likely hire you, if you were interested."

"I'm not so sure about that," Rachel said with a small laugh. "He already has a talented team of designers. Besides which, everything I've done has been with the goal of making a career at Lakeside Industries." She gave Conall a helpless look. "It's where my family has worked for generations."

Conall nodded. "I understand."

Realizing they had reached an impasse, Rachel leaned toward him, feeling the need to explain her decision. He had to see that she couldn't remain in Ireland, no matter how much she might be tempted. There were too many factors that played into such a big decision. "Even if I were to consider staying here, I'd still need to formally present my thesis and graduate, and I would need to go back to Chicago to do that."

"But that's just a formality at this point, yeah?"

"Well, yes," she acknowledged. "But I would hate to let my uncle down, after everything he's done to help me. He's promised me a position on the design team and I think he would be disappointed if I changed my mind now. Not to mention I'd be leaving Lori in the lurch with the apartment."

Conall studied her. "Your family means a lot to you, don't they?"

"I suppose so. Yours means a lot to you too. You said you're very close."

"We are, but they'd never expect me to live my life according to their expectations."

"I'm not—"

"That wasn't a criticism," Conall soothed. "I admire what you're doing, and how much you love your family. And

I understand why you might not be able to just pick up and relocate to another country. I tried it, and I couldn't do it."

Rachel recalled what Fiona had told her. "Australia?" she ventured. "You said you'd lived there for a short time."

"A very short time," he admitted, his tone wry. "I met a girl from Melbourne during college and while I'd hoped she would stay in Ireland, she returned to Australia. I fancied myself in love and stayed here just long enough to finish my studies before I packed my bags and followed her over there."

Rachel listened, even as something sharp and painful twisted inside her. "What happened?"

Conall shrugged. "I don't think she expected I would actually come after her. I hadn't told her I was coming over—I wanted to surprise her; sweep her off her feet with my grand gesture." He swirled the wine in his glass, his expression inscrutable. "But my unexpected arrival threw a monkey wrench into her plans to move to Brisbane, which is almost two thousand miles north of Melbourne."

"You didn't know she was planning to move?"

"She hadn't wanted to say anything until it was official. If she'd known I was coming over, she would have told me. In the end, our efforts to surprise each other backfired."

"So what did you do?" Rachel asked.

"I'd already accepted a job with a Melbourne clinic, so I stayed in Melbourne and she moved to Brisbane. We tried to make it work, but we might as well have been on different continents." He shrugged. "We barely saw each other and, after six months, I had to accept that it wasn't going to work, and I returned home. I won't lie—it was a tough decision and for a long time I wondered if I'd done the right thing. But I didn't leave only because of her; I missed Ireland. I missed my family. I wanted to come back."

"Have you seen each other since?"

Conall gave a brief laugh. "No. I heard through a mutual friend that she's married now."

Rachel digested what he had told her, feeling inexplicably sad, both for Conall and for herself.

Conall set his wineglass down, and a rueful smile tugged at his mouth. "Just bad timing, isn't it?"

Rachel didn't pretend to misunderstand. "Yes."

Chapter Twelve

"So . . . how was dinner with the marathon man?"

Rachel and Lori were finishing a late breakfast at the hotel restaurant, where Conall would soon pick them up for their weekend visit to Galway.

"It was great," Rachel said. "He made an amazing seafood casserole served with mashed potatoes that, honestly, was the best thing I've tasted in a long time."

"Wow!" Lori took a sip of her coffee, her eyes sparkling over the rim of her cup. "A man who's good-looking, financially independent, and can cook." She gave Rachel a wink. "If you don't want him, I'll take him. So did you . . . you know, do the deed?"

Rachel gave her cousin a reproving look. "I'd tell you that's none of your business, but you'd take it as proof that something happened. Which it didn't. Well, not much, anyway."

Lori's mouth drooped in disappointment. "You're such a prude. Would it kill you to have a little fun while you're here?"

"I am having fun!" Rachel protested. "I love spending

time with Conall, but every minute we're together just makes it harder to keep things casual. I can't afford to get emotionally involved with him, Lori, although part of me wonders if it isn't already too late."

"You really like him." Lori stared at her in growing wonder. "As in *like* like him!"

Rachel groaned. "I do. And it's terrible because he's practically perfect, but it would never work between us. He admitted he doesn't want to leave Ireland, and there's no way I can stay."

"Maybe it's just not meant to be," Lori said sympathetically. "Which is sad, because he's so cute and he seems to really like you too."

Rachel thought again of their dinner on the patio, and how they'd watched the sun sink over the ocean. When it had grown chilly, Conall had lit a fire in the firepit and loaned her one of his thick, cabled sweaters. They'd sat close together and talked quietly into the night until the fire had burned down to embers. Only then had he driven her back to the B&B, but true to his word, he hadn't kissed her goodnight. Instead, he'd kept his hands shoved into his front pockets and leaned against the fender of his car. In the end, she'd been the one to kiss him, standing on tiptoe to press her mouth against his, gratified when he groaned softly and hauled her into his arms. The kiss had gone on and on, and she'd slid her hands under the hem of his sweater to find the warm skin beneath, until finally he'd set her away from him and urged her to go into the house and get some sleep. Only when she'd reached her room did she realize she still wore his sweater. She'd taken it to bed with her and buried her face in it, breathing in the familiar scents of wool and the warm, tangy spices of his soap. It had been a long time before she'd fallen asleep.

"What about you?" she asked, deliberately changing the subject. "How was your day with Flynn?"

Lori shrugged, but Rachel knew her cousin too well, and recognized the gesture as a weak attempt to pretend her day with the big Irishman had been no big deal. "Oh, you know . . . you've seen one waterfall, you've seen them all."

"Because you've seen so many," Rachel said drily. "C'mon, tell me how it went. Was he a gentleman?"

Lori scowled. "No. Just the opposite, in fact. Honestly, I've never met a man as infuriating as Flynn O'Rourke. He wants to argue about everything and, when he's not trying to annoy me, he takes a perverse pleasure in teasing me!" She leaned forward. "It's no wonder he's still single—I don't think he has any clue about women. Good looks will only get you so far."

Rachel lifted her coffee cup to hide her smile. "Mm-hmm. And how far did he get?" To her astonishment, Lori's face turned red. "Oh. My. God. You totally made out with him, didn't you?"

"I might have let him kiss me. It was no big deal, and it meant nothing."

"Uh-huh. Sure."

Lori scowled. "I know you don't believe me, but he's not my type. Even you have to admit that."

Rachel thought about the guys Lori had dated over the years. Like Seth Bieler, they had all been polished and professional, and she couldn't imagine any of them working outside or with animals, or allowing their hands to get dirty. She certainly couldn't picture them shearing a sheep or working in a peat bog.

"Okay, I'll admit he's not your usual style, but there is a certain charm to him."

"Yeah, if you like a guy who manhandles helpless creatures."

"Are you referring to yourself?" Rachel asked with a smirk. "Because I happen to know there's nothing helpless about you."

"Ha-ha." Lori waved a hand. "Anyway, enough about that. I'm really looking forward to seeing Galway." Suddenly, her eyes widened and she shrank down in her chair, staring over Rachel's shoulder toward the entrance to the restaurant. "Oh, no," she muttered.

Turning, Rachel saw Conall enter the restaurant, followed by Flynn O'Rourke. She spun back toward Lori. "Did you invite him to come to Galway with us?"

Lori made a face. "I might have mentioned something, but I honestly didn't think he'd be interested."

Rachel laughed softly. "Oh, I think he's definitely interested."

If anything, Lori looked even more miserable. "Maybe he just ran into Conall and decided to come by and say hello."

"Good morning," Conall said as he and Flynn approached their table. "Flynn is going to join us on our Galway adventure."

"That's wonderful!" Rachel said, beaming up at both men. "Now Conall won't feel so outnumbered by us women."

"I couldn't let him have all the fun, could I?" Flynn asked, and his gaze slid to Lori in what looked like a gentle challenge.

"I'm surprised you could get away from the farm for two days," Lori said sweetly. "All those sheep that need shearing . . ."

"It was no trouble," he assured her with a grin. "I have two brothers, after all. Thank you for inviting me to tag along."

"Did I, though?" Lori asked, narrowing her eyes at him. "I seem to recall saying something to the effect that I sympathized with Conall, spending his weekend shepherding four women around Galway."

"Exactly," Flynn said. "Which is why I'm here. So when you ladies decide to explore Shop Street, Conall won't have to sit alone in a pub, nursing a pint." He spread his arms. "It's a win-win for everyone."

"Where is Fiona?" Rachel asked, glancing toward the entrance. "Is she waiting for us outside?"

"Fiona is taking her own car," Conall replied. "She likes to be master of her own destiny and this way she's not locked into our schedule. We'll meet up with her and Mary-Kate in Galway."

Rachel nodded, but exchanged a quick, troubled glance with Lori. This weekend was turning into something she had not anticipated. Instead of a group getaway, it was feeling more and more like a couple's retreat.

"Look, I know what you're thinking," Conall said quickly. "But we're having lunch with them when we arrive, and then we'll get checked into the hotel. After that, I have business at my shop for the rest of the day, so I won't see you until later tonight. You'll have the afternoon to explore on your own."

"What about you?" Lori asked, looking at Flynn. "What are your plans?"

"I'm actually going to nip out and meet some of my mates for a football match this afternoon," he said. "I went to university in Galway and I have a number of friends who still live there." He gave her a conspiratorial wink. "Don't worry. I won't expect you to entertain me, as charming as that sounds."

"You play football?" Lori eyed him with renewed interest.

"I do, but it's not American football. It's Gaelic football."

"I'm not familiar with that."

"You should come by, then."

"Maybe I will."

Rachel pushed her chair back. "We're ready to go. We left our bags at the front desk."

After retrieving their overnight bags, they left the hotel and climbed into the Range Rover.

"Your father doesn't mind giving up his vehicle for the weekend?" Rachel asked as they pulled away from the hotel.

"Not at all," Conall said, meeting her gaze in the rearview mirror. "He and my mum enjoy the convertible, and I wouldn't be surprised if they do a little touring of their own this weekend."

"What about Quinn?" she asked.

"He's staying with my parents. They'll spoil him and probably undo all the progress he's made." But his voice lacked any real censure or concern.

The drive to Galway took them through picturesque farmland and small villages, and along the coast toward Sligo. Both Rachel and Lori stared in wonder at the jutting mountains and rocky coastline that characterized the region.

"That's Ben Bulben," Flynn said, pointing to an enormous, flat-topped rock formation in the distance that looked like the prow of a massive ship. The majestic peak dominated the landscape and could be seen for miles. "We're in Yeats country now. 'Under bare Ben Bulben's head / In Drumcliff churchyard Yeats is laid.'" He broke off with an embarrassed laugh. "I used to know the entire poem, but that's all I can recall at the moment."

"Very good," Conall said, grinning at his friend. "I'd no idea you could spout poetry."

"Obviously, I can't," Flynn said ruefully. "At least, not very well."

They arrived in Galway just before noon and, as they drove through the narrow streets, Rachel was charmed by the small city and the central park with its enormous fountain and sculptures. After checking into the hotel, they met in the lobby.

"I told Fiona and Mary-Kate we'd meet them at the restaurant," Conall said, glancing at his watch. "Flynn, will you join us?"

"Sorry, I can't. I'm due at the sports field in thirty minutes, but I'll catch up with you later."

After he left, they walked with Conall across the park, where the warm weather had drawn dozens of people outdoors. They reached Shop Street, a long, cobblestoned pedestrian district of brightly colored shops and restaurants, thronging with crowds of tourists. Overhead, festive bunting fluttered in the breeze. Music swelled on every street corner as performers played fiddles, harmonicas, and accordions. Shop windows featured woolens, fine clothing, gold claddagh jewelry, and Irish souvenirs. Restaurant seating spilled onto the street, and Rachel breathed in the aromas of fried seafood, pizza, and grilled steak.

"Here we are," Conall said. "And there are Mary-Kate and Fiona."

They had reached a restaurant with outdoor tables surrounded by tall pots of flowers, and Rachel saw Fiona and her sister were already seated. After Lori had been introduced to Mary-Kate, they ordered pints of beer and fish and chips. They ate and talked, and watched the crowds of people go past, and every so often, Rachel would catch Conall's glance, and he would smile at her as if they shared a secret, which made her feel warm all over.

"Well," he said when they had finished and paid the bill. "I'm off. Let's plan to meet at the hotel around half seven, yeah?"

"I'll show the girls around, shall I?" Mary-Kate offered. She leaned toward Rachel. "Most tourists don't venture too far from Shop Street, but there are loads of fabulous bargains to be had on the side streets and across the river."

"Have fun," Conall said, grinning. "I think it's a good thing we brought the big car! More space for your purchases."

After he left, the four of them spent several hours exploring Shop Street and the quiet alleyways, then ventured out to see the Spanish Arch and the River Corrib, which ran through the center of town and out to the ocean. They had tea and pastries at a quaint tea shop overlooking the water before deciding to call it a day.

"Yes, I'd say we did a good job of it today," Mary-Kate

said as they made their way back to the hotel. "Was there anything else you wanted to look for while we're here?"

"Actually," Rachel ventured, "Conall said your aunt Eileen has a shop here in Galway. Would it be possible to stop in? I'd love to see her work."

"We could do," Fiona said. "But her shop isn't located in Galway. She belongs to a craft consortium in Connemara, so we'd need the car to get there. It's only a twenty-minute drive, but too far to walk."

"Oh." Disappointment swamped Rachel. She had hoped to meet Eileen McDermott, ask if she had known her father, and find out if the pattern he'd designed might have been named after her.

"I'm sure you could go tomorrow," Mary-Kate said gently. "It's not that far, and it's in the direction you'd be heading to go home. Besides, you can't come this far and not take a drive through Connemara. It's gorgeous country."

"Oh, I'd love to go," Lori said, struggling under the burden of her purchases. "Sounds like a perfect place to get some handmade gifts to bring home."

"I'd say you've done enough damage," Rachel said, eyeing her purchases with a grin. "Any more gifts, and you're going to need another suitcase."

They reached the hotel and, after the McDermott sisters took the elevator to their room, Rachel and Lori lingered over a display of tourist brochures near the entrance.

"What time are we heading back tomorrow?" Lori asked,

studying a brochure about the Cliffs of Moher.

"I don't think we have a set schedule. If you really want to see the cliffs, I'm sure Conall and Flynn won't mind."

"Oh, that's okay." Lori replaced the glossy pamphlet. "There's no reason to go out of our way to see the Cliffs of Moher. Flynn said he would take me out to see some other cliffs, closer to Ballylahane."

"Oh, so, suddenly, he's not so annoying?" Rachel suppressed a smile as she slid a sideways glance at her cousin.

"Oh, he is definitely the most exasperating man I've ever met," Lori replied cheerfully. "I'm thinking of a second date as payback."

"Admitting, of course, that your first outing was, in fact, a date," Rachel said teasingly.

Lori made a scoffing sound. "As if I would ever *date* a guy like that."

Before Rachel could respond, the glass entrance doors slid smoothly open and two men stepped into the lobby. She spotted Conall's bright hair and did a double-take. How was it that each time she saw him, she was struck again by his good looks? His gaze found hers and he smiled at her in a way that made her feel as if he'd been waiting all afternoon for just this moment, when he would see her again. She had a nearly overwhelming urge to move into his arms and kiss him, which in itself was startling enough to keep her rooted in place.

Flynn followed behind him, and in contrast, looked both

intimidating and more than a little tough. He wore a sports jersey that was both dirt- and grass-stained, and his black hair was sweat-soaked. But his eyes were alight with humor and he broke into a broad grin when he saw Rachel and Lori.

"Hello, ladies," he said. "I didn't see you at the match, so I guess the shopping was good?"

Lori eyed him with interest, and Rachel didn't miss how her gaze lingered on his impressive shoulders and chest. Her cousin might deny her attraction to the big Irishman, but there was no denying the feminine admiration in her eyes.

"I'd say it was very good," Conall agreed, indicating the small mountain of shopping bags nearby. He stopped so close to Rachel that she could smell the unique woodsy scent that she had come to associate with him. "Did you enjoy yourselves?"

"We had a great time," Lori assured him.

Conall looked at Rachel. "So, what do you think of Galway?"

Rachel stared into his blue eyes and answered honestly. "I think I'm in love."

Chapter Thirteen

A N HOUR LATER, when they reconvened in the lobby, Rachel was still mentally kicking herself for her impulsive remark. Even though she'd hurried to amend her statement, saying she was in love with *Galway*, she couldn't help but feel she'd given herself away. Which was ridiculous, because she wasn't in love with Conall.

She *couldn't* be in love with him. She'd known him for only a couple of weeks.

Aside from a slight widening of his eyes, Conall hadn't reacted to her words. And when she'd hastened to clarify that it was Galway she was in love with, he'd surprised her by slinging an arm around her shoulders and pulling her close.

"Good," he'd said quietly against her ear, and then he'd pressed a brief kiss against her hair before releasing her. "I'm glad."

That brief exchange had unsettled her even more because she had the distinct feeling he had deliberately misunderstood her. They left the hotel as a group and made their way back to Shop Street, where they visited several different pubs. Mary-Kate was in high spirits and eager to share her favorite places with them, although Rachel suspected none of the pubs were unfamiliar to either Conall or Flynn, and probably not Fiona, either. By the time they reached the third pub, Rachel had determined she wouldn't have another pint; two was her limit, and she was already feeling her inhibitions beginning to slip. But as they stepped through the front door, she saw the pub was small and unusually quiet in comparison to the previous places they'd visited. Three elderly gentlemen sat at the bar, nursing their beers as they chatted with the bartender. Irish fiddle music piped in through two small speakers over the bar, which had only five stools and three high-top tables near the window, all of them unoccupied.

"You actually come here?" Lori asked Mary-Kate in surprise. "This doesn't seem like a happening place for college students, unless you want to meet older men." She slid a meaningful glance at the grizzled man nodding over his pint. "He looks promising."

Mary-Kate grinned. "Follow me."

Rachel glanced at Conall, who indicated she should precede him through a doorway at the back of the tiny pub. Following Mary-Kate, they found themselves in a room with yet another bar, this one larger and busier than the first. The lighting here was dim, but Rachel had an impression of dark wood and intimate booths filled with young people. But Mary-Kate didn't stop and continued through yet another door that led to an even bigger room. Here, the massive bar took up most of the space, and young people stood three-deep, waiting to place their drink orders. Behind the bar, ornately carved shelves held bottles that gleamed under gold lamps, and the perimeter of the room was lined with plush, purple benches and small tables. Loud music reverberated through the room, heavy with bass, and a small dance floor teemed with people.

"C'mon, this way!" Mary-Kate had to shout to be heard, and pointed to a curving staircase at the back of the room.

"This place is like a maze!" Rachel said to Conall.

"It is, yeah," he agreed, and put a hand at the small of her back to guide her through the crowd. "Most of the pubs in Galway are like this!"

They climbed the staircase to another room that featured high, arched ceilings inlaid with intricate tin tiles and soft, gold lighting, and an even longer bar with rich, carved paneling and dozens of stools, and an enormous dance floor overflowing with gyrating bodies. There were so many people crammed into the space that Rachel was grateful when Conall put his arm around her to steer her through the crowd and ensure she didn't get trampled. They found a cubbyhole in a corner that resembled a grotto, with an arched opening and stone walls and a table big enough for the six of them. The bench seating was upholstered in the same deep-purple leather and Rachel slid in, grateful to be out of the crush.

"That was insane!" Fiona exclaimed when they had all

been seated. "I can't believe I once thought this was fun! I must really be getting old."

"You had me completely fooled," Rachel said, leaning forward to look at Mary-Kate. "I thought you were bringing us to a pub for old folks!"

Mary-Kate laughed, clearly delighted to have fooled them. "Yes, it's deceiving when you first come in. A lot of the pubs are like this, with a place for the old-timers near the front, but the deeper you go, the more insane it gets."

"This place is huge," Lori agreed, looking around in wonder. "I've never seen anything like it."

Conall ordered a round of beer for everyone and, not wanting to look like a prude, Rachel made no objection but decided to nurse hers. She couldn't afford to let her guard down, not when Conall looked tempting in a blue jersey that matched his eyes and emphasized the broad thrust of his shoulders. With their unusual height and good looks, both he and Flynn had drawn the attention of more than a few women as they'd made their way through the crowd. Rachel and Lori sat on the inside of the booth, bracketed by Conall and Flynn, while Fiona and Mary-Kate sat on either end. Conversation was almost impossible given the noise level inside, so they sat and people-watched until a popular song began to play and Conall looked expectantly at Rachel.

"Dance?"

Rachel shook her head. "No, I'm not much good."

"Oh, come on," Flynn insisted, leaning forward to look

at her. "Lori and I are hitting the dance floor."

Lori gave him a doubtful look. "We are?"

"Most definitely," he said and slid out of the booth, pulling her behind him. Lori cast one beseeching glance back at Rachel before she and Flynn were swallowed by the crowd.

"Okay," she said, glancing at Conall. The tempo of the music was upbeat and lively and even Fiona and Mary-Kate had gotten up to dance. "One dance."

But no sooner had they made their way onto the dance floor than the music turned into a slow, pulsing love song. Immediately, Rachel turned to go back to the table, but Conall caught her hand.

"Don't run away," he said, pulling her back toward him. "Dance with me."

Glancing around, she saw other couples making their way onto the floor and spied Lori clasped loosely in Flynn's arms. Then Conall swung her into his arms and the only thing she was aware of was him. She placed one hand on his shoulder and he caught her other hand in his and curled it against his chest. With his free hand at the small of her back, he maintained just enough space between their bodies so they weren't actually touching, but Rachel could feel his every move as they glided together.

"I thought about you today," he said, his warm breath stirring her hair. "Did you have fun?"

She leaned back to look at him and her heart skipped a beat as his gaze traveled leisurely over her features and lingered on her mouth. Reflexively, she moistened her lips with her tongue, not missing how he seemed riveted by the small action.

"I did. Fiona and Mary-Kate were wonderful, but—" She broke off, realizing she'd been about to tell him she would have enjoyed the day more if he'd been there. The music swelled around them and Rachel felt the seductive pull of it in her veins.

"I don't have to go back to the shop tomorrow," he said, reading her thoughts. "We can do whatever you want."

"I have no expectations," she assured him. "But I'm hoping that on our way home, maybe we can stop by your aunt's shop. Fiona said it's in Connemara."

"We can, sure," he said. "She'll be thrilled to see us."

He eased her closer, sliding his hand up to rest between her shoulder blades. The movement brought her body into full contact with his, so that she could feel his warmth and strength. Beneath her palm, his shoulder muscles bunched and relaxed with each movement he made. Without conscious thought, Rachel rested her cheek against his chest. She could hear the strong, steady beat of his heart and she breathed in his familiar scent. She felt his lips against her temple and inched a little closer to him. All too soon, the song ended and the music changed.

Conall released her but kept her hand clasped warmly in his own as they made their way back to the table. The others were already there, and Rachel didn't miss how Fiona's gaze flicked from their joined hands to their faces, or how her mouth flattened into a disapproving line. Ignoring her, Rachel slid in next to Lori, whose eyes were alight in her flushed face.

"Have fun?" she asked, bumping her shoulder against the other woman's.

"I did, actually." Lori lowered her voice. "I guess I don't need to ask you if you had a good time, since it was pretty obvious."

Rachel avoided eye contact. "Was it?"

Lori picked up her drink and took a sip but didn't say anything, her eyes dancing.

"So, where to next?" Fiona asked. "This place is a little loud for my tastes."

"You're getting old," Mary-Kate complained.

"She's right," Flynn said. "There was a time when you loved this place, and we couldn't drag you home until dawn."

Rachel leaned forward to look past Lori at Flynn. "When was this?"

"Back when we were at university," Conall said. "We were all here at the same time. You wouldn't know it, but back then, Fiona loved the nightlife in Galway."

Fiona frowned. "No more than any other college student. Besides, what do you know? You were so wrapped up in your Australian girlfriend, I'm surprised you noticed. At least some things never change."

There was a moment of strained silence.

"Wait." Lori glanced between Fiona and Conall. "You had an Australian girlfriend?" She glanced at Rachel as if to ask, *Did you know this?*

"It was a long time ago," Conall muttered. "It didn't work out."

"Do you keep in touch with her?" Lori asked.

Conall frowned. "No, of course not. Why would I?"

"Just asking," Lori said.

"I haven't seen or spoken to her in over five years."

"You don't need to explain to anyone," Rachel said, feeling the need to defend him, and more than a little annoyed with Fiona for putting him on the spot.

"Apparently, I do," he retorted, sending Fiona a dark look.

"Ah, let's just forget it," Flynn said, leaning his brawny arms on the table. "It's not worth discussing. Like Conall said, it was a long time ago and we're all entitled to make mistakes."

"I'm just trying to prevent him making another one," Fiona muttered.

"If you're implying that my cousin—" Lori began hotly, but Fiona forestalled whatever else she might have said by throwing up her hands.

"I'm sorry. It's none of my business and I shouldn't have said anything," she interjected. "I think I'll go back to the hotel. I've had too much to drink and I'm obviously putting a damper on the evening." She stood up and gathered her purse and jacket. "Sorry, Conall. Sorry, Rachel, I didn't mean any offense."

"Please don't leave," Rachel said, feeling as if the entire night had just been ruined. She didn't want to be at odds with Fiona, especially since they had to work together, but there was a part of her that resented her interference.

"No, it's alright, really. I'm tired and I just want to sleep," Fiona insisted.

Flynn stood up. "I'll walk you back."

"No, there's no need, honestly."

"I'll go with her," Mary-Kate said, standing up. "You guys go on ahead to Salthill."

"What about you?" Conall asked, frowning. "Will you join us later?"

"I can hear trad music anytime," Mary-Kate replied. "I'll see you at breakfast, yeah?"

"I feel bad that Fiona felt she had to leave," Rachel said after the two sisters had left. There was no denying a distinct pall had fallen over the table in their absence.

"Don't." Conall rubbed a hand over his eyes. "She means well, but she needs to learn to mind her own business."

Privately, Rachel agreed.

"So, who was this other girl?" Lori asked, ignoring Rachel's pointed warning look.

"Just a girl I dated in college. Really, it's no big deal," Conall said. "Fiona talks too much."

Conall was deliberately making light of the relationship in order to avoid further discussion. Clearly, he didn't want to talk about it and neither did Rachel, knowing how hurt he had been. Lori didn't even know the half of it—that Conall had actually moved to Australia in the hope of making the relationship work. But she also knew Fiona hadn't been entirely wrong in trying to protect Conall from heartbreak, because every minute Rachel spent in his company made her fall a little bit more in love with him. Maybe they weren't serious yet, but everything about him appealed to her. It wouldn't take much for her to completely lose her heart, and that would be the worst thing that could happen. Because when her internship ended, so would their relationship. Conall wouldn't make the same mistake twice.

"Hey, let's get a move on and head over to Salthill," Flynn said, breaking the silence. "The music will be starting soon and we want to get a seat."

They stood and gathered their belongings, and Conall took a moment to pull Rachel aside. "Look," he said quietly, glancing over her shoulder at Flynn and Lori, who were moving toward the exit. "I hope Fiona didn't upset you. She had no business saying what she did."

"But what if she's right?" Rachel asked. "What if our spending time together is a mistake?"

"And what if it isn't?" A smile lifted on each side of his generous mouth. "You can't live your life always playing it safe, Rachel. Remember what I said the first day we met? If you don't get off the beaten path, you'll miss all the best parts. Take a chance, yeah?"

She was mesmerized by the expression in his blue eyes and knew then it was too late. She loved him. She almost blurted the truth to him, but bit her tongue instead and simply nodded.

"Okay." He seemed almost relieved, as if he'd half expected her to refuse. She was unprepared when he stepped close and pressed a brief, fierce kiss against her mouth. "Let's go listen to some trad music."

She followed him, too surprised to protest. She moistened her lips reflexively, still feeling the pressure of his mouth against hers. As they stepped outside, he caught her hand and linked his fingers through hers. The sun had set and the cobbled street was illuminated by hundreds of tiny lights that had been strung across the road. The restaurants and pubs and sidewalk cafés were doing a brisk business and the crowds had not thinned from earlier in the day. From a nearby alley came the haunting strains of a violin. Ahead of them, Flynn and Lori had all but vanished into the crowd and Rachel was grateful for Conall's solid bulk beside her.

They reached the bridge over the River Corrib, where they found Flynn and Lori leaning on the stone railing as they watched the water rush beneath them. Rachel surreptitiously released Conall's hand, but she knew it was too late. The expression on her cousin's face told her she had already seen the intimate gesture.

"I thought we'd lost you," Lori said.

"We could see Flynn the entire time," Rachel assured her, linking her arm through Lori's, as Conall and Flynn fell into step behind them.

"I thought maybe you two ditched us."

"Seriously?" Rachel looked at her cousin in surprise. "Why would you even think that?"

Lori leaned her head toward Rachel and dropped her voice. "If you could see how you look at each other, you'd understand."

Recalling the brief kiss, Rachel found her face growing warm, but she had no response except to give Lori's arm a reassuring squeeze. "I'm sorry if you were nervous."

"Me? Nervous?" Lori gave a soft laugh. "Not likely. I was completely safe. For all his size and arrogance, Flynn's actually very considerate."

"Oh!" Rachel gave the other woman a teasing look. "Are we developing an attachment?"

"Definitely not," Lori said, emphatic. "Unlike some people I know, when it's time for me to go home, I won't be leaving any broken hearts behind—mine or anyone else's."

Chapter Fourteen

T HEY DIDN'T RETURN to the hotel until after midnight and, while Rachel had enjoyed the evening of tradition-al Irish music, she'd slept poorly. The result was that she woke up the following morning feeling tired and cranky.

"I don't think it's the late night that has you grumpy," Lori observed as they made their way to the hotel breakfast room. "I think it's because someone didn't kiss you good-night."

Rachel directed a sour look at her friend even as she tried to ignore the ring of truth in her words. She didn't know what she had expected, but after Conall's declaration that he still had time to make her change her mind about going home, she had thought he might at least try to kiss her again. The brief kiss in the pub didn't count, since she hadn't been prepared and hadn't had a chance to participate.

But while he'd been attentive and friendly as they'd lis-tened to the lively music, he hadn't touched her again. Even during the walk back to the hotel, when Flynn and Lori had walked ahead of them, Conall had kept his hands pushed into his front pockets. At the hotel, he'd simply wished her good-night and had joined Flynn in the small hotel pub.

Rachel shrugged. "It's probably for the best. It's all well and good to say he's going to change my mind about staying here in Ireland, or that I should take a chance on him, but in the end it won't matter because I need to go back to Chicago."

"Why?"

For a moment, Rachel thought her cousin was joking. "Lori, everything I've done—my studies, my travel to India and Pakistan, my master's degree, my thesis—it's all been so I can work at Lakeside Industries. You know that."

"But why?" Lori persisted. "You don't *have* to work there. You're a talented textile designer and soon you'll have the credentials to get a job anywhere. You could even work here, in Ireland. I mean, c'mon, this place is gorgeous. Who wouldn't want to live here?" She gave Rachel a sly look. "Flynn said he hasn't seen Conall this happy in a long time, and he said it's only been since he met you. He said he hasn't had a serious relationship in forever."

"We aren't in a serious relationship, and you probably shouldn't be telling me this." But even as the words left her mouth, she wanted to hear more. As if reading her thoughts, Lori leaned closer, her expression earnest.

"Flynn said he's extremely smart and has always been an overachiever. But these last few years, he's driven himself even harder, opening more stores and pushing himself and his staff to be the best." When Rachel would have said

210

something, Lori held up a hand to forestall her. "The only reason I even mention it is because Flynn was so surprised that Conall has been taking time off work. Apparently, he never does that."

"So you think I should throw everything away and stay here, because Conall seems happy?"

"You seem happy too," Lori observed. "But who says you'd be throwing everything away? You'd still have your education and experience and"—she gestured expansively toward the sliding glass doors of the lobby—"all of this, and Conall too! It seems like a no-brainer to me."

They had reached the lobby. Beyond the hotel lay the River Corrib and the brightly colored houses that marched along its banks. Rachel could see the ocean on the horizon and the distant hills. She didn't want to admit how tempted she was, but Lori didn't understand how important it was for her to go back to Chicago and literally pick up where her father had left off.

"I'm sure it's not as easy as you think to move overseas and there's probably all kinds of red tape. Besides, it means a lot to me to follow in my dad's footsteps. In a way, it's like keeping his dreams alive—keeping *him* alive."

"All I'm saying is think about it," Lori said quietly. "I'm sorry you lost your dad so young, but just look at everything you've accomplished. You're a strong and independent woman as a result."

Rachel gave her cousin an amused glance. "And you're

not?"

To her surprise, Lori didn't respond with a humorous rejoinder or her usual laughter. "I'm suffocating under the expectations of my family," she replied. "My father says he wants me to work for him, but he won't trust me with the same level of responsibility he gives my brothers. He just wants to keep me close, as if I'm still a little girl, and placates me with promises that never materialize."

"You're his only daughter," Rachel soothed. "It's only natural for him to feel protective."

"I've done everything I can to prove myself to him," Lori continued, as if Rachel hadn't spoken. "Even this trip—" She broke abruptly off, as if she'd said too much.

"What?" Rachel asked, curious. Through the doors to the breakfast room, she could see Flynn and Conall sitting at a table. But she couldn't shake the sense that whatever Lori had been about to say was important. "Tell me. What about this trip?"

"Nothing," Lori muttered. "Let's just say you have options that I don't have."

She turned and walked into the breakfast room and, by the time Rachel reached their table, any sign of Lori's inner distress was gone. She was smiling at the two men and saying something that had them both laughing.

"Good morning," Conall said, pulling a chair out for her. He wore a pair of jeans and a crisp white shirt with the sleeves pushed back over his forearms. His hair was still damp from his shower and, as she sat down, she caught enticing whiffs of his soap. He watched her intently, and Rachel knew he didn't miss the faint shadows beneath her eyes. "I hope you don't mind, but I ordered for you both. It was either the full Irish breakfast or the buffet, so I went with the buffet. You'll feel reinvigorated after some food and coffee."

"I feel fine," she fibbed. "Have you been waiting long?"

"Not long at all."

"We've already been for a nice ten-mile run," Flynn added.

"Really?" Rachel said in admiration. "I'm impressed."

"We're in training," Flynn said. "Will you be coming to the marathon next weekend?"

"Of course," she assured him. "We wouldn't miss it. Where are Fiona and Mary-Kate?"

"Mary-Kate rang my room last night to say they were going to sleep in this morning, and to head out without them."

Rachel accepted a proffered mug of coffee with a murmured thanks, but inwardly she worried that perhaps Fiona was avoiding her. "I hope she's not upset about last night," she said, voicing her concern aloud. They still had to work together for the remainder of her internship, and she still had so much to learn from the other woman.

"She's not," Conall assured her. "Fiona tends to be over-protective, but she doesn't have a mean bone in her body."

"He's right," Flynn added. "Fiona's just projecting her own unwanted emotions onto you and Conall. It's a classic defense mechanism."

Both Rachel and Lori looked at the big man in surprise.

"What?" he demanded. "I'm more than just a pretty face!"

Lori gave a snort of laughter.

"She and my brother were pretty serious about each other, once," Flynn continued. "But they couldn't make it work because she wanted to be in Dublin and he wouldn't leave the farm. If anyone knows a thing or two about broken hearts, it's Fiona McDermott. Cut her some slack."

"Wow," Lori said, looking impressed. "A man who understands sheep *and* women. I'm sure there's a joke in there somewhere, but I can't remember the punch line."

Flynn threw her a look that promised retribution, but before he could reply, their breakfast arrived and Rachel and Lori walked over to the buffet to help themselves to yogurt and fruit. When they returned to the table, the conversation moved on to another topic, much to Rachel's relief.

"So, what's on the agenda for today?" Lori asked after they had finished eating.

"We'll drive to the Spiddal Crafts Village and visit my aunt," Conall said, glancing at Rachel. "But before we go there, there's a little town I want you to see. You'll just have to trust me."

"Oh, a mystery drive," Rachel said, smiling. "That

sounds like fun."

After checking out of the hotel and retrieving the car, they left Galway and drove north until they arrived in a small village called Cong. They parked and walked the short distance to the village center, which consisted of a pub and restaurant, a tea shop, and a post office. Across the street stood a bronze statue of a man in an Irish Scally cap carrying a woman in his arms.

"You and Lori will appreciate this," Conall said, crossing the street toward the statue.

As they drew closer, Rachel realized the statue was of John Wayne and Maureen O'Hara. "This is where they filmed *The Quiet Man?*" she asked in astonishment. "I remember watching it with my father when I was young! He loved that movie, and he must have told me a dozen times how he visited this town. I think I even have a photo of him standing next to this statue."

They were silent for a moment.

"Yeah, I've never heard of that movie," Lori admitted, breaking the silence and causing them all to laugh.

Rachel pulled her camera out of her backpack. "It's an oldie but goodie. Here, take my picture!"

They took turns posing in front of the statue, and Conall surprised Rachel by lifting her in his arms and holding her the same way John Wayne was holding Maureen O'Hara.

"Oh, Flynn, I want a picture like that!" Lori exclaimed, giving him a pleading look.

"Well, then you can ask Conall."

"Not with Conall," she said, exasperated. "Oh, fine!"

She handed the camera to Rachel, but before she could say anything to Conall, Flynn swept her up in his arms. She shrieked and clutched his broad shoulders, and Rachel swiftly snapped several pictures as Flynn pretended to stagger under her weight.

After that, they wandered over to the ruins of a nearby church and explored the ancient graveyard. Rachel took photos of the beautifully carved arches that marked doorways and windows, devoid now of wood or glass. Behind the church was a long swathe of green grass and, beyond that, a deep forest.

"There's a walking path through the woods," Conall said, "and a tower that may once have belonged to Rapunzel."

Both Rachel and Lori looked at him in disbelief.

"Okay," he conceded with a rueful grin. "It was actually built by the Guinness family, but I swear it looks like Rapunzel's tower."

They followed a path over a small bridge and into the woods. At the entrance to the forest, they passed beneath a stone archway with a man's head carved into the rock. With his flowing beard and mustache and regal crown, he looked to be an ancient king.

"That's Rory O'Connor, the last high king of Ireland," Conall said.

Rachel snapped more pictures, enchanted by the other-worldly feel of the place. The forest was deep and cool, the trees covered with lichen and moss. They passed small glens where the ground was thick with snowdrops and patches of sun-dappled clover.

"Here we are," Conall said as they rounded a bend in the trail.

Ahead of them, rising among the dense trees, was a magnificent square tower that looked as if it had been guarding this part of the forest for centuries. As they drew closer, Rachel saw an arched doorway at the base of the tower, and narrow windows marching toward the crenellated top. If a long, thick braid had suddenly dropped from the highest window, Rachel wouldn't have been at all surprised. Rapunzel's tower, indeed.

"This is amazing," she said. "I can't imagine too many people even know about this place. It's so off the beaten path—" She stopped, realizing what she had said, and gave Conall a chagrined look. "You were right."

"Can we climb up to the top?" Lori asked.

"I think so, but it's narrow at the top. You two go on up, and we'll wait and go up after you."

They watched as Lori and Flynn entered the tower and a few minutes later, they heard a muffled shriek from inside, as if Flynn had deliberately frightened Lori.

"I think she actually likes him," Rachel said as she peered through the lens of her camera, waiting for Lori and Flynn to appear at the top of the tower.

"Yeah, he's the best sort of mate," Conall said.

Lowering her camera, Rachel looked at him. "But you thought I would be attracted to him."

Conall sucked his teeth and rubbed the back of his head, looking sheepish. "I did, yeah, with good reason. Most women are."

"He's very good-looking," she acknowledged. "But he's not my type."

Conall's gaze sharpened on her. "No? And what is your type?"

Emboldened by the heat she saw banked in his blue eyes, she stepped closer. "I think you know. I like a guy with red hair and a great smile who can make me laugh. I like a guy who can pull a girl out of a boghole as easily as he can throw together a delicious fish pie."

She was close enough now that only the camera around her neck separated them. As he looked down at her, there was no laughter in eyes, only a fierce intensity that made her heart beat faster and warmth bloom low in her womb.

"Oh, yeah?"

"Yes."

Reaching up, he carefully pulled the camera strap over her head and hitched it over his own shoulder, and then slid his hand along her jaw until he cupped her nape. Dipping his head, he captured her mouth in a kiss so sweet and so devastatingly thorough that her legs went a little mushy.

Conall made an incoherent sound of need, something between a groan and a growl, and pulled her fully into his arms. Rachel gave in to the desire that swamped her, kissing him back as she slid her arms around him, reveling in the solid bulk of muscle and bone beneath her fingers. His mouth slanted over hers, exploring her with deep, soft sweeps of his tongue as he buried one hand in her hair, and pressed the other hand against her lower back. Urged against him, she could feel his heat and strength, and how much he wanted her.

A piercing whistle rent the air and they broke apart, breathless. Glancing up, they saw Flynn and Lori leaning over the ramparts of the tower, grinning down at them. Conall gave a huff of laughter and bent his forehead to Rachel's.

"I've been dying to do that since last night," he said softly.

"I wished last night you had," she replied.

"I know you're feeling confused about us, so I wanted to give you some space."

"Oh." Moved beyond words, Rachel could only stare at him, wanting to admit there was no confusion about the way she felt.

Ignoring Flynn's catcalls, Conall ran the pad of his thumb over her lower lip and then bent his head for a lingering kiss that left Rachel clinging to him. When they finally pulled apart, his eyes were a soft, hot blue.

"I don't think you two should go into the tower," Flynn said as he and Lori emerged through the arched door.

"Why not?"

Flynn gave Rachel a cheeky wink. "Because you obviously can't be trusted on your own, and we still have things to do and places to go today."

"There's a castle through the woods," Lori exclaimed. "We could see it from the top of the tower."

"Yeah, that would be Ashford Castle," Conall confirmed. "We can walk over, if you'd like."

They followed the forest path until the trees fell away and ahead of them was an ancient stone bridge that crossed the river. On the far side, they passed beneath a massive stone archway until they stood on the grounds of the castle, staring in awe at the sprawling medieval structure. The magnificent castle boasted towers and battlements and turrets, and arched windows nearly obscured by climbing ivy.

"Let's walk around to the front of the castle," Conall suggested. "That's the best part."

"Better than this?" Rachel asked. "I feel as if I've walked into a fairy tale."

They crossed the immaculate, manicured grass and made their way around the other side of the castle. Green lawns, intersected by gravel pathways, swept down to a large lake, where swans glided on the mirrored surface. An enormous fountain in the center of the lawn spouted plumes of water, and small groups of people wandered the paths. From their vantage, Rachel could appreciate how enormous the castle was, with a wing that extended toward the water, and a gothic-style conservatory that enclosed an indoor swimming pool and spa.

"Who lives here?" Lori asked, staring around her in awe.

"It's actually a hotel," Conall said. "You could stay here, if you wanted."

"Maybe if I come back, I will," Lori mused.

"They offer falconry, fishing, horse riding, shooting, and archery," Conall said, "in addition to afternoon tea and spa services, so there really is something for everyone."

"It's such a beautiful spot for a special event," Rachel said. "I'd love to spend my honeymoon here."

There was a moment of silence.

"Well, I hope you intend to marry someone rich," Flynn said. "A night's stay here would set you back at least a week's salary, probably more."

"Well, maybe a week's salary for you," Lori teased, nudging him. "Unless sheep farming is more lucrative than I realized."

For just an instant, Flynn's eyes clouded. Rachel doubted anyone else had even noticed, it was gone so quickly, replaced by his usual buoyant spirit. But it was enough to make her wonder if perhaps he did have some financial concerns.

"My future wife isn't going to care where we spend our

honeymoon," he said, puffing his chest out and walking with an exaggerated swagger.

"Oh, really?" Lori cast him a curious look. "Why is that?"

"Why do you think?" He gave her a wink.

Lori rolled her eyes, but Rachel noted how her cheeks grew pink at the suggestion in his voice. She exchanged an amused glance with Conall, who shrugged and fell into step beside her as they made their way back toward the bridge.

"If my wife wanted to stay here, I'd make it happen," he said.

"That's because you don't have what I have," Flynn retorted, grinning.

"What? An enormous ego?" Conall asked, laughing.

They made their way back to the car park, walking along the river. From Cong, it was a quick drive out to the coast to the Spiddal Crafts Village, a small grouping of a dozen small cottages, each featuring a different artist. The village was located directly across the street from the ocean, and Rachel took several moments to just breathe in the salty air and watch the seabirds as they dipped and wheeled on the air currents.

"This never gets old," she said as Conall came to stand beside her.

"Yeah, a bit different than Chicago, I'm thinking."

"Well, Lake Michigan is certainly large enough that you can fool yourself into believing you're on the ocean, but it doesn't smell like this or sound like this."

The brightly painted cottages were organized around a central park where benches and picnic tables with umbrellas had been placed for visitors. The parking lot was full, and dozens of people sat outside, enjoying the weather. They browsed the artists' workshops, admiring handwoven baskets, paintings, stained glass, pottery, and Celtic jewelry. Both Rachel and Lori took the opportunity to purchase small gifts, and inside the last small shop, Rachel lingered over a display of Celtic necklaces.

"This one is pretty," Lori said, fingering a delicate chain with an interwoven Celtic knot.

"That's the Good Luck Knot," Conall said, leaning in to take a closer look. He indicated another necklace with a triangular-shaped pendant. "This one is the Trinity Knot, which is probably the most common and easily recognized."

"What about this one?" Rachel asked, lifting a gold pendant that featured two interlocked hearts.

"Ah, that's the Celtic Love Knot. It's believed early Celts exchanged these knots the way we exchange rings."

Rachel studied the necklace before reluctantly dropping it back into place. "It's lovely, but a bit beyond my budget."

"Hey, this looks a lot like the necklace you have," Lori said, indicating a rectangular pendant.

"That's the Sailor's Knot," Conall said. "Woven by sailors for their loved ones while they were away at sea. You have a similar one?"

Reaching into the opening of her blouse, Rachel withdrew the heavy gold necklace that had belonged to her father. Resting in her palm was a Sailor's Knot. While not as refined as those on display, the chunky, masculine version was no less beautiful.

"Where did you get that?"

They looked up to see a woman standing behind the counter, staring at the necklace as if she had seen a ghost. Somewhere around fifty years old, she had long, red hair that fell nearly to her hips, and blue eyes that were wide now with disbelief.

In that instant, Rachel knew this was the Eileen she'd been looking for.

"Aunt Isla, this is Rachel Woods from America." He put an arm around Rachel's shoulders. "She's doing an internship at the mill. Are you okay?"

The woman's face cleared and she seemed to recollect herself. Smiling, she leaned across the counter to cup Conall's face in her hands and kiss his cheek. "Of course, love. It's grand to see you. I didn't know you'd be down this way."

"I couldn't come to Galway and not stop in to say hello to my favorite aunt," he said. He turned toward Rachel and Lori. "This is Rachel's cousin, Lori."

Isla looked at Rachel and her face softened. "You're Roger's daughter. Even without seeing the necklace, I would have known. You're the very spit of him."

"You knew him?"

Isla laughed. "I did. I made that necklace for him more than thirty years ago, before he left to go back to America."

Astonished, Rachel studied the necklace again. "He never told me where he got it."

"Well, he wouldn't have, would he?" Isla asked. "It's not my best work, but I was just learning the art of goldsmithing. I thought it quite good at the time."

"It's beautiful," Rachel said. "He always wore it. He never took it off."

Isla's blue eyes seemed to mist. "I was sorry to hear of his passing. He was a very special man."

"Did you two date?" Conall asked, dropping his hand to curl his fingers around Rachel's and give them a reassuring squeeze.

"Date?" Isla laughed. "We were engaged to be married."

Rachel and Lori both gasped.

"What happened?" Rachel asked. "Why didn't he ever mention it?"

Isla sighed. "Let's head up to the café and get a coffee. I think I need to be sitting down to tell this story." She looked at Rachel again. "It really is lovely to meet you, Rachel. It's like seeing him again."

After telling her shop assistant that she was taking a break, the five of them made their way to a small café, which was part of the crafts village, and sat at an outdoor table while Flynn and Lori ducked inside to order coffee.

"You were really engaged to be married?" Rachel asked.

"We were. Oh, it was all unofficial, and I don't think too many people knew we were in love." She gave Rachel a sympathetic smile. "I hope this isn't hard for you to hear."

"No, of course not," Rachel murmured. As if sensing she wasn't being entirely truthful, Conall placed a reassuring hand on her back to gently knead the hard knot of tension that she hadn't realized was there until that moment. "What happened? Why didn't you get married?"

Isla shrugged. "He left, promising to return as soon as he could. But time went by and we grew more distant, both literally and figuratively. We were both absorbed in our careers, and neither of us had the money to travel to where the other person was. There was no internet then, or the ability to video chat, and overseas phone calls were quite costly." She shrugged. "The fruit withered on the vine, so to speak. I suppose it was inevitable."

Her tone was matter-of-fact, but Rachel detected an underlying sadness in her green eyes and suspected she wasn't as emotionless as she appeared. The fact that she had never married or, according to Conall, been romantically linked to anyone, indicated she might have continued to carry a torch for Roger Woods even after their romance had ended.

"I'm so sorry," Rachel murmured. "I think he must have cared deeply for you, as he never took this necklace off."

"That's kind of you to say. May I see it?"

"Of course." Removing the necklace, she glanced at Conall, whose expression was inscrutable. She dropped the pendant into Isla's hand.

"I remember making this for him," Isla said, smiling softly. "I melted down every bit of gold jewelry I owned and then some."

"You should keep it," Rachel said, on impulse. "I'm sure he would want you to have it."

"Thank you, love, but I must refuse." Isla placed the necklace back in Rachel's hand.

Flynn and Lori returned with a tray of coffee and pastries for each of them. "Here we are," Lori said, plopping down next to Rachel. "What did we miss?"

"I was just telling your cousin that I can't accept the necklace I made for her father," Isla said.

"Why? Is it worth a lot of money?" Lori asked.

"Well, considering gold is worth five times what it was in 1992, I'd say it has certainly appreciated in value," Isla said.

"I found the tweed pattern that my father named after you," Rachel said, changing the subject. "But he named it Eileen, not Isla."

Isla laughed. "Yes, he was the only one who ever called me by my given name. He gave me five meters of the fabric and a gorgeous shawl that I still wear on occasion."

"What did you do with the fabric?"

"Oh, it's wrapped in tissue paper and tucked away in a cedar chest," Isla said. "After it became apparent we were finished, I couldn't bring myself to use it for anything, even as lovely as it is."

"I wonder," Rachel said, "if you might be willing to exchange the necklace for some of the fabric." She hefted the Celtic knot in her hand. "You could melt this down again and make something else."

Isla waved a hand and shook her head. "It's a very generous offer, but I couldn't."

"But it belongs to you," Rachel insisted quietly. "My father would want you to have it, and it would mean so much to me to have some of the fabric he designed, even just a meter or two. Please."

Isla picked up the necklace and closed her fingers around the pendant. "In that case, I accept. How much longer are you in Ireland?"

"I'll be in Ballylahane until the end of June."

"I'll mail the tweed to Conall and he can give it to you." She glanced at Conall. "Would that be alright?"

"Of course," he replied. His expression was shuttered, and Rachel knew he was thinking that history was destined to repeat itself, and she would eventually return to America, as her father had. She knew he was thinking it, because the same dismal thoughts were running through her own head.

"I'm still not sure this is a good idea," Isla said. "I think I may be getting the better part of the bargain."

"I disagree," Rachel replied. "McDermott tweed can sell for as much as four hundred euros per meter, but the fact that this particular tweed was designed by my father makes it worth its weight in gold."

Chapter Fifteen

RACHEL TOOK A step back from her laptop to critically study the pattern she had just put the finishing touches on. A week had passed since they'd returned from Galway and Rachel had thrown herself into the work of designing a pattern that was uniquely hers. Looking now at the digital image, she felt satisfied. She only hoped Seamus liked it.

With a base color of soft lichen green, she'd incorporated a triple windowpane plaid of forest green, deep fuchsia, and pale lavender, and then blended alternating bands of dark purple, light blue, and white throughout the pattern. The result was a lovely green tweed with pink and purple accents, softened by the pale blue and white bands. The digital program she'd used made the colors appear bolder than they would be in reality and failed to capture the tones and textures of the yarns she had selected, but overall, she felt the image was a good representation of what she had set out to create.

"Why, Rachel, that's quite nice."

She turned to see Seamus and Fiona had entered the room behind her and were now admiring the pattern.

"Thank you," she replied. "I think I can safely say I've finished this design."

"May I see the yarns you've selected?" Seamus asked.

Rachel indicated the design table, where her selection of yarns was laid out. Setting down the thick binder he carried, Seamus picked up a skein of green yarn.

"Cashmere," he mused. "Very nice."

"Very expensive," Fiona countered, studying the selection.

"Only the green yarn is cashmere," Rachel hastened to explain. "Enough to lend the fabric softness, but I did try to keep the material costs down."

"Well, let's load it into the system and get it scheduled for production," Seamus said. "What do you think, Fiona? Two hundred meters?"

"I actually think it will be quite popular," Fiona said, glancing at Rachel. "It evokes the green of Ireland, while hinting at wildflowers and the sea. Let's do three hundred meters."

Seamus nodded. "I agree. I know we're scheduled out at least three months, so check with Liam in production to see if we can fit this into the lineup before you return to America."

Rachel felt a rush of excitement at the prospect of seeing her fabric come to life on the power loom. "Thank you, Seamus."

His cell phone began to buzz and he pulled it out of his

pocket and checked the display. "Ah, I need to take this call. Good job, Rachel, and congratulations." He glanced at Fiona. "You should be part of this meeting. Come along to my office."

Fiona turned to follow Seamus, but then hesitated. "Nice work, Rachel. At this rate, you'll be able to design another half-dozen patterns before you head home. If they're as beautiful as this one, expect my father to try to convince you to stay. We could use another designer like yourself."

"Thank you. But even if what you say is true, I couldn't accept. My plan has always been to go back to Chicago."

"What about Conall?"

For a moment, Rachel was too surprised to respond. "I've never misled him," she finally said. "I would think you'd be happy knowing I'm not going to stick around."

"I never said I was against you and Conall as a couple," Fiona said, sounding mildly exasperated. "I just said I didn't want to see him get hurt. But honestly, it's been a long time since I've seen him looking as happy as he does when he's with you."

Rachel flushed, feeling equal rushes of pleasure and guilt. Pleasure, because she felt the same happiness whenever she was with Conall, and guilt because she had done nothing to discourage him, even knowing it couldn't last.

"I mentioned that I met your aunt Isla the last day we were in Galway," she offered. "But I didn't tell you what she shared with me. She and my father were romantically involved. Did you know he named his pattern after her? She said he was the only one who called her Eileen and not Isla."

Fiona nodded. "I heard stories, growing up, that she'd fallen in love with an American, and that he had broken her heart. I think my father has always felt bad about it, since he's the one who introduced them."

Rachel bristled and jumped to her father's defense. "I think it was mutual. I believe they really did love each other, but they couldn't find a way to make it work. That can happen."

"Sorry, but I'm not buying it. I think if you really love someone, you'll figure out a way to be together." She glanced at her watch. "Well, I shouldn't keep my father waiting. We'll speak to Liam in the morning about scheduling the production run."

Her words hung in the air after she was gone, and Rachel hated how they resonated within her. Was she only kidding herself by thinking she and Conall could never have more than these few months together? She didn't think so. She couldn't seriously contemplate anything more, because that would mean staying in Ireland, which wasn't possible. Her entire life was back in Chicago, and Conall had already said he wouldn't leave Ireland. No matter how she tried to work it out, their relationship was like a Rubik's Cube. If there was a solution, she couldn't find it.

Fiona had been gone scant moments when Lori poked her head through the door.

"Knock, knock," she said softly. "Permission to enter the premises?"

"Lori!" Rachel exclaimed, unaccountably glad to see her cousin. "I'm so glad to see you. I finished designing my first tweed pattern and Seamus likes it."

"Oh, it's beautiful," Lori gushed, looking at the image on the laptop screen. "I love the colors you used."

"Thanks," Rachel said. "I can see this as a woman's jacket or suit—"

"Or drapes or pillows," Lori interjected, prowling around the table as she studied the skeins of yarn and the photos Rachel had pinned to her mood board. "Even an upholstered chair or sofa."

Rachel gave her a bemused look. "As in, home textiles?"

Lori shrugged. "Sure, why not?"

"I guess I've never really thought about tweeds that way," Rachel mused. "I suppose there might be a market for it."

"I think there definitely is." Lori opened the binder that Seamus had left behind and flipped through several pages. "In fact—oh, look, Rachel, these are the sales numbers for the past quarter!"

Rachel cast an uneasy glance toward the door. "I'm sure Seamus wouldn't want us looking through that."

"Did you know McDermott Mills sells to Versace and Vera Wang?" Her voice held a note of awe.

Reaching out, Rachel closed the binder and pushed it toward the end of the table. "I don't think—"

"Ah, there it is!" Seamus sailed into the room and grabbed up the binder. "I knew I set it down somewhere, and I need this for my meeting."

When he had left again, Rachel and Lori exchanged a meaningful glance. "That was close," Rachel said. "I would have hated to explain why we were snooping through his papers."

"Versace, Vera Wang *and* Dior," Lori said with excitement. "There were more, but you closed it too fast for me to see."

Bracing a hand on one hip, Rachel looked suspiciously at Lori. "Why are you so interested in McDermott's business partners? Is there something you're not telling me?"

"No. I just didn't realize Parisian fashion houses were into Donegal tweed," Lori said defensively. "It's interesting, that's all. So now that we know they do buy McDermott tweed, you need to create something sensational that they'll want to incorporate into their fashion line. Imagine, your designs could be showcased at Paris Fashion Week!"

Rachel laughed. "I'm not sure about that, but I'll do my best."

"What time are we heading north?" Lori asked.

The marathon along the northern coast would take place the following day, and Conall and Flynn wanted to drive up that evening in order to register for the event. Conall's parents would drive up the following morning, and Rachel found herself feeling nervous about meeting them despite the fact there was no reason to. Hadn't she spent most of the week convincing herself that she and Conall weren't in a serious relationship?

Even if they had spent every evening together since they'd returned from Galway.

Even if she couldn't seem to stop thinking about him when they were apart.

Even if their relationship had recently gained a new intensity, as if they were both all too aware their time together was slipping away.

Rachel glanced at her phone, surprised to see it was nearly three o'clock. "Conall said they would pick us up at four, so we should probably get going."

"I can't believe this is my last adventure before I head home," Lori said.

"Have you had fun?" Lori's flight was scheduled to leave on Tuesday, which was coming up too fast for Rachel's liking.

"I've had a ball," Lori replied. "I love being the third wheel to you and Conall."

"You weren't!" Rachel cried. "Besides, Flynn was with us almost every night this week, and don't think I didn't notice you flirting with him."

Lori shrugged. "Well, you work with what you have available."

"Oh, come on. What's not to like about Flynn? He's gorgeous, smart, athletic—"

"He's a sheep farmer," Lori said darkly. "Why couldn't he have a normal career like Conall? No, scratch that—why can't he live in Chicago instead of Ireland? My father would lose his mind if I told him I was staying here to be with a sheep farmer." She gave a humorless laugh. "Things wouldn't go well. Can you even imagine what life would be like on a sheep farm, with the entire O'Rourke family within shouting distance?" She gave a dramatic shudder. "No, thank you. Besides which, he and I are completely incompatible. Even you must see that. We're like oil and water. Like fire and ice. Like—"

"Okay, I get it," Rachel said, laughing. "Even if I don't entirely agree with you."

They made their way out of the mill and began walking through town toward the hotel, where Rachel had left her weekend bag in anticipation of Conall picking them up.

"Well, it's good that you're going home," Rachel said with a grin. "I'm sure Seth will be delighted to have you back."

"Ha. He's probably so busy ingratiating himself to my father that he hasn't even noticed I'm gone."

"I doubt that's true," Rachel said, linking her arm through Lori's. "I'd say you're pretty unforgettable." She waved one arm dramatically. "You are a woman among sheep!"

Lori punched her playfully on the shoulder. They reached the hotel and, as they walked through the lobby,

Lori withdrew her room key and handed it to Rachel. "I have to make a quick phone call," she said. "Go on up and make yourself comfortable, and I'll be right up."

"Why don't I just wait here for you?" Rachel asked, taking the key. "I can order us both some coffee or tea while you make your call."

"No, I won't be long. Why don't you go up and pick out the clothes I should bring? I have no idea what people wear to a marathon event."

Rachel narrowed her eyes at her cousin. "I'm pretty sure that would be jeans and sneakers."

"Great. I should have some in the closet." She gave Rachel a pleading look. "I just need a little privacy for this call. Please?"

Bemused, Rachel threw up her hands. "Fine. I'll be in your room. But if you get to Northern Ireland and discover I've only packed your underwear, you'll have no one to blame but yourself."

"Thank you." Lori beamed, leaning forward to plant a kiss on Rachel's cheek. "You're the best! I'll be right up!"

As Rachel made her way to the elevator, she glanced back at Lori, who now had her phone pressed to her ear. Seeing Rachel watching her, she gave a happy wave and then turned away. Frowning, Rachel stepped into the elevator. Who was Lori calling, and why was it such a secret that she couldn't talk in front of Rachel? Her instincts told her it had to do with the binder Seamus had left in the design room, which led to another, more serious question: why was Lori so interested in McDermott Mills and their business dealings? Donegal tweed was about as far a cry from luxury home textiles as you could possibly get.

Once inside Lori's hotel room, Rachel pulled her own phone out of her backpack and quickly dialed her uncle's number at Lakeside Industries. Almost immediately, his office manager picked up.

"Hi, Pam, it's Rachel Woods. Is my uncle available?"

"Rachel, it's so good to hear from you! How are you enjoying Ireland?"

"Very much, thanks. I really need to talk to Uncle Jack. Is he free?"

"No. In fact, he's on the other line talking to Lori. Isn't she with you?"

"Er, not at the moment," Rachel said, her suspicions confirmed. "Just let Uncle Jack know I called, okay? It's not urgent."

"Of course. I'm sure he's anxious to speak with you, considering what's happened."

That gave Rachel pause. "Why? What has happened?"

"Linda Morse got engaged!"

Linda was one of the lead designers at the home textile company and had worked there for years. "That's wonderful!"

"Well," Pam said in a conspiratorial tone, "yes and no. Her fiancé just took a job in Los Angeles, and they're both moving there within the next few months. Which means there will soon be a position open and rumor has it, Jack wants you to have it."

"Me?" Rachel asked in astonishment. "I know he said I'd make a great lead designer, but I figured it wouldn't happen for several years, maybe longer."

"I guess he thinks you're qualified now."

Rachel could hardly think straight. This was her dream job, the position she'd hoped might one day be hers, but not this quickly. "But I'm not ready," she protested. "I still have my master's thesis to finish."

"Your uncle must believe you can manage both." Pam lowered her voice. "Please don't let on that I told you about this, okay? He may have wanted to tell you himself, so when he does call you, act surprised. Please?"

"Of course," Rachel said, still stunned. "I won't say a thing."

"Thank you. I'll let him know you called. Enjoy the rest of your time in Ireland!"

After Rachel hung up, she sat on the edge of Lori's bed and considered what she had just learned. Did her uncle expect her to cut her internship short and return to Chicago right away, or did she still have some time? Her chest felt tight and achy with the knowledge that she could be leaving Ireland sooner than she thought. Overriding any excitement she felt about obtaining a lead design position at Lakeside Industries was the realization that she wasn't ready to go home.

She didn't want to leave Conall.

The door opened and Lori breezed in. "Sorry about that! I forgot there was something I wanted to talk to my dad about. Nothing urgent, but I didn't want to wait until after the weekend." She paused and then looked around in bemusement. "What's wrong? I thought you'd jump at the chance to pack my overnight bag for me. You know, mixing stripes and plaids, so I'd really stand out?"

Rachel forced a smile. "I'm fine. Just a bit of a headache, suddenly. How is Uncle Jack doing?"

"He's doing well," she said, studying Rachel. "Better than you. Are you sure you're okay? You look like you're going to be sick."

"No, I'm okay, really." Rachel wasn't ready to share the news she'd received from Pam. Not yet. Not until she knew for certain that her uncle intended to offer her the job. There was a chance Pam could be wrong. Then there was the issue of Lori's secretive call to her father. "Are you sure there's nothing you want to tell me? Because I can't help but feel as if your call to Uncle Jack had something to do with McDermott Mills."

There was no mistaking the swift flash of guilt in Lori's eyes before she schooled her features into a mask of innocence. "Why would you think that?"

"So I'm right!" Rachel said in triumph. "Please tell me Uncle Jack isn't trying to take over the mill, or do something that would hurt the McDermott business."

"What?" Lori asked in unfeigned astonishment. "No! Trust me, it's nothing like that. I can't tell you *exactly* what's going on, but I can tell you it's nothing nefarious." Reaching out, she grabbed one of Rachel's hands. "Trust me, okay?"

Rachel searched her cousin's eyes. "Why can't you tell me?"

"Because I made a promise to not say anything, at least for now," Lori said, her voice earnest. "As soon as I can tell you, I will. Just trust me."

After a moment, Rachel reluctantly nodded. "Okay, as long as you swear it's nothing bad."

Lori hooked her little finger around Rachel's, the same way she had done since they'd been little girls. "Pinky swear, pinky promise."

A reluctant smile tugged at Rachel's mouth, knowing the childish promise carried the weight of their friendship. "Fine. Now let's take a look at your wardrobe and make sure you pack something practical."

"Says the woman who fell into a boghole wearing a pair of leopard-print ballet flats," Lori retorted, smiling to take any sting out of her words.

"Well," Rachel said weakly, "it was the only way I could think of to meet a cute guy."

Lori laughed. "So you're saying I should wear something entirely impractical? That should be fun. Flynn will no doubt have a field day at my expense."

But as she watched Lori pack her suitcase, she couldn't help wondering why her uncle might be interested in McDermott Mills, and what, if anything, it had to do with Lakeside Industries—and herself.

～

"I'M GLAD YOU brought Quinn," Rachel said as they drove north toward the Causeway Coast. The border collie sat on the seat between her and Lori, watching the road with all the alertness of a back seat driver. "I can watch him while you and Flynn run."

Conall met her gaze in the rearview mirror. "Thanks, but there's no need. He'll run with me."

Lori leaned forward, her expression one of concern. "For twenty-six miles? That sounds like animal abuse to me."

Instead of looking offended, Conall laughed softly. "Nah, he's bred to go all day long. border collies have a high tolerance for endurance activities. Besides, he's been training with me. If I didn't think he could do it—and enjoy it—I wouldn't bring him."

"What will you do if he quits halfway?" Lori persisted.

"He won't," Conall assured her. "But my parents will drive to several different viewing spots along the marathon route, so if he looks like he's flagging, I can send him off with them."

Rachel stroked the dog's thick fur. "But you're not going

to quit, are you? You're going to win the medal for best four-legged marathoner."

As if in agreement, Quinn thumped his tail against the seat. Impulsively, Rachel hugged the dog, burying her face in his soft ruff. She would miss Quinn when it came time to return home. She would miss all of this.

For most of the three-hour drive, she'd been consumed with her own thoughts. She'd never felt so conflicted in her life. No matter how many times she told herself that everything she'd ever wanted was finally falling into place, she felt no joy. Pulling away from Quinn, she saw Conall watching her in the rearview mirror, his eyes registering concern.

"You've been very quiet," he observed. "Everything okay?"

"Just tired," she fibbed. But when he turned his attention back to the road, Rachel continued to study his reflection, committing it to memory. She would miss him most of all. Maybe, given time and distance, the memory of him would fade. Maybe she would become like Isla and one day look back on their time together with a mixture of sadness and regret. Did she want that?

Rachel opened her window and turned her face into the wind, hoping the gusty blasts of sea air would help clear her muddled thoughts. Until she'd received the news about the lead designer position, she'd counted on staying until the end of June in Ballylahane. But if Pam was right, her uncle might want her back sooner, which meant she needed to treasure whatever time she had left. She should be ecstatic at the thought of returning to Chicago to secure her dream job, but the thought of leaving Conall made her chest ache and a lump form in her throat.

They arrived at their hotel, a sprawling four-story structure overlooking a small bay. After they checked in, Rachel and Lori explored the common areas while they waited for Conall and Flynn. The dining room featured enormous glass windows and doors that led to an expansive terrace with numerous tables and umbrellas. At Lori's request, they were seated at an outside table, where they each ordered a lemonade.

"Okay, out with it," Lori said when they were alone. "You've been moping since we left Ballylahane. What's going on?"

Rachel gave her a tolerant look. "Don't pretend you don't know. I talked with Pam this afternoon and she told me about Linda Morse."

Lori looked blank. "I have no idea what you're talking about."

"Seriously?" Seeing her cousin's expression, she realized Lori really didn't know. "Linda is leaving the company. Pam thinks your father is going to offer me the lead design position."

"Ah, now I understand. Here's your big opportunity, being offered to you on a silver platter, but—" Lori shrugged. "I already told you my thoughts. Nothing says you have to work at Lakeside Industries. My father would understand. Of course, he'd throw a fit first, tell you all the reasons why you should stay and take the job, but eventually, he would understand."

"I never expected to be offered the position of lead designer straight out of college. I always thought that would come later—a lot later. That Uncle Jack believes I'm capable of handling that kind of responsibility now—well, it would be hard to turn it down. Opportunities like this only come along once in a lifetime."

"I guess you have some soul-searching to do," Lori said. "Because guys like Conall McDermott might come along once in a lifetime too."

Before Rachel could respond, they were interrupted by Quinn, who bounded onto the patio and made a beeline toward their table.

"Down, Quinn," Conall said as he and Flynn approached. With a soft whine, Quinn obediently dropped to the ground and rested his chin on his front paws. "Good boy."

"Wow," Lori said. "I'm impressed."

"He's a good dog. He only needed a bit of positive reinforcement." Conall pulled out the chair nearest to Rachel and sat down. "How's your room?"

"It's lovely," Rachel assured him. "We even have a view of the water. What about you?"

Flynn grimaced. "They stuck us in an older room on the

ground floor, well away from the other guests, overlooking the dumpsters." He slanted a look at Lori. "I'd say management is not as impressed with Quinn as you are."

"Maybe Quinn isn't the reason they put you in a room away from the other guests," Lori suggested with an impish grin.

"Ha. You're a wit," Flynn retorted.

"What about the marathon route?" Rachel asked, changing the subject. "Did you want to check it out?"

"No, I don't think so," Conall said. "Both Flynn and I have run this marathon before. Most of the route is along the beaches or the cliffs. Very little of it is visible from the road, so there's not much sense in trying to scope it out."

"Then let's have something to eat and have an early night," Rachel suggested. "Lori and I don't want to be the reason you guys come in dead last tomorrow."

Conall laughed, his blue eyes filled with suggestion. "I can't think of a better reason to lose."

"At least then, I'd have an excuse," Flynn muttered.

Lori looked at him in surprise. "You don't expect to do well?"

"I'm just here for the free swag," he quipped.

"Don't believe him," Conall said. "He's a natural."

"I'm out of practice," Flynn admitted. "The farm has kept me too busy to properly train, so I'm just hoping to finish."

"I'm sure you'll both represent Ballylahane very well,"

Rachel said.

They ordered dinner and lingered at the table long after the meal was over, talking and laughing, until Flynn pushed his chair back and stood up. "Sorry to be a spoilsport, but I think I'm going to turn in."

Lori rose to her feet as well. "I think I'll do the same. What time does the fun start tomorrow?"

"The race starts at half nine, but we'll be at the starting line before nine," Conall said.

"That early?"

Flynn rolled his eyes. "Come on, princess. I'll see you safe to your room."

After they left, Conall stood. "Feel like a walk?"

"Yes, actually," Rachel said, grateful for the opportunity to spend more time with him.

They made their way along a well-lit path that led to the bay, where they stood at the water's edge, listening to the surf as it washed up and pulled the pebbles back with a soft rattling sound.

"You've been quiet today," Conall said, looking at her. "Sure everything is okay?"

"There's a chance my uncle may offer me a lead design position at Lakeside Industries," she said. "I wasn't going to say anything until I was sure, but . . ."

"I see," he said, his voice quiet.

Rachel knew he was thinking that history was repeating itself, which was why she'd made the decision to tell him about the possible job offer, even though it wasn't yet a sure thing. She didn't want him to be blindsided the way he'd been once before.

"Do you know when you'd need to return?"

"No," she admitted. "I'm not even one hundred percent sure it will happen, but I wanted you to know. Just in case."

He turned fully to face her. "Will you accept?"

"I think so."

Reaching out, Conall pushed a tendril of her hair back from her face. "You know I only want good things for you, Rachel. I want you to be happy."

"Thank you," she murmured.

"But I'm also selfish enough to want you to stay," he continued. "I think we have something special, and we owe it to ourselves to explore it and see where it leads. I'd like you to stay here with me."

"Conall—"

"I think you'd like to stay, as well, but you're letting obligation and nostalgia dictate your decisions."

Rachel heard the frustration in his tone. "I'm not—"

"You are. You could stay, Rachel, if you wanted to."

She was silent for a long moment, recalling that Lori had said something similar. "I want to stay. I just don't see how I can without letting people down. People I care about."

Conall blew out a hard breath. "I don't know how to respond to that because your work ethic, your commitment to your beliefs, and the way you put your family first are just some of the qualities I love about you."

"Oh . . ." Rachel stared at him, her heart beating fast. He hadn't said he loved her, but that's what she heard, and the world seemed to tilt sideways for an instant.

"At least finish your internship here." His gaze drifted over her face and lingered on her mouth. "Given another month or so, I'm hoping I can change your mind."

Rachel was certain he could. Without conscious thought, she moved into his arms and dropped her forehead against his chest. "That sounds nice."

With one finger beneath her chin, Conall lifted her face and searched her eyes. "We'll figure it out."

"Yes," she agreed, but in her heart, she didn't see how they could. She didn't want to talk anymore. "Kiss me, please."

He did.

Chapter Sixteen

THE MORNING OF the race dawned clear and cool, with a salty breeze that blew in from the North Atlantic. Rachel sat on the outside terrace with a mug of steaming coffee cupped in her hands as she watched Conall and Flynn apply surgical tape to their bare feet. Quinn lay on the grass, watching the activity with interest. At the tables nearby, other runners were going through similar motions.

"Does that really work?" she asked.

"Yeah, it does," Conall replied. "I always tape up before a marathon. It massively reduces blisters."

"Where's your sidekick this morning?" Flynn asked, glancing up.

Rachel laughed softly. "You're kidding, right? It's barely eight o'clock. You won't see her until at least eight thirty."

Flynn scowled. "The race starts at half nine and we have to be in place by nine, which means we need to leave here by half eight."

Conall glanced at his friend in surprise and then gave Rachel a wink. "Don't fret. She'll be at the finish line."

"I never fret," Flynn growled. "If she wants to sleep the

day away, it's nothing to do with me."

Behind his back, Conall's eyebrows shot up, and he grinned at Rachel, because clearly, Flynn was bothered by Lori's absence.

"Maybe I should wake her up," Rachel said.

"No, don't bother," Flynn retorted, tearing off a strip of tape with excessive force.

"Don't bother with what?"

They looked up to see Lori step onto the terrace looking effortlessly pretty and pulled together, although Rachel knew for a fact she'd been sound asleep just thirty minutes earlier. She didn't miss how Flynn's gaze swept over the other woman, missing no detail of her appearance, from her black jeggings and oversized sweater to her pretty matching headband and leather ankle boots. As she watched, his entire posture relaxed, and Rachel thought she saw something like satisfaction in his silver eyes before he quickly bent back to his task.

"There you are," Rachel said, indicating a nearby chair. "Come have some coffee while the guys get ready. Do you want to order breakfast?"

"Maybe just some toast and jam," she said, watching Flynn.

"That's not a breakfast," Flynn scoffed. "You need protein, like eggs and bacon."

Lori's face screwed itself into an expression of distaste. "Ew, no. I can't even face food until I've been up for at least an hour, and I never eat a big breakfast. I prefer toast, or maybe fruit and yogurt."

Rachel slid her a mug of coffee. "Here, start with this."

"What about you guys?" Lori asked. "Have you eaten?"

"They each had a banana with peanut butter and toast with jam," Rachel laughed. "I didn't see so much as a single egg or slice of bacon."

"And you're lecturing me?" Lori looked at Flynn with astonishment.

"We go mostly for carbs or something simple before a race," Conall explained.

Once their feet were taped, they pulled on two pairs of socks and then laced up their sneakers before moving to a grassy area to stretch. Rachel paused in the act of raising her coffee mug. They each wore stretchy running shorts and shirts, and Rachel couldn't stop looking at how the fabric clung to the strong muscles of Conall's thighs and backside. His body was limber and graceful, his muscles sleek and toned. She glanced at Lori, who was watching Flynn with equal intensity.

"Breakfast and a show," Lori murmured, smiling at Rachel over the rim of her coffee mug. "I wish I'd woken up earlier."

After Lori had finished her toast and coffee, they made their way to where the race would start, on a wide beach beneath the local boat club. The harbor of Portballintrae had been transformed into a festival that teemed with people, fest tents, music, and food. The beach itself was swarming with runners, while cars and buses jammed the nearby roads.

"This is crazy!" Rachel said, hanging on to Quinn's leash lest he decide to bolt in the crowd.

"It is, yeah," Conall agreed. "There are more than one thousand runners participating in five different events today, so it's bound to be a bit congested. My shop is hosting a tent here, but I'm not sure where it's located. Michael came up yesterday and got it set up."

"Your running shop?" Rachel asked.

"Yes. We're selling running shoes and accessories and giving away some prizes. We're also handing out some discount coupons for anyone who visits one of the shops in person within the next six months."

Flynn called to them, and they followed him and Lori to the boat club, where Conall found the other members of his local running club. Like Conall and Flynn, they wore matching jerseys and each of them carried a small hydration pack.

"Listen," Conall said, pulling Rachel and Lori aside. "My parents should be here soon, and they offered to drive you to the halfway point in Ballintoy, and then back here to the finish line. We're going to head down to the beach now, so I'll see you when it's over, yeah?"

"Are you excited?" Rachel asked, handing him the leash.

"I'm pretty stoked," he confirmed. He unhooked Quinn's leash and handed it back to Rachel. "This is one of the best marathons in Ireland, in my opinion, and not your traditional route. We'll be running on the beach, along the cliffs, over rocks, and up steep trails."

"Break a leg!" Lori called out cheerfully.

"Yeah, that should probably be reserved for the theater," Conall retorted.

"Just be careful," Rachel said. "I read a little about the marathon last night, and it seems like a particularly difficult run."

Conall's face creased into a smile, and he pulled her up against him. "I've run this marathon before and I know the challenges. But I appreciate your concern. Don't worry, Rachel. I'll be fine."

"Are you hoping to win?" Lori asked.

Conall laughed. "No, I'm hoping to finish. If I beat my time from last year, I'll be happy." He released Rachel and lifted a hand in greeting. "There are my folks now."

Rachel turned to see an older couple walking toward them. Even if Rachel hadn't known the man was Conall's father, there was no mistaking the similar build and the same bright hair. He reminded her a bit of Seamus. Conall's mother was slender and attractive, with black hair, blue eyes, and a ready smile.

"These are my parents, Daniel and Ava," Conall said. "Mum, Dad . . . meet Rachel and Lori Woods."

Ava took Rachel's hand and, although her smile was friendly, Rachel could see the speculation in her blue eyes.

"So, you're Rachel. I've heard your name quite a bit over the past few weeks."

"Mum," Conall said warningly.

"It's lovely to meet you," Ava continued, ignoring her son.

"I'm surprised you and I haven't already met," Daniel said, stepping forward. "Welcome to Ireland and to McDermott Mills, Rachel. Seamus tells me you're a keen designer."

"I do enjoy it," Rachel said, instantly liking both of them. "Thank you for taking us under your wing today."

"Oh, it's our pleasure," Daniel said. "We'll leave a bit before the race begins so you can see some of the terrain the runners have to negotiate. We should be back here at the finish line in plenty of time to see the lads come across."

"Okay, we've gotta run," Conall said. "Quite literally."

"Good luck." Rachel rose to her feet and watched as he pulled a beanie over his bright hair.

"A good-luck kiss wouldn't hurt," he said, and before she guessed his intent, he drew her into his arms and lowered his head, covering her mouth with his own. She was only distantly aware of Quinn barking in excitement. As kisses went, it was brief, but so thorough that when he stepped away, Rachel felt a little unbalanced.

When Flynn made as if he would do the same to Lori, she put up a hand to ward him off. "Don't even think about it, buster," she said. "Unless you want to complete this race in a wheelchair."

"Right." Unfazed by her rejection, he gave her a broad wink, and then they were gone, sprinting down to the beach with Quinn hard at their heels, where hundreds of other runners were already congregated.

"Okay, ladies," Daniel said, his eyes bright with speculation and amusement. "Let's head toward Ballintoy, with a couple of stops along the way."

"Conall tells me you're a marathon runner too," Rachel said when they were in the car and on their way out of Portballintrae.

"I am, yeah," he said, glancing at her in the rearview mirror. "But I don't run the Causeway Coast marathon. The locals call it the 'beaches, bays, and cliffs marathon.' It's a difficult trail and, although the scenery is spectacular, the run is quite treacherous in places."

"How long will it take Conall and Flynn to reach the finish line?"

"Nearly four hours, I should think."

Ava turned in her seat and smiled. "Plenty of time for us to see the sights and get to know one another."

Rachel didn't miss the gentle challenge in the other woman's eyes and wondered just what Conall had told his parents about her.

"I've heard a lot of nice things about you these past few weeks," she continued, as if reading Rachel's thoughts. "Conall's not one to talk much about his personal life, so I knew you must be special."

"Oh," Rachel said, uncertain how to respond. Did his mother guess just how much they liked each other? More importantly, did she approve? Even knowing her relationship with Conall might not last, she didn't want his parents to think badly of her. "You must be very proud of him."

"Oh, yes," his mother said with a smile. "Even when he decided to quit medicine and pursue running, I wasn't worried." She laughed. "Well, not much, anyway. He's a smart lad, and he's always been a bit of a marketing geek. When he told us he could make a go of a running store, I knew he wasn't just talking."

"Did you know his shop won an award for the Best Small Business in western Ireland?" Daniel asked, glancing at her in the rearview mirror.

"No, he never said," Rachel replied. "That's quite an accomplishment."

"He never does anything unless he's fully committed," Ava said. "He's a man who knows what he wants and goes after it."

"Yes, I can see that about him," Rachel said weakly. Next to her, Lori gave her foot a hard nudge as if to say, *I told you so.*

"Have you seen the Giant's Causeway?" Daniel asked. "No? Well, you can't very well visit the northern coast and not see that."

Their first stop was at the Giant's Causeway and Visitor

Centre where they managed to find a parking spot.

"Looks like we're not the only ones with this idea," Ava said. "How long before the first runners come through here?"

"Not long," Daniel confirmed. "Step lively, girls."

They followed Daniel along a steep, paved path that led from the Centre down to the ocean, where Rachel had her first glimpse of the basalt columns that made the region famous. Rising majestically out of the water, the top of the hexagonal columns formed stepping stones that led from the towering cliffs down into the ocean. After snapping a dozen or more photos, they chose a rock formation and sat down to wait. Around them, other people were doing the same thing.

"What causes the rock to be shaped like this?" Lori asked.

"Well, legend has it, an Irish giant named Finn McCool was challenged to a fight by a Scottish giant called Benandonner. Finn accepted the challenge and built the causeway across the North Channel so the two giants could meet. Finn defeated Benandonner, who fled back to Scotland and destroyed the causeway behind him so that Finn would be unable to chase him down." Daniel peered at them. "Across the sea, there are identical basalt columns in Scotland, so the story must be true."

"Here they come," Ava said, shielding her eyes.

Even as she said the words, Rachel saw the first group of runners making their way down the path toward them. The onlookers began to clap and cheer as the runners picked their way across the basalt columns and crossed the rocky beach to a distant trail that ascended steeply in a series of dizzying switchbacks to the top of the cliffs.

"They have to climb *that*?" Lori gasped.

"Once they reach that path, halfway up the cliff, there are one hundred and sixty-two steps to the top, called the Shepherd's Steps," Daniel said. "And that's just the beginning."

"Oh, there they are!" Rachel cried. Conall and Flynn were easy to spot as they ran in a group with others from their club, their long strides making it look effortless. Quinn bounded beside them, clearly in his element. Conall lifted a hand in greeting as they ran past, and Rachel watched him until he vanished among the mass of other runners making their way up the cliff trail.

"He makes it look so simple," Ava said, her eyes following the runners. "But then, that's typical of Conall, isn't it? No matter how difficult something might be, he rarely lets on if he's struggling."

"He's very independent, that's true," Daniel said.

"Has he had many struggles?" Rachel asked, curious. "I only ask because you seem like such a close-knit family, and I'm sure he knows everyone in the local community. He doesn't seem to lack a support system."

"Yes, I'd say that's true," Ava replied. "As a child, he was small and slight and we sent him to an all-boys boarding school where he endured his share of bullying. If anything, it made him more determined to succeed. By the time he graduated, he was top of his class and captain of the football team, and he still keeps in touch with his old classmates."

"He went to boarding school?" Rachel asked. "I had no idea."

She'd also attended boarding school in Chicago, but the experience had only been positive.

"Yes, he was quite determined to go, since that's where Flynn and his brothers went, *and* they had the best sports teams in the county," Ava said. "Conall has been mad about sports since he was small. Even when he couldn't play well, he was determined to participate. I should have guessed then he would choose running over—" She broke off with a rueful smile. "Well, it all worked out in the end, I'd say."

"That's it then," Daniel said, his tone putting an end to the discussion. "Time to move on. We can catch the lads again at the Carrick-a-Rede rope bridge, although there are likely to be even more spectators there. Then it's on to Ballintoy and back again to the starting line."

As Ava and Daniel moved away, Lori leaned in toward Rachel and lowered her voice. "Why do I suddenly feel like we're the ones running a marathon?"

Rachel chuckled. "I know what you mean. I told Conall I wasn't much of an outdoors person, but I don't think he believed me."

"Well, it's a good thing you're going back to Chicago, isn't it? I mean, who needs all this fresh air and scenery, anyway?" She gave Rachel a long look. "We're city girls, born and raised, right?"

"Right," Rachel agreed, but her words sounded weak and unconvincing, even to her own ears.

THREE HOURS LATER, they watched Conall and Flynn cross the finish line and Rachel's throat felt hoarse from cheering so loudly. Daniel and Ava had secured a picnic table for them near the festival tents, as Rachel and Lori made their way to where the runners were accepting their medals. She saw Conall before he noticed her, and she took the opportunity to snap some photos of him while he was unaware. He was laughing at something Flynn and another runner were saying as he emptied a full bottle of water over his head and then shook it, spraying droplets everywhere. Quinn lay sprawled on the ground by his feet with his tongue lolling out, a bowl of water nearby. Conall had removed his hydration pack and his beanie, and both his legs and sneakers were covered in splashes of mud and sand.

As if he sensed her presence, he turned toward her, and his face creased into a smile. Sunlight slanted across his features and made his blue eyes glow, and Rachel found herself lowering the camera and moving toward him, filled with a sense that she had finally come home.

"You're not taking photos of me, are you?" he asked,

smiling down at her. "I look like something the cat just dragged in."

"No," she said, her gaze traveling over his sunburned face. "You look like a guy who just won a marathon."

"I didn't win, sweetheart. But I finished, and that's all that matters."

"Thank you for including me," she said. "I'm so glad I came. I had no idea it would be like this."

Conall tipped his head. "Like what?"

"So exciting, so fun." She spread her arms wide. "There are people here from all over the world, and yet it feels like a private club where everybody knows each other. It's amazing!"

"It is, yeah, but I'm not going to lie—I'm glad it's over." He looked beyond her. "Where are Mam and Dad?"

"They're saving a table for us. They brought a picnic lunch, if you're hungry."

"Starving, actually." Reaching over, he whacked Flynn on the shoulder. "Hey, mate, let's go eat."

They made their way to the table where Ava had spread a picnic lunch consisting of thick ham sandwiches, coleslaw, fresh strawberries, cold sausage rolls, and potato salad, with scones and lemon curd for dessert. They listened as Conall and Flynn recounted the race, describing some of the more difficult terrain in a way that had them all laughing. Halfway through the meal, Conall's assistant, Michael, joined them and handed Conall a thick envelope.

"How did it go today?" Conall asked, folding and tucking the envelope into his waist pack.

Michael grinned. "We sold out on nearly everything. I think we may have a half-dozen runners left, and those are in the smaller sizes. I packed everything up and brought it to the car."

Conall shook the younger man's hand. "Good job, mate. Thanks a million."

After they had eaten, they visited the fest tents where vendors were selling race memorabilia, including shirts, jackets, and running accessories, as well as food. On impulse, Rachel purchased a graphic poster of the Giant's Causeway, depicting a colorful line of marathoners running up the cliff trail toward the Shepherd's Steps.

"To remember this day," she explained to Conall, tucking the mailing tube into her backpack. "I don't want to forget."

He gave her a quizzical look and, regardless of the knowing looks he drew from his parents, slung an arm around her shoulders and pressed a kiss against her hair. "I hope you don't need a poster for that."

Rachel didn't reply and didn't object when he kept his arm around her while they continued to walk through the festival. The day had taken on a dreamlike quality and she didn't believe she would forget any of it, but she had a sinking feeling that aside from the poster and the photos she'd taken, memories would be all she had.

Chapter Seventeen

"I STILL CAN'T believe you're leaving tomorrow," Rachel said.

She sat on Lori's bed and watched her sort through her belongings, organizing everything into neat piles.

"It's been a fabulous ten days," Lori said. "But it's time for me to return to the real world." She turned to look at Rachel. "What about you?"

Rachel pretended to misunderstand. "What about me?"

"You're determined to give all this up?"

"I can't stay, even if I want to. My visa is only good for three months."

"That's not what I'm talking about and you know it." Throwing an item of clothing into her suitcase, she came and sat down next to Rachel. "You're totally in love with Conall."

Rachel drew in a shaky breath, unable to deny it. "Is it that obvious?"

"Only to anyone with eyes." She covered Rachel's hand with her own. "You should at least tell him how you feel."

"Why? So I can completely break his heart? Or worse,

find out he doesn't feel the same way?"

"So you do love him."

Rachel looked helplessly at her cousin. "How can I not? He's an amazing guy, and the way he makes me feel—" She broke off, unable to admit to Lori that her greatest fear was never again feeling the way she did when she was with Conall.

With him, she felt completely alive and hopeful about all the possibilities the future might hold. She found herself daydreaming about a life in his whitewashed cottage by the edge of the sea and of beautiful red-haired babies with blue eyes.

"You're crying," Lori said softly.

Rachel swiped at her damp cheeks. "How can I possibly leave him?"

"The real question is, why would you? He loves you . . . I can tell. It's there in the way he looks at you, like he can't quite believe you're real. He can barely keep himself from touching you whenever you're together. He's a great guy, Rachel, one in a million."

"You think I don't realize that?" She dragged in an uneven breath and gave a groan. "But this isn't what I planned! None of this was supposed to happen. I'm meant to return to Chicago, finish my degree, and work at Lakeside Industries. It's what I've worked so hard for."

"Is it?"

Before Rachel could reply, her phone began to vibrate.

Pulling it out, she looked at the display and then turned wide eyes to Lori. "It's your father."

Lori put her hand over the phone, her expression earnest. "Don't answer it."

"No, I have to." She hesitated. "Besides, I think we both know what he wants."

Lori stood up and walked to the door. "I'll give you some privacy. Tell Dad I'll call him later. I'll meet you downstairs when you're finished."

Twenty minutes later, Rachel made her way to the hotel lobby, feeling numb. As she had suspected, her uncle had offered her the position of lead designer at Lakeside Industries, since Linda Morse would soon be leaving the company. Rachel knew she should be ecstatic, but she'd never felt more like crying. Even now, her chest felt tight and her throat ached with the effort not to burst into tears.

Lori was sitting at a table by the window, chewing the side of her finger, but she jumped to her feet when she saw Rachel.

"Are you okay?" she asked, her expression wary.

Rachel shrugged. "Pam was right. He offered me the job of lead designer, but said if I want it, I need to come back right away. He bought me a ticket for the same flight you're taking home tomorrow."

Lori's mouth compressed in sympathy. "I'm so sorry. Did he say why you need to return so soon?"

"Apparently, Linda is leaving at the end of the month

and he wants a *smooth workload transition*." She used air quotes to emphasize the words. "He said he already spoke to Seamus about it, so it's all been decided."

"But that's not fair," Lori protested. "What about your internship?"

"He said my work at Lakeside Industries would meet the internship requirement."

"What are you going to do?"

Rachel looked helplessly at her cousin. "What choice do I have? If I don't take the position now, it could be years before I have another opportunity."

Lori leaned forward, her expression intent. "You always have a choice, Rachel. What if you could work here, in Ballylahane? Would you stay? My father wouldn't care; he's only ever wanted you to be happy. He could find another designer if you told him you want to stay here."

Rachel shook her head. "No. I could never ask Seamus for a job. I wouldn't want him to hire me out of pity or some sense of obligation."

Lori drew back, looking disappointed. "You're so stubborn. You have been for as long as I can remember. You're like a dog with a bone. Once you set your mind to something, you don't give it up, even when there's something infinitely better within your reach."

"You can't possibly understand," Rachel retorted, knowing her words were harsh. Lori had been striving for years to prove herself to her father, hoping he would give her the position of commodities manager, but knowing he would likely pass her over in favor of Seth Bieler.

"Okay, whatever," Lori said. "I guess that's it, then." She stood up. "I'm going to my room to finish packing since the bus leaves for the airport pretty early tomorrow morning. You should probably do the same. But do me a favor and at least let Conall know why you're leaving, and why he isn't enough for you. He deserves that much."

With her back rigid, she walked away.

RACHEL STOOD ON the beach and looked at the cottage where Conall lived, although there was no sign of him. She had procrastinated seeking him out, telling herself she didn't want to break the news to him at his shop. But the running store had been closed now for more than an hour and she could see Conall's small car parked at the side of the cottage. If he was at home, he must be indoors.

Drawing in a deep breath, she made her way along the path through the dunes, and opened the gate that led to his patio. In her hands, she carried the sweater he had loaned her the last time she'd been here, when they'd had dinner on the patio and had watched the sun sink into the sea. She'd slept with it each night since. Now her heart pounded in her chest, and she thought there was nothing she wanted to do less than tell Conall she was leaving in the morning. Gathering her faltering courage, she rapped on the door, but there was no answer. After knocking again without a response, she made her way to the small table on the patio and sat down.

She didn't have to wait long. As she gazed out at the beach, she saw the figures of a man and a dog running along the shore. Quinn reached the house first, bounding easily over the low stone wall to greet Rachel enthusiastically. As Conall opened the gate and came closer, she reluctantly stood. As always, he nearly took her breath away with his vitality. His hair was damp and disheveled and color rode high on his cheeks from his exertions, but his blue eyes glowed warmly when he saw her.

"Hey," he said, clearly pleased. "This is a nice surprise."

Stripping his shirt over his head, he used it to wipe the perspiration from his face and chest, while Rachel swallowed hard. His chest and shoulders were honed to perfection and his stomach was cobbled with muscles. Her fingers ached to trace the deep groove that bisected his chest and traveled down to his navel.

"I, um—" She cleared her throat. "We need to talk."

"This sounds serious." His gaze fell on the sweater she had placed on the nearby chair, and his smile faltered. "Come into the house and let me get you something to drink while I take a quick shower. I'd hug you, but I'm not fit to be touched."

"No, that's okay. I think it's better if we stay outside."

She didn't want to go indoors, where it would feel more

intimate. She didn't want to hear the shower running, or envision him naked beneath the spray of water. Her imagination was already running wild, just seeing him without his shirt. The truth was, she was a coward and her resistance was low. She didn't want to admit, even to herself, that she was on the fence about returning home. If she gave Conall an opportunity to change her mind, she would fold faster than a lawn chair. She didn't doubt that he could make her happy, but what if the day came when she regretted not following her dream? What if she eventually grew to resent Conall? She didn't want that to happen, which was why it was better to just end it now, on a high note.

"You look wrecked," Conall said, his brows pulling together. "Come, sit down and tell me what's upset you."

He pulled out a chair and Rachel sat on the edge, feeling nervous and sick to her stomach. "I don't know how to say it," she confessed. "I'm still trying to process it myself."

"Just say it."

She searched his eyes. "I'm leaving tomorrow."

He was quiet for a moment, his face intent. "Tomorrow," he repeated quietly. "Is there a reason why you need to leave so soon?"

"My uncle offered me the lead design position, but I have to go back right away."

Conall looked down at the shirt he held in his hands. "I see."

Rachel dipped her head to look into his eyes. "You know

why I need to go. If I don't take this job, I may never get another chance."

Conall nodded. "Yeah, of course. You have to do what you feel is right." He looked at her then, his expression stark. "So that's it then."

"I'm sorry." She drew in a shaky breath. "For what it's worth, I'll never forget you, or this past month."

Conall gave a huff of bitter laughter. "Thanks."

Feeling inadequate and on the verge of tears, she stood. "I should go."

Conall rose to his feet. "Hang on. I have something for you."

Before she could say anything, he vanished inside the house and then reappeared a moment later wearing a clean shirt and carrying a package wrapped in brown paper. "This arrived this morning. I was going to bring it by after I took a shower, but since you're already here . . ."

He handed Rachel the package. It felt soft and heavy in her arms. Placing it on the patio table, she undid the string and opened the paper. There, nestled inside layers of tissue paper, was a folded length of rich, Donegal tweed—the same tweed her father had designed and given to Eileen McDermott. Rachel didn't realize she was crying until a tear plopped onto the paper. Swiftly, she wiped her eyes.

"Thank you. This means so much to me," she said, not looking at Conall.

"There's something else," he said. She felt him come up

behind her, and then his hands were on her shoulders, turning her gently to face him. "I asked her to make this for me. For you."

He pressed a small box into her hands, the kind of box reserved for fine jewelry.

"No, whatever this is, it's too much," she protested.

"Just open it, Rachel."

Glancing up at him, she saw his jaw was set and his blue eyes were shuttered. Carefully, she opened the box and a small gasp escaped her. There, startlingly bright against the backdrop of black velvet, was a necklace with a Celtic knot. Wrought in gold, the pendant was delicate and feminine. Taking the box from her hands, Conall lifted the necklace out.

"This is the Celtic Love Knot," he said, pulling her hair to one side so that he could fasten it around her neck. "It's your father's necklace, melted down and remade. It represents the love between two people."

Rachel lifted the pendant, looked at the two intertwined hearts, and then raised her gaze to Conall. "It's the most beautiful thing anyone has ever given me."

Conall cupped her face in his hands, his eyes searching hers. He swallowed hard. "I love you, Rachel Woods. I think I fell in love with you the instant I saw you tumble into that boghole. Please don't go. There's nothing wrong in forging your own path, one that's different from your father's. He would be proud of you regardless of what you do. Please stay here in Ireland. Choose me. I promise you'll never regret it."

His image began to blur and swim, and she pulled away because in another second she would throw herself against him, and she knew that if he kissed her—if he held her—she would never leave.

"I can't," she said thickly. "I have to go. For what it's worth, I love you too, Conall McDermott, *so much*. But I have to leave. I'm sorry."

Swiftly, before she could change her mind, she picked up the bolt of fabric and fled through the gate and across the beach. Only when she reached the seawall near town did she risk a glance back. He hadn't followed her. She was completely alone on the beach. She could just make out the small house behind the dunes, but there was no man or dog in sight.

RACHEL AND LORI boarded the big coach bus at six thirty the following morning in front of the hotel. Even at that early hour, the bus was half-full of people headed in the direction of Donegal. They slid into two seats near the front of the bus and waited as the driver stashed their suitcases in the cargo hold. Rachel had checked out of the B&B the night before and had stayed with Lori at the hotel, due to their early morning departure. She hadn't slept, and her eyes felt gritty and tired. Her entire body ached, as if an enormous weight had settled onto her shoulders. She'd spent most of the night scrolling through her camera footage at the dozens—no, hundreds—of photos she had taken during her short time in Ireland. So many of them were pictures of Conall, but there were pictures of her too. Pictures that Conall had taken at the cliffs and other pictures he'd taken when she'd been unaware. Pictures that Flynn had taken during their visit to the farm. Each of them seemed to reveal something she hadn't been aware of until then. When she'd finally fallen asleep with the camera in her hands, she dreamed of Ireland and Conall.

Now, sitting on the bus, the prospect of going back to Chicago held no joy for her, and she couldn't even summon any enthusiasm about the coveted position that awaited her there. No matter how she tried, she couldn't stop thinking about Conall, or his face as she'd left.

"Did you say goodbye to Flynn?" she asked, trying to rouse herself for Lori's sake.

But Lori had her face turned toward the window and refused to look at Rachel. When she spoke, her voice was wooden. "We said our goodbyes when we came back from Northern Ireland."

"Oh." Rachel hesitated. "Are you going to ignore me the whole way to Chicago?"

"No, just to Dublin." Lori shifted in her seat to look at Rachel, opened her mouth to say something else, and then abruptly closed it again. Whatever she had been about to say died on her lips as she studied Rachel's face. Her expression softened and she reached over to hold Rachel's hand.

"I'm sorry," she said. "I've been so upset I haven't really considered how hard this is for you." She dropped Rachel's hand. "Even though it's all your doing."

Rachel sighed as the bus pulled away from the curb. "I have no choice, Lori. Things don't always have an easy solution, despite what you believe."

"Rachel, working in Chicago was your father's dream, but it doesn't have to be yours, not when it's clear you belong here in Ballylahane."

"Now you sound like Conall. That's what he said too."

Lori considered her for a moment. "What if I told you there might be a way for you to still work for Lakeside Industries and also stay here in Ireland?"

Rachel narrowed her eyes in suspicion. "I'd say you should have told me this last night, before I went and broke Conall's heart."

"I couldn't," Lori said. "I was—*I am*—under strict orders not to say anything. But I think you need to know."

"What do you mean? Does this have anything to do with your excessive interest in Seamus's business dealings?"

Lori's expression turned guilty.

"Lori!" Rachel hissed. "I knew it! Please tell me you were not spying on McDermott Mills for Uncle Jack! If he thinks he can just buy Seamus out, he has another think coming. The McDermotts would never relinquish control of their company."

"No, of course my father doesn't want to buy McDermott Mills! He wants to establish a partnership with them."

Rachel stared at her, bemused. "What? How would that even work?"

Quickly, Lori explained how they would import luxury Donegal tweed for their Chicago-based store and also sell to top European designers for their home design collections.

"Don't you see? It would expand McDermott's sales and give us a way into the European luxury home goods market."

The bus had left the main road of Ballylahane and turned onto the road toward the cliffs where Rachel and Conall had first walked together. The sun was just rising to the east, bathing the fields in a warm, golden glow. Rachel felt her chest tighten, knowing that in a few short moments, they would leave Ballylahane behind forever.

"Why couldn't you tell me all this before?" she demanded. "I wouldn't have said anything."

"My father made me promise," Lori said. "Until we knew a partnership was feasible, I was told to make an assessment of the McDermott factory, find out what I could about their capabilities and marketing, and keep the plans under wraps until a partnership is officially approved. I couldn't even tell you about it. I'm sorry."

"And is it? Officially approved?"

"Well, the lawyers are drafting up the papers, so I have to believe it's going to happen. Once a partnership between the two companies is finalized, we'll need someone in Ireland to help oversee the design and selection of tweeds."

Standing up, Rachel reached for her backpack. "Driver," she called, "stop the bus, please! I need to get off!"

The bus pulled to the side of the road with a hiss of air brakes and the driver rose from his seat.

Lori laughed in astonishment. "What are you doing?"

Leaning down, Rachel kissed her cousin's cheek. "They say home is where the heart is, and my heart is here in Ireland. I can't go back to Chicago. Tell Uncle Jack I'm sorry, but I can't accept the position of lead designer. I'll work for him from here, if he'll let me, or for Seamus. Even if neither option works, I'm staying. How could I ever leave?"

Laughing, Lori stood and hugged her hard. "I knew you'd come to your senses in time."

"You'll come back and visit, won't you?"

Lori gave her a secretive smile. "Oh, I think I can safely say I'll be back. After all, I now have several very good reasons for wanting to visit Ballylahane."

"Miss?" The bus driver opened the door. "Will you be wanting to get off, or have you changed your mind?"

"I have definitely made up my mind," Rachel said, "to stay!"

Clambering down from the bus, she waited as the driver dragged her suitcases to the side of the road. Rachel waved to Lori until the big green bus disappeared from sight. After a moment's consideration, she pulled her heaviest suitcase into the ditch where it would be less likely to attract attention, and then set out across the fields in the direction of Ballyla-hane, carrying her smaller suitcase, which contained her father's precious tweed.

The sun was higher now, and she carefully picked her way through the first field, glad she had worn her new runners. At least she now knew to avoid bogholes. Within minutes, her shoulders ached with the effort of lugging her suitcase. She climbed over a second livestock gate and saw the Ballylahane church spire in the distance. She was almost there. Hefting her suitcase, she began trudging up the hill when she heard the familiar sound of a dog barking. Looking up, she saw a border collie careening toward her.

"Quinn!"

He nearly bowled her over in his excitement and then ran in boisterous circles around her, his tail wagging happily. She looked past him expectantly and saw a lone runner appear over the crest of the hill. Seeing her, he abruptly stopped.

Rachel couldn't breathe as her heart leaped in her chest. Even from a distance, she recognized the lean figure and could just make out the astonished expression on his face. Dropping her suitcase, she began to run toward him. He met her halfway, catching her in his arms and holding her tightly as Quinn barked with excitement.

"I can't believe you're here," she said when she could finally speak.

Conall's blue eyes were suspiciously bright as he pulled back and searched her face. "I woke up and realized I was completely mad to let you go. I ran to the hotel but you had just left. I came running in the hopes of catching your bus, because I wanted to tell you that if I need to relocate to the States in order for us to be together, I'll do it."

Rachel stared at him in astonishment. "What?"

"I may have to travel back and forth to Ireland each quarter to visit the shops, but I can manage it." He spoke quickly, his voice earnest and his expression hopeful. "If you want to live in Chicago, I'll come with you. I haven't worked out all the details yet, but I've made up my mind."

He would live in Chicago, if that's what she wanted.

The realization that he was ready to give up everything in order to be with her made her feel both deeply humbled and profoundly grateful that she had found such an incredible man.

"No," she said. "You don't need to do that."

"I want to," he insisted. His blue eyes clouded. "Unless you don't want me to."

"I want you with all my heart, but you don't need to move to the States because I'm staying! I'm staying here," Rachel said breathlessly as his strong arms came around her. She was crying and laughing all at the same time, hugging him and pressing kisses against his face and mouth. "I was crazy to think I could ever leave you. I love you, Conall. I choose you!"

He kissed her deeply, stopping just long enough to say, "I love you, Rachel Woods. Welcome home."

And as he kissed her, Rachel realized she had finally found her own path, and her way home.

The End

Don't miss the next book in the Love Always, Ireland series, *Love Me Beneath the Irish Moon*!

Join Tule Publishing's newsletter for more great reads and weekly deals!

If you enjoyed *Kiss Me Under the Irish Sky,*
you'll love the next book in the…

Love Always, Ireland series

Book 1: *Kiss Me Under the Irish Sky*

Book 2: *Love Me Beneath the Irish Moon*
Coming in May 2023

Available now at your favorite online retailer!

More Books by Karen Foley

The Riverrun Ranch series

Book 1: *Swipe Right for a Cowboy*

Book 2: *Counting on the Cowboy*

Book 3: *How to Catch a Cowboy*

The Glacier Creek series

Book 1: *A Hummingbird Christmas*

Book 2: *Montana Defender*

Book 3: *Montana Firefighter*

Book 4: *Montana Protector*

Available now at your favorite online retailer!

About the Author

Karen Foley admits to being an incurable romantic. When she's not working for the Department of Defense, she loves writing sexy stories about alpha heroes and strong heroines. Karen lives in New England with her husband, two daughters, and a houseful of pets.

Thank you for reading

Kiss Me Under the Irish Sky

If you enjoyed this book, you can find more from all our great authors at TulePublishing.com, or from your favorite online retailer.

Made in the USA
Middletown, DE
09 May 2023

30314411R00175